Death Prescription

Jeffrey B. Martin Jr.

Published by Waldorf Publishing
2140 Hall Johnson Road
#102-345
Grapevine, Texas 76051
www.WaldorfPublishing.com

Death's Prescription

ISBN: 978-1-64136-857-5

Library of Congress Control Number: 2020937461

Copyright © 2020

Design by Baris Celik

Table of Contents

Chapter 1

Anatomy of a Killer

Darkness and death were comfortable roommates for the stranger hidden in the dense foliage. The downpour that spewed from the heavens scattered the masses in various directions, as they sought refuge from the Almighty's wrath. *Outstanding*! The art show was the perfect venue for him to collect his next victim. Rubbing the coin between his fingers, the man cherished the preciousness of the moment.

The death of the young woman made him *powerful,* almost like he was deemed to be untouchable by mere mortals. Murder was how he chose to define the nickname his mother had labeled him with when disciplining him so many years earlier. *Lucifer.* She taunted him with the name for *so* long.

He recalled his *first* "masterpiece" as he prepared to kill again. That night had been similar to this, with one exception; the rain had been gently bouncing off the streets in a way that seemed acrobatic. A tall, young woman named Angela Deeds carried a dark umbrella in one hand and a set of keys in the other. Her light blue pantsuit hugged her figure like a second skin, which left nothing to the imagination. She ran towards her yellow sports car, trying to avoid the raindrops. *The least of your worries.* The destiny of this female was to be his first masterpiece in a line of many that would follow. There had been a previous death, but it was not worthy of the effort. He watched her approach the vehicle, close to where he was hidden. All the muscles in his body tensed.

The two instruments he had chosen to start his new craft with seemed to weigh down his hands. *Get a hold of yourself.*

He peeked through the bushes and remembered how exquisite she looked. Angela's hair was the silkiest and shiniest he'd ever seen, like those unattainable women advertising shampoo in a television commercial. Lucifer was excited as he tightened his hands around that night's weapons of choice, a small syringe full of his paralytic concoction and the silver nickel-plated 9mm semi-automatic handgun. He hadn't held a firearm for many years and wanted to use it *just* as an alternative.

He had planned the assault in his mind for many days. Her arrival and departure times were predictable to say the least. On several occasions, Lucifer made it a point to walk past Angela's place of business and just *once,* he purchased items from a lingerie store across the street from her office. Yesterday, he went even further and approached her at the coffee shop adjacent her apartment complex and tried to engage the girl in small talk. She of course, ignored him, which surprised the killer.

His future victim was a few short feet away. Angela tried to hold the umbrella and open her car door at the same time. The combination of weather and the urge to multi-task caused the keys to slip from her hand and clatter to the ground.

Divine intervention. Lucifer slipped out from the darkness and approached her undetected. A sudden movement later, it was too late. The young woman tumbled to the cold wet pavement and landed on her back. She looked up. Lucifer noticed the anguish in her eyes and relished the fact Angela seemed to recognize him from *somewhere,* but with the onset of paralysis, time had run out for cognitive thought. Angela Deeds' breath was labored, and she clutched at her throat, in search of that last bite of air. *Almost the end.*

Lucifer towered over his victim; the sudden of stream of headlights forced his hand. *Damn them*! *Oh, well.* He pulled the silver slide back, as the sound of the bullet being chambered into position thrilled him. Lowering the firearm, he pointed it between her eyes. Passionately, the man gazed into them and beamed with delight when her pupils dilated. Lucifer eased the trigger back. An explosion erupted,propelling the blunt projectile through the front of her skull. The impact of the small round scattered her brain matter upon the saturated pavement.

Lucifer was pleased with his performance and how his victim had been unable to react. He fingered through all of her belongings, and located several coins scattered in the bottom of her blood-spattered purse. He placed one in his pocket. *"This is how I'll honor all victims.* That was the first day of his *new* life. Lucifer would keep the fifty-cent piece with him always, to commemorate that day—until the day he died.

* * *

Lucifer finished his performance for *this* evening as well. The killer had returned to his apartment and stood at the kitchen sink washing the remnants of human carnage from his hands. *Unexpected deaths.* Lucifer hadn't considered two other people would be in the park, but so be it. He improvised, and now *they* would also be enshrined in his collection of "masterpieces." Cleaning off the battle-axe and drunk with excitement, he stared at the wooden table. "Ah, three new prize possessions*,"* Lucifer whispered.

He picked up the first item. It was a worn silver Zippo lighter with the initials *J.P.* etched on the right side of the lid. He held it for a few seconds, careful to return it to the proper place. Ah, this second treasure had come from his youngest victim… *ever*. Lucifer was pleased the plastic neon band had been spared from the violence. He tapped the bright face of the timepiece. Raising it to his ear, he could still hear the repetitive sound of a battery. Lucifer set it back on the table and smiled.

The third and final article would, hands down, be the most cherished of all his new tokens. He ran his fingers along the canvas, careful not to damage the small masterpiece. The artist had created a wonderful work, which Lucifer admired. *I have the perfect place!* He decided to hang it on the wall in the cramped closet that held his "collection." *What a productive night.* Lucifer was skilled with many of the tools reserved in the creation of pain and torture. Tonight's performance was no exception. This sample of work was but a preview of what was to come. Tomorrow, he would start his hunt for another victim, and become one with his prey. But now, even the killer needed to rest.

Chapter 2

Introducing Brian

"Brian, what the hell are you doing?"

Sarah's yelling at me again, thought Brian Jeffers. He was tired. This was supposed to be his day off. He rolled over and glared at the alarm clock on the nightstand. He groaned as he answered his wife. "Nothing, honey, I'm just trying to sleep."

"Get your butt up, Brian! The girls have soccer practice in twenty minutes, and *you're* taking them."

"Yes, dear," he said with little emotion. He tried to roll from his bed, but the sudden movement, caused pain to radiate through his left arm.

"Damn!" He exhaled and rubbed the area. Several years earlier, a bullet from a local drug dealer's gun pierced his bicep and the agony he endured was a constant reminder, of the almost fatal mistake. "Thirty-five years old, and I feel like eighty," Brian said to himself. *I'm also way too young to retire.*

He had worked for Valentine that long; the recent promotion to the Homicide Division would place him into the top tier of salary when he *did* decide to retire. The mid-sized city was located about fifty miles west of Lincoln, Nebraska. It had seen its share of murders in the last twenty years, but so did any other its size. There were two major reasons Brian decided to become a law enforcement officer here. First, Brian and Sarah both liked the school system. It was better than average, especially in *this* day and age. Second, the cost of expenses was *very* affordable for a police officer and his part-time-working wife.

He heard the floorboards, as the sound of his persistent wife reverberated through his head. "Stop daydreaming and get down here now. I don't want to have to explain to three little girls why *their* daddy's too busy to spend any time with them."

Ouch…anything to make me feel guilty. Careful not to aggravate his injury further, he slipped out of the bed. Brian was unaware his wife had repositioned the vanity mirror and almost did a double-take as his reflection greeted him. *Ugh*! Many people often described him as the typical law enforcement type. His hair was jet black with shades of gray. His deep-brown, eyes made women notice him and criminals fear him. He also had gained several pounds on his six-foot–four frame from Sarah's excellent home cooking. Rubbing a hand over his new-found girth, Brian shook his head. He needed to hit the gym, but between case files and the girls, time was short for any activity that involved time-consuming exercises and sweating. *Oh, shit*! Brian threw on his clothes in realization, a third reminder from his beloved spouse would land him on the couch, and the doghouse was just around the corner. *I really don't need that.*

   * * *

Brian had driven the girls to the Valentine sports complex for their weekend soccer extravaganza. They didn't like to compete against other kids; they just wanted to run around outside and be free from any household chores. He watched the girls finish up practice; relieved the activity produced only sore muscles and minor bruises versus the compilation of broken bones.

The group made a quick but unhealthy stop at the local Jake's Hamburger Spot, where Brian ordered what he always did: a double cheeseburger with extra jalapenos. He loved the jalapenos; they always made everything taste better. The girls usually got the kid's pack. Chicken strips, macaroni and cheese, and orange soda. Before Brian could sit down and enjoy his high-fat and nutritionally extinct meal, he received a buzz on his weekend-ending pager. The digital display had the all-too-familiar number listed on it. *Not now*. He knew it was not going to be easy to explain to his family why he was summoned to work on the weekend… *again*.

"Kids, I have to drop you off at home. Daddy's work needs to see him."

The girls were very intelligent for their respective ages of five, seven, and nine. They knew what the sound of *that* pager meant.

"Not again, Dad. It's Saturday… you promised to play with us," whined Melissa, the oldest and the loudest of the three. As usual, the others started in right away.

"Daddy, no, I want to see you," Victoria cried, the remains of macaroni and cheese scattered all over her face.

"This is stupid, Dad," Alyssa said. This was the gang-up-on-Daddy trio; they knew how to play this game.

"Now, girls, I'll hurry as fast as I can and come see you when I'm done."

They *knew* better and also realized they could punish him with silent treatment. He glanced in the rearview and noticed they *all* displayed the all-too familiar look of disappointment.

Fuck me!

Chapter 3

The Discovery

The silence was even more noticeable after he dropped off the girls, but sometimes, that's the way life is. If Brian wanted a nine-to-five job where he could sit behind a cozy desk and punch numbers into a database, then he would have taken *that* career path. *This* is what he'd chosen and was born to do. Brian had just pulled into the back lot of district office on Balboa Street when he felt the vibration of his cell phone.

"Detective Jeffers here."

"This is Barnum. Get your ass to 1449 Marketplace Avenue as fast as that piece-of-shit off-duty car can get you here."

The Supervisor from Hades. "Okay, Bossman."

This always made Barnum upset. Brian often referred to him as Bossman for how the man treated the underlings in his office, like that of a plantation owner.

"Fuck you, Jeffers. Just get here."

Brian laughed. *It never hurts to have a little fun with people.*

When he arrived at 1449 Marketplace Avenue, Brian noticed a multitude of Valentine Police marked patrol units. He spotted the brand-new unmarked blue Impala that belonged to Commander Alex Barnum. The hard-nosed authoritarian had been with the Valentine Police Department for what seemed like *way* too long. He was fifty-five years old and looked every year of it. Alex was over three hundred pounds of pure fatty tissue and lacked enough hair on his head to even complete a comb over. *Nice*. When Barnum came into view, Brian found it difficult to maintain a straight face. He wore a black pin-stripe suit, which may have fit when he was one hundred pounds lighter. The seams of the clothing were in obvious protest as they appeared to be stretched even beyond their limitations. Brian squinted. *Is he running?*

He winked at the uniformed officer, who was busy with traffic detail. "Man that guy better not fall over, or he may roll all the way down the hill."

The officer nodded, but refrained from any comments.

"Jeffers." Barnum stopped a few feet from him and was having obvious difficulty catching his breath. "I need you to follow me now. This is some shit, Mr. Homicide Detective. A couple was walking through the park and discovered the bodies."

* * *

One-four-four-nine Marketplace was the official address of Glade Center Park. The venue had the required playground its moniker would suggest, but the center was home to a large amphitheater. This held many types of events which ranged from, concerts to weekly art and trade shows. Today, however, it lacked the normal flow of Saturday morning visitors. Even the pigeons that counted on their staple of nourishment had disappeared. Following Barnum past the amphitheater and through several rows of bushes, Brian Jeffers noticed a grassy clearing. Barnum wiped his brow and pointed. "Look!"

Brian stood motionless for a few seconds and witnessed what he considered to be the most gruesome, sick, and twisted scene he ever laid eyes on. *Oh, fuck.*

The ground was soaked with a dark red tint which appeared to be the entire blood supply of three naked, mutilated bodies, positioned side-by-side. All were decapitated, and the heads were placed on top of their torsos. Brian inched closer, and observed carved letters in the fleshy portion of each victim's forehead. *Ritualistic killings?*

The first of the deceased was a man in his mid-forties, of medium build and lightly muscled. Whoever was responsible for this was powerful. His damaged face also showed distinct signs of aging by the assortment of various sunspots and wrinkles that peppered his skin. The inscription *LUC* was sculpted into his forehead and a brown wallet sat in the palm of his right hand. There were countless lacerations on his body, each wound a doorway. Brian guessed it was a good possibility the male victim was already dead before the beheading occurred. He stepped to the next in line. *Bastard.* She was a young, female around Brian's eldest daughter's age. She, too, possessed many cavernous slashes on her petite, mutilated body. The letters *IF* were engraved on her freckled forehead. It made Brian sick to see she had suffered like this. *Fucking lunatic!* Stepping around evidence markers, Brian stopped in front of the last of the dead. She was blonde, appeared to be in her mid-forties and very fit. Brian clenched his jaw. The killer had removed both her arms and placed them in an *X* on top of her stomach. He didn't realize it at first, but now understood she held her own severed appendage. The look on her blood-drained face said it all. The eyes were sunk back into her skull and her mouth lay wide open, the remains of a scream that was never to be. The letters *ER* were embedded into her flesh, as she seemed to possess the final letters needed to finish whatever the killer meant to say.

Brian glared at the sculpted lettering. *A fucking*

cryptic message. The inscription spelled out the word: LUC-IF-ER. Brian was awestruck at the horrific attacks. He took a deep breath and glanced at his supervisor. Worry and fear encompassed the man's face. This was the worst murder scene Valentine Law Enforcement had ever experienced. Brian studied the unbelievable devastation, which made him think about his own family. He would make sure to call Sarah and the girls and tell them he loved them. That would put things in perspective, once this day was over.

Chapter 4

A Common Thread

One of the crime scene team members stopped Brian Jeffers and handed him a plastic evidence bag which contained the male victim's wallet. The driver's license identified him as, Justin Paul. The man had lived at 1254 Kirkwood Avenue in Valentine. It also contained several of his business cards. Justin Paul worked for A.P. Lodfig as a Marketing Consultant. This man could demand a high-dollar salary with his position in the prosperous company. A.P. Lodfig was known to hire the best and brightest. The organization's headquarters was in the metro area. They were a strong supporter of local charities in the community and would often donate to the police department and its various programs. Brian motioned to a uniformed patrol officer he recognized as, Kyle Douglas.

"Kyle, do me a favor and keep this road blocked off until after the medical examiner arrives at the scene. We don't want the news media near this area yet."

"No problem. I'll make sure we keep them out until you give the okay," Officer Douglas said.

"One more thing. Do you have the names of the people who discovered our victims?" Brian removed his notebook from his suit jacket pocket.

"I think Officer Rhodes was the first one here. I'll get with him and forward you the information, sir."

"Thanks. I appreciate it."

Brian stopped in front of his supervisor. "Any luck?"

Barnum stared at the collected evidence bags. "Just

this shit!"

Brian leaned closer. *Two packs of cigarettes*. He walked the scene. *Cigarettes, but no lighter or matches? Strange, maybe the guy was trying to quit.* Barnum stood up and bypassed him without an even glance in his direction. He gave commands to a few of the uniformed officers and then turned towards the junior investigator.

"So what do you think, Mr. Homicide Detective?"

"Besides the cigarettes?

"You know what the fuck I mean!" Barnum eyed him with contempt. *Here it goes.* "The letters carved into the victims' foreheads say it all. If you add them in order, they spell the word *LUCIFER*."

Barnum raised his eyebrows. "Lucifer? As in the devil and Jesus and all that happy religious stuff? Oh shit, Jeffers… are you talking about satanic cult shit or *anything* like that?" Barnum gnashed his teeth.

Brian held up his hand. "Hold up—"

Barnum turned red. "The fucking media would have a field day talking about this topic on the news. Can you imagine the headlines? "Local Killing Spree by Satanic Cult Plagues the Midwestern City of Valentine."

"I didn't say Satanic—"

Barnum raised a finger. "I don't want to even hear you mention something like *that* again. You're giving me gray hair thinking about it!"

Brian hesitated. "This is the beginning of something…just don't know what…"

Barnum wiped at his face. "Whoever slaughtered these people is fucked in the head, but it's your job to find out who this freak show is. A case indeed, *Mr. Detective Extraordinaire.* But unless you can goddamn well prove it, I don't want to hear the words satanic ritual, cult, or anything else like that!"

"Again, I didn't say cult, you did." Brian spat. *This guy so sucks*!

"Not again, you understand?" His supervisor stormed off, shaking his head.

Brian called out after him. "I'll check for vehicles registered in Paul's name and send out an all-points bulletin to see if there's someone driving around in them." *Why bother*?

He knew Barnum had stopped paying attention to him. Whoever was responsible for these murders wasn't going to steal the dead man's car and drive it through town. At least if he was halfway smart. And the mere fact they didn't have the killer in custody proved he was.

"Okay, Jeffers, do what you do!" Barnum barked from fifty feet away. He resumed the conversation with the uniformed officers.

Brian returned to the area where his unmarked patrol car was parked. He punched the ignition button ready to leave, when a voice pleaded for his attention. "Detective!" A young uniformed patrol officer raced across the lot.

Brian rolled down the window. "Yes, Officer?"

"Sir, I'm Steve Rhodes. Officer Douglas said you needed the names of the two people who found those bodies?"

"Good. I'm in a hurry to get back to the station. Give them to me and I'll call when I can." Brian reached into his suit jacket pocket and pulled out a pen and notebook.

Officer Rhodes opened his uniform shirt pocket, and hauled out the exact same style of notebook. He flipped through the pages and located the one he needed. "Sir, here you go." Ripping out sheet of paper, he handed it to the investigator.

"Thanks for the information. Did you get a chance to talk to them?"

"Yes, but only for a few minutes. I haven't had a chance to write my report yet, but I told the women, a detective will be contacting them with a follow-up."

"Good work, Rhodes. Commander Barnum or I will get in touch with them." Brian pulled away from the curb as he headed off to get some much-needed information.

 * * *

The administrative assistant for the Valentine Police Department was an intelligent former newspaper editor named, Cynthia Cornerstone. She was the brightest and most knowledgeable woman in law enforcement administration since the city had created the position. Although she neared forty-seven years old, her features didn't show it. Cynthia had shoulder-length dark brown hair and blue eyes that made men quiver when she looked at them. She was dark-skinned and sported an athletic physique, not the norm for a woman who bore three children.

"Cynthia, where is my one and only lifesaver?" Brian entered the police administration offices.

The space that headquartered the detective and homicide bureaus was pristine. Each displayed hand-crafted oak furniture and top-of-the-line leather chairs to create a Fortune 500 type setting. The walls were covered in paintings from a famous local artist named, Bell Willows, who was gracious enough to still send the newest designs to the department and the Chief of Police was more than happy to display them. Brian brushed his hand over one of the works as he stopped at Cynthia's desk. "Nice, eh?"

She raised her glasses. "If you like that sort of thing?

And by the way young man, I'm your one and only female employee who can *type*, so I guess in a way I am your lifesaver." Cornerstone smiled "What do you need, Brian dear?"

"Glad you asked. I need you to research everything available about the deceased Justin Paul. Concentrate mainly on his past criminal history, if he has one."

She nodded. "Anything else?"

"I would also really appreciate it if you could find out what vehicles he has registered in his name. I know Barnum was sending a couple of uniformed officers over to his house to look for anything with an address of possible next of kin."

"Brian, do you know which officers are going over to the house?"

Brian shook his head. "Go ahead and give the dispatcher a call to find who was tasked."

"Okay." She readied her pen for more instructions.

Brian winked. "Should be it. Barnum and I couldn't find any identification on the other two victims, but I'm pretty certain they were related…not three random strangers."

"I'll work on it. Let me know if there is anything else?" Cornerstone said with sincerity in her voice.

Brian stopped at his assigned office. He gazed at the stenciling on the glass door. *Detective Brian Jeffers-Homicide Division.* Even though he had been in the position for a while, the writing made it seem more official. Inside the office, a cool breeze from above, assaulted his skin, as goose bumps formed on unprotected flesh. It was always too cold, even in the summer. For all the money the department spent with the executive offices, they should have thought about a cooling system upgrade. *Probably knew this one was mine.*

Cynthia Cornerstone tapped on the frame of his door. "Officer Petrie wanted me to give you these." She dropped a stack of paperwork onto the desk.

He flipped through the pages. "Whoa, not one latent print at the scene, there's no fucking way."

Cynthia shook her head. "That's exactly what Officer Petrie said." She scowled and left Brian alone with the paperwork.

Too much blood spilled for there to be nothing. Opening the four-drawer gray filing cabinet, he felt drained. Brian sorted through various files, until he found several unsolved homicide cases from years long before he was hired. He thumbed through each of the attached photos. *No prints and lots of blood. All of these seem to look like our case.*

The five victims were murdered in brutal fashion, but not one shred of evidence was discovered at the scene in any of them. Evidence techs and homicide investigators alike scoured each scene, as the investigation lacked both witnesses and suspects. Brian analyzed the files several times, determining that this case had some of the same elements. Except today, there were a few witnesses and he was hopeful they could provide information to catch this monster. The hair stood up on his neck. He got the distinct sense some unseen evil was present, and the Glade Park Killings was just a taste of what was to come.

Chapter 5

August & Tamia

August Dellano was in his home away from home; the Daltry Hotel. What a great sexual experience he'd just had with Tamia Stevens. She was his Thursday to Sunday lover. The other days of the week he would re-side with his very plain wife Janice. The differences were superficial, no emotion required. It was as simple as that.

Tamia was a young twenty-three-year-old cover model with the cookie-cutter looks most women in her profession displayed. She had long golden hair, ocean blue eyes with blonde eyelashes, and a very full set of non-collagen injected lips. She had long, tanned, toned legs, which led to the most perfect ass; which alone was enough to attract August Dellano to this vixen.

He was twenty years older and was very grateful for the time he was allowed to spend with her. August looked every bit his age, mostly from indulging in alco-hol and the daily habit of Putro cigars. The six-course Italian meals Janice prepared might have played a part in his overall appearance. He considered himself a little heavy, not obese like his acquaintances at the country club would tell everyone within earshot. His black hair had turned a serious shade of gray, and his dark-skinned face showed the signs of over exposure. Although he liked Tamia, he knew his wife would murder him if she ever found out. He didn't want to think what would hap-pen to this poor girl if Janice ever caught them. But right now, August was happy for the night. Pulling on his Ar-mani suit pants, he praised his mistress.

"Baby, you were hot tonight. I wish I could marry you."

Tamia wasn't the stereotypical dumb blonde and wasn't going to fall for the, Mr. Director-has-a-part-for-you-in-this-movie line. "Well, you don't have to go that far, but you could invest some money into a new vehicle. My Navigator is getting a little old."

"Just what I like about you. Not only do you have a great ass, but you're smart, too." August laughed.

Tamia looked him in the eye. "Yeah, you know *me*, smart and sexy model meets forty-year-old Italian pizza man."

"Now wait a minute," cried August. "I'm thirty-nine and own a high-profile restaurant in this Godforsaken Midwestern city."

"Whatever you say, Lover Boy," she teased. She used her attitude to get to him.

"All right, enough teasing the Italian for tonight. See you after your shoot in Chicago." August purred.

"Of course, anything for my sugar daddy." Tamia rubbed the back of his neck.

Both dressed in quick-like fashion and were silent for the remainder of their stay.

     * * *

As the couple exited the room, neither seemed to notice the tall man; he stood just off to the right of the hallway entrance. For the past two days, he was learning the routine of his next victims. Lucifer ran the fifty-cent piece through the fingers on his right hand, ready for another addition to his collection. Silently, he watched the sinful couple exit room 101 and walk out to their respective vehicles. The male would get into a light blue sports car. The female owned a black, older-model sports utility vehicle with a sunroof.

Hmm… a perfect place for her death. Lucifer was excited and eager to collect the rewards from these two future masterpieces. He slipped out the rear door of the hotel as the two lovers drove out of the lot. He stopped. The all too familiar voice of his mother echoed in his head. It was ages since the woman spoke to him; he wasn't too happy she chose to engage him now. The voice was unbearable, ever more scolding, but with distinct clarity.

"You're a fool, Lucifer. No woman would ever want to be with you. You're too stupid to even know how to be with a female. All you do all day long is read those horror magazines. Get out in the real world where people have to work for a living!" The repetitive rant of his guardian caused him to place his hands over his ears. He never understood why she chose to criticize him again and again. No wonder she met her end at his hands, and then, he heard that voice, too…

"What are you doing, you ungrateful demon-spawn child? Put down that knife, and get your lazy ass out of my house! Oh my God, no!" That was the last time his mother ever spoke. The son disposed of this hurtful and spiteful woman forever.

The knife felt good in his hands. Lucifer was an artist creating his masterpiece. The blood dripped down his forearm as she stood there frozen, her eyes wide open. He was almost surprised with his quickness and skill as he struck with the blade. He smiled as the vicious woman grabbed at her throat, trying to cover up the deep gash across her jugular. The blood poured from the wound and onto the dirty, tiled, cockroach-infested floor. Lucifer laughed. This nightmare he lived all of his young life was over.

The sound of the Navigator's engine, brought the killer back to the present. Hidden behind the door of the hotel, Lucifer was covered in sweat, a nervous high-school boy in the throes of his first sexual encounter.

As the two left the lot, he grabbed the handle of the door, and hurried out. Lucifer looked back several times, wondering if he was discovered as he crept into the night. *Nobody saw me*. His mother's voice had quieted, hopefully, it would never return. Somehow, Lucifer doubted that was the case. When he returned home, he needed to make sure he had his medication. This was paramount for continued success. He'd been so preoccupied in preparation to resurrect his craft; he missed the importance of the needed prescription. Lucifer couldn't afford any mistakes when he knew the ultimate masterpiece was yet to come. Goosebumps populated his skin, telling him it was almost time for another conquest.

Chapter 6

The Medical Examiner

Brian Jeffers finished with the files and thought about Sarah. The sound of her voice would be comfort, even though she would be less than thrilled this might be an all-nighter. Sarah was used to this; the late shifts were a part of their lives when he was rookie and even *now*, they weren't able to escape the vicious cycle. He almost felt guilty when he told her this promotion might be more family oriented and for once there would be consistency. Well, so far, that hadn't worked out the way he anticipated. *Here it goes.* He picked up the handset, tapping the *1 key.

" Um…hello."

"Hey, baby. It's been a long day, wanted to let you know I'm sorry I couldn't be with you and the girls."

She was sympathetic. "The girls will get over it, but you owe me a nice, expensive—and I mean *expensive*—dinner at the restaurant of my choosing."

Brian smiled. *That's too easy. No yelling or arguing, just bartering. Do not say the wrong thing now.*

"Okay, I owe you. Is everything ok?

"Not really…but "I'll see you when you get home—" She hung up.

Definitely pissed. Brian continued to pack away the file folders when his cell phone vibrated. *Time for a better shot at an apology*. "Hey, I'm glad you called back.—"

"Detective, this is Alan Sanderson with the Dunlap County Coroner's Office. I was just finishing up the autopsy on the eldest female victim and the DNA is positive. All the deceased are blood related."

Oops… and I fucking knew it. Just like he thought, these were not random strangers in the wrong place at the wrong time. *At least it's official.*

"Thank you, Doc. I'll coordinate with the uniform guys and get the next of kin from this family to identify them."

The medical examiner hesitated. "I also found something quite odd while examining the bodies. There appear to be puncture marks on all three victims. I'm not sure *why* that is, but I'll check the toxicology screen for any drugs that your victims could have in their system."

Puncture marks? Brian didn't want to jump to any conclusions, but this could be the reason all the victims were unclothed without noticeable defense wounds. *Drugged before the slaughter?* This case had become more sinister with each moment.

"Give me a call as soon as you find out, Dr. Sanderson."

Brian remembered an unsolved murder years ago that mentioned usage of paralyzing drug, but he couldn't recall all the particulars. The murder was committed in the Calmine County jurisdiction. It was forty miles south of Valentine, and only two investigators were employed in the sheriff's department. One was his best friend, Toby Wall. He was the lead investigator for the last few years. The two had known each other since attending the state law enforcement academy. They became good friends while there and continued the friendship when they returned to their respective duty locations. If anyone had insight for a case as heinous as this, Toby would be the man to contact. He grabbed a post-it-note and scribbled a few lines.

Brian was at the edge of exhaustion and a few hours of rest would rejuvenate his investigative juices. Tomorrow he would call Toby, and maybe, just maybe, his friend could provide some important details about what type of killer might be on the loose in Brian's backyard.

Chapter 7

Watching and Waiting

Several miles from where Brian Jeffers was doing his research, so was Lucifer. He was perched in a back booth of a downtown bar named, *The Sports Page*. Luckily, he was unnoticed by the luscious model, who stood at the main bar, surrounded by several young men. Tamia Stevens left the hotel hours ago and stopped at her place just long enough for a change of clothes. Lucifer caught her as he pulled out of the alley. Tamia had led him to this meat market; he wasn't impressed with her choice of drinking establishments. She had just consumed her fourth Long Island Iced Tea as the men bought one after the other in the hopes to satisfy their primal urges. He was amused at their tactics. This woman already had all the attention she needed from that Italian slob, August Dellano.

Bitch loves the alcohol. Lucifer sipped his lone drink; it was the traditional whiskey, accompanied with a small portion of citrus soda. A drink he'd enjoyed since the young age of eighteen, this was the only alcohol he would consume because of his required medication.

Tamia ran her hand through the hair of a body-builder bartender. *Likes the muscles.* The goliath appeared to be consumed by her; to give her credit, so was every other man. Lucifer observed the combination of her strong sensuality coupled with her physical appearance and almost had second thoughts. But this dissipated within a few seconds, and he focused on the task at hand. Tamia would die just as planned. Lucifer was not in the business of reprieve, or mercy, for that matter.

The creation of wonderful and unique masterpieces was his singular agenda. Sympathy could not be earned or was ever to be warranted. Tamia was soon joined by another young male with long, unkempt hair. He slid next to her and pushed between several other men. Lucifer heard him raise his voice over everyone else in the crowd. "Tamia, baby, come over here and sit on my lap." The man knocked over one of the other's drinks.

Even from where Lucifer sat, he was able to smell strong, pungent odors of marijuana and booze. *What a combination. Two dependencies to nurse.* He didn't believe this was her type of guy. Maybe he should kill him and rid society of another possible drug-addicted fool. Lucifer figured the disheveled loser would die from whatever disease the two addictions could offer, so he decided not to waste his ability on such a nuisance. Time would be better spent on the preparation of Tamia Steven's final performance. *Concentrate.* The model loved all the attention; soon, she would have his. Tamia was known to the whole bar as the local hottie who got a break, and she made it a point to rub her popularity in these men's faces. Lucifer believed a pretty girl like this knew how to get anything she desired and did. For example, take the rich Italian cheater. He was married, and Tamia didn't shy away from him. This girl wanted to use him for some reason other than his pitiful lovemaking, that Lucifer doubted August Dellano's skill set was even at that level. *What a waste*. It didn't matter. Tamia would die within a few days, and then he would move on to her sugar daddy.

The excitement gave him chills. Lucifer wasn't sure if the alcohol was responsible, but he didn't think so. As he pushed away from the table, a very attractive young redhead forced herself into the seat across from him. She was dressed in a tight red crop-top, which did very little to hide her natural gifts. The skin-tight blue jeans accentuated her well-defined posterior. He snickered. *The smell of her perfume was intoxicating.*

"Hey there," she said with a large smile across her very tan face.

"Hi, yourself." For all his evil and inward hate, Lucifer was an attractive man. He was tall and muscular with long brown hair, soft brown eyes, and a chiseled physique. He knew many women found him irresistible, and most of the time, that worked to his advantage.

"I think you're sexy." She brushed her hair aside so he could see her face.

Nice. "Thank you, and I like your attire, and nice um…smile…as well. What's your name?"

"Krista." She edged closer to him. "What's yours?"

Lucifer was careful not to give a name even close to his own. He could smell her perfume in its full effect. Smiling, he reached over and stroked her long, red hair.

"Call me Patrick." In his head, he was formulating a plan that would involve her painful death and another addition to his collection. He was turned on for the first time in years. He decided she would agree to help him satisfy that forgotten urge, since she approached him.

She smiled and grabbed his hand while he stroked her hair. Krista planted a lingering kiss on the back of his hand. "Well, Mr. Patrick, buy me a drink, and let's talk about what we are going to do later."

She again kissed his hand; Lucifer was aroused.

I'll have to kill her but not tonight. Tension relieving sex will be good, especially with a girl like this. His next sentence provoked her. "Let's skip the formalities, and get the fuck out of here." He winked.

Krista reached across the table and caressed Lucifer's neck and ran her fingers up along his face. "I like your thinking...walk me to my car?"

"We will take mine," Lucifer said. He enjoyed control and would never relinquish this to anyone. Krista shook her head in a provocative manner that told Lucifer she was interested in one thing. Lucifer had seen this look in many women's eyes and knew how to handle her.

* * *

Lucifer and Krista went back to her cozy, one-bedroom apartment on Veridian Avenue and made some unimportant small talk. She gave the killer all the information he would need to add her to his collection. Her name was Krista Meade, and she worked as an advertisement executive with A.P. Lodfig. *How very interesting*, Lucifer thought. *Well, they would be two employees short for work next week.*

Finished with the menial dump of informational bullshit, Lucifer's appetite for sex was soon satisfied. He could tell Krista enjoyed his skill in the bedroom; this pleased him to no end. After they finished, the buxom redhead fell asleep in his arms. He continued to study her throughout the hours of darkness. He didn't dare kill her now, at least not in her own apartment. This was *not* his style. He would choose the perfect place for the cherished event.

Lucifer didn't take the creation of masterpieces without deep thought, except for the unexpected man and child that were in the park that lucky night. He knew it was better to study and plan for his prey, and he would with this redheaded slut as well. She would be kept around until he felt the time was right to end her existence. He thought of Tamia Stevens and how soon her life was going to end. So far, this week had turned out better than he had anticipated. *I will steal her last breath, making her a part of my collection forever.* The combination of sex and a well-planned murder made Lucifer feel fulfilled, indeed.

Chapter 8

A Friend's Help

Brian Jeffers didn't get much sleep and left the house before Sarah and the girls awoke for Sunday morning church. Earlier, he had e-mailed his long-time friend, Toby Wall, and within a few minutes Toby inquired about the demographics of the case and the possible usage of an unknown drug. Toby summoned him to his residence for some one-on-one intelligence sharing. The drive wasn't too long, and besides, Brian could listen to his favorite satellite radio channel without the girls requesting a change of music every two minutes.

The two agreed to meet at Toby's house in rural Sacred Bay. The town was just outside the county limits of Dunlap. It was a one-traffic-light sized jurisdiction with little crime, except for the occasional unleashed canine. Brian used to tease his best friend about being a lone ranger in a town of country folk. Toby loved living in the country; he always told Brian he felt it was better for concentrating. Brian himself wouldn't be caught dead living in a small community. He thought modern day society couldn't operate without a twenty-four-hour gas station and the essential all-night conglomerate discount store.

When the two were training at the academy, he would rib Toby about becoming the only law enforcement officer in the state with a John Deere tractor and a pasture full of cows. Brian hadn't talked to his friend in a few months and felt a little guilty about not staying in touch. Toby never let small things like that bother him, but there could always be a first time, and Brian was prepared with an apology.

He was turning onto the interstate when he received a phone call on his ever-reliable two-way. He rolled his eyes. "Yes, Bossman."

"Where are you at?" Barnum sounded like urgency was on the agenda.

In most cases, Brian didn't tell Barnum his daily itinerary, but this weekend was definitely not the usual. "I'm following the yellow brick road. What have you got?"

"I have the next of kin for Justin Paul flying in from Sacramento at three o'clock this afternoon. You *need* to be here for that face to face."

That was quick, Brian thought. He hadn't even been informed who the next of kin was; much less that he was having a meeting with them. This made him upset with Barnum, but he decided not to mention it right now.

"I'll be out of town in Calmine County, checking with an investigator. There was an unsolved murder case there a few years ago, and a paralytic drug may have been used on the victim before he was murdered."

"Okay, you think the murder there and the one we're investigating may be connected. I get it, but why? Get a tip or something *you* didn't share with me?"

Doesn't listen well. "Dr. Sanderson called me late last night and informed me that all of our victims had puncture marks located in the same spot. It appears the killer injected them with something, perhaps before he committed the despicable acts."

Barnum paused for a long moment. "Okay, it sounds like you may have hit on something, but get your ass back from *wherever* you are by three p.m. You understand, amigo?"

Brian didn't want to argue, but added a little sarcasm to the reply. "Yes, sir. I should have all the cotton picked and ready to place at the master's feet by that time."

"Just shut up and be here."

Brian enjoyed being a pain in Barnum's ass. It was just easier than conforming to standards which were fucked up... at least for "normal" law enforcement protocols. Besides, he didn't like him anyway and was counting the days until the man retired, so he could run the investigation division like it was *supposed* to be.

Brian turned off of Highway 92 onto an unnamed gravel road. Beyond a doubt, he was in the middle of nowhere. He was glad he had his firearm with him. *You can never be too careful.* Several miles later, along with a few near-misses with deer, he spotted the outline of his friend's house. *It looks like something from an oil painting set in the 1800s.*

Pulling into the long driveway, he gazed in amazement. *Wow!* Most would have considered it more like a mansion than anything else. It was a large, three-story Victorian-style residence with a cluster of mythological sculptures that decorated both, the front and back. Attached to the rear of the home, was a four-car garage. Toby never owned more than one vehicle and that made Brian laugh. If Brian didn't know his best friend lived here, he would think someone with very high stature in the community would own such an expensive piece of real estate. The investigator had inherited this wonderful property from his grandfather and had done a masterful job to keep it in the pristine condition of his predecessor.

Brian rang the bell. The echo of cathedral chimes greeted him. He smiled as the door opened; his friend cocked his head, sporting a wide-eyed grin. Toby was a former high school teacher and didn't fit the law enforcement prototype. He was lanky with a medium build and short, cropped hair. Toby also wore the *most* unattractive dark-rimmed glasses available for purchase. If the word "geek" had a picture next to it in the dictionary, *he* would be the visual representation. Today, he was wearing a football jersey and black sweatpants.

"Good morning, sunshine."

"Hey, dude, good to see ya." Toby always talked like he was a surfing pro out of Huntington Beach.

"Good to see you, too. Wish it was under better circumstances." He paused. "Hey, sorry I haven't spoken to you in a while." Brian blurted out the apology.

"Well, shit happens. We all get busy. No more with that crap." He playfully punched Brian in the chest. "Come in, and we'll look at what you got. Maybe we can see if there's something that will hook us up with the answer, my brother."

Brian followed his friend and stared at the beautiful paintings throughout the large corridor which led to Toby's den. His friend had spent a small fortune in keeping the interior of the residence as breathtaking as the exterior. The house was full of expensive leather furniture, and many designer paintings lined the walls. The dining room was home to a large, oak banquet table that would seat at least eight people. Brian gawked in envy. He hadn't been here in a while, but he enjoyed the ambience of this house.

Toby escorted his friend through an adjacent corridor until the two faced a set of mahogany double doors. He pushed on the handle. "Welcome to my sanctuary of solitude."

The den was double the size of most, and it was filled with enormous bookshelves that appeared to be the refuge for thousands of hardcover books. *The rows seem to go forever*. Brian raised his eyebrows in amazement. In the center of the room was a state-of-the-art metallic desk with a sixty-five inch flat-screen monitor set into the metal frame. A compact tower component was neatly stacked on the right side accompanied by a set of two stereo surround-sound speakers. The king-sized leather chair that overshadowed the desk was almost comical. Toby noticed his buddy staring at the chair and laughed. "Yeah, I see you're a speechless dude. I know it's humongous, but man, it's cool beans. You haven't been here forever, and I decided to upgrade everything."

"Wow, you really have decked it out since the last time I was here," Brian said with a bit of jealousy in his voice.

"Yeah, I spent some of my money on things I needed to be a real cop, versus the brand new Lexus I wanted." He laughed.

"You seem to have everything you need to be the next CEO of a corporation. By the way, if you are offering, *I* could use a new Lexus." Brian poked him in the ribs. A hint of jealousness escaped the investigator.

"Ha! I don't think my future is with corporate America, and the answer about the Lexus is… no way, dude. My ex-wife gets enough of my payroll. I don't need to be contributing to the detective-with-a-minivan fund."

Brian shrugged in defeat. "Worth a try?"

Toby's divorce, which happened shortly after Brian had been shot was almost another chronicle in a Lifetime channel original. Michelle was his ex-wife. They *never* quite fit. She was a lab assistant in the local county hospital; she didn't like the law enforcement type. This had been very apparent to Brian from this first day he met her. Michelle told Toby that she *hoped* he would get killed in the line of duty, giving her the estate without a divorce. The final straw came a few days after Brian was hospitalized. Toby came home after visiting him to find Michelle and all her personal items gone, and on the kitchen table was the "Dear Toby" letter. It was quite heartless, saying she was leaving because she didn't want to live with a man she didn't truly love, and Brian the super cop deserved what he got. Toby was very upset by the break-up and was forced to seek help from a therapist to get him back on track. Months later, he had arisen from the land of the walking dead and returned to the crime fighter mentality. Toby snapped his fingers, which awakened Brian to this reality. "Dude, let's cross reference these cases and show you what kind of drug you might be looking for. You never know…it might be a common denominator for both of our cases. Let me grab the file."

Toby sat down behind the desk and opened up the file cabinet and pulled out a colossal, dust-covered brown folder and placed it in front of him. Toby ushered Brian to pull up one of the small chairs sitting next to a coffee table by the picture window. As he slid in beside his friend, Toby opened the folder. Brian was more than eager to see if the drug used could be the same. Uneasiness stole over him as his friend narrowed his eyes and spoke in a whisper. "Seeing what's in *here* is fucked up beyond words, partner. Are you ready?"

Chapter 9

A Devious Plot

The sun was bright on this windy Sunday morning as Lucifer jogged through the Valentine City Park. There were few people on the trail, which was optimal. He needed the privacy to think, so he could concentrate on his next target. For several years, he had conducted himself this way. Jogging was a necessary evil for two reasons. First, it helped him clear his head and prepare for creating more brilliant masterpieces. Second, it kept him in a high state of physical conditioning. Lucifer needed to remain stronger than all of the prey he would add to his collection. He stepped up his pace as he exited the trail and entered city streets.

Several police patrol cars drove by; one officer even waved at the killer while he was stopped at a traffic device. This made him chuckle. He continued his run until he made a complete circle around the park. He glanced down at his watch. *Pretty good time*. Lucifer slowed his pace as he watched several children playing on the sand-filled playground.

These kids have no idea a killer like me is only a few feet from them...their biggest concern is what flavor of ice cream they are going to buy today. He laughed out loud and finished the last of the three-mile run. With a final glimpse at the stopwatch, he cursed the display. "Twenty-two minutes and thirteen seconds!" Lucifer was over his regular time by four minutes. He averaged completion of the course in eighteen or less. *Tomorrow, I will work harder*. He thought about the girl he had sex with the night before. *She was an excellent lay. I may keep her around for a few more sessions.* Lucifer swallowed; his throat was very dry, so he decided to quench his thirst.

The green water fountain was on a cement slab in the center of the playground. When he was about twenty feet away, his interest was piqued, as three young girls were taking their respective turns partaking in the cool water from the spout. He watched; his eyes fixed on the oldest one who helped the other two up to the fountain and then took a drink herself.

"Alyssa, I think you've had enough water. It's my turn now," bellowed the annoyed Melissa.

"No, I'm thirsty, and it's getting hot. I need more water," Alyssa said.

Victoria started in as well. "I want water, too." She was the youngest of the three but was also the most demanding.

"Sissy wants water, too, Alyssa." Melissa tried to stand up for the smallest of the three.

"No! I was here first."

"Okay, hurry up, so everyone can get some." Melissa crossed her arms.

"Girls, let's have this picnic. Don't make a mess over there. I have plenty of soda for you!" Sarah Jeffers yelled. She had been watching the three sisters argue from a small picnic area within earshot of the children. All three responded in unison.

Melissa called out. "Give me a second, Mom; I have to get the sand out of my shoes."

Lucifer took his time and had taken interest in the mother of the innocent youngsters. She was very appealing. She had mid-shoulder length blonde hair, and for a woman who had given birth at least three times, she possessed a very shapely body, and long, athletic legs.

"Hmm, very nice, very nice." He mouthed this out loud, in hopes none of the young children had heard him. Lucifer alternated looking down at his stopwatch and quick glances at the mother. Although he wasn't sure why his woman looked familiar, he recognized her from somewhere. Approaching the fountain, he watched as the other two girls left their sister behind. They ran at full speed in the direction of the picnic area. Lucifer stopped where the oldest Jeffers child was dumping sand from her shoes onto the grass. She shook the remaining particles off her white summer shorts and stood up. Melissa Jeffers tried to turn the knob on the fountain by pushing at it with her right leg, while at the same time trying to put her sand-encrusted hands under the spout. Lucifer laughed to himself as he spoke in a sly voice. "Hi. Do you need some help?"

Melissa was a true extrovert and too naïve to understand when it was appropriate to engage strangers. She knew her dad didn't like her approaching everybody, but she didn't care and decided to take the man's help. She smiled. "Thank you."

Lucifer turned the knob on the faucet. Melissa placed both her hands under the spout, cleaning them as he kept a tight grip. The killer split his concentration between Melissa and the three others at the picnic table; his mind raced with evil thoughts. Melissa shook the leftover droplets off her hands.

"What is your name, mister?"

Lucifer didn't expect the girl to ask him any questions, especially his name, but figured the one he utilized to manipulate Krista Meade would suffice. "You're welcome, young lady. I'm Patrick. May I ask what yours is?"

Melissa didn't hesitate to answer the question; a deep grin sprawled throughout her freckled face. She extended her scrawny hand. "Melissa Katelyn Jeffers. I'm glad you were nice and helped me clean my yucky hands."

This girl is too innocent for her own good. He didn't say anything else but sort of waved to her as she ran back to join her other family members. Lucifer walked the opposite direction and cut through the trees to the graveled parking lot adjacent to the park. He scanned the newly paved lot and noticed two vehicles were still in the spacious area. It was quiet, and the regular traffic of park visitors didn't show up until much later. *Easy peasy.*

Lucifer laid his eyes on a four-door white Ford Taurus. He peeked inside and couldn't see the required child restraint devices needed for the two children *No good*! He sneered, and approached the other conveyance; a black minivan. On the rear window, was a police sticker for the local police association. Lucifer scanned over each shoulder, ensuring his presence hadn't been discovered. He used caution as he pretended to stretch out and took a peek inside the van. *Wonderful.* Two pink car seats, small toys, and fast food wrappers told him this was his jackpot. Smiling the familiar grin he used when he planned something most people would consider horrendous and unconscionable, Lucifer recorded the minivan's plate in his mind—743 EFG—and repeated it several times out loud, as well.

Tomorrow, he would check on the registration plate at the local Department of Transportation office. It was *time to create a recipe for death. Time…indeed.*

Chapter 10

Propaganician

Detective Brian Jeffers and Toby Wall stared at the case files sprawled atop the desk. Toby viewed Brian's current group of homicides while Brian studied the file from the murder years earlier. He flipped to the investigator's notes stapled inside the rear page of the file. *Not everything is listed.* A quizzical look filled his face. "What's missing?" Brian tapped the file.

Toby motioned for the folder, a look of uncertainty overtook one normally full of confidence.

"Mr. Dead Guy in the photos is former used car dealership owner, Ross Bosworth. He made plenty of people upset with the pieces of shit cars he sold. I would be surprised to see who *didn't* want to jack his ass."

Brian stared at the pictures. He read the notes on the scene but wasn't convinced they told the whole story. "What were the other circumstances regarding his death… and *you* know, what I mean." Brian's eyes fixated on his friend.

Toby leaned back and smirked. "Well, this dude was walking out to his vehicle, and someone snatched him before he made it to the parking lot. We didn't find the body for like three days. When we did, he was naked, and his stomach entrails were being chewed on by the local wildlife. Hands were tied behind his back, and he's gutted like someone was trying to show off their hunting prowess. Guess what the craziest thing about this was?"

Brian recalled the horrific crime scene from yesterday and was slow to respond. "Being gutted is fucking crazy in itself."

Toby raised his eyebrows. "This guy's heart was missing out of his freaking chest, dude. I mean like… poof the fuck gone. The psycho responsible was very skilled, and I thought for weeks after that it might be some pissed-off doctor who bought a lemon from Bosworth."

Brian reviewed the file, but didn't see in the notes anything about collecting witness statements from Bosworth's clients.

"Was there anyone on the sold vehicle inventory roster that even showed up as suspicious?" Brian dug for more information.

"You know this area. Most of Bosworth's clients consisted of poor farmers and local manufacturing workers trying to get by. A lot of them needed a vehicle but didn't have the major credit to secure a cherry. I would say after spending time investigating this…the person responsible for carving him up wasn't these country folk. Till this day, I always thought it was some type of medical specialist. I still think it is!" Toby almost jumped from his seat.

Brian agreed with his friend, knowing the unsolved murder of this loser used car dealership owner was more than likely planned. The killer didn't seem like some avenger on a crusade for the people Bosworth allegedly scammed.

"Makes some sense." Brian leaned over the file. "Tell me about this drug you e-mailed me on this morning. Do you think this killer may have a connection to both of our investigations?" Brian didn't like how that sounded, even as it came spilling from his mouth. He wanted no part of a serial murderer, especially after seeing what this Lucifer son-of-a bitch had done less than forty-eight hours ago.

Toby rubbed his chin. "Here's the deal. If you look at crime scene photo attachment J, you'll see a large puncture wound underneath the right armpit. The toxicology screen on this came up weird, and the coroner said this guy was paralyzed from the drug. Bosworth probably couldn't move while he was being murdered. From what you told me, it sounds like the puncture marks are in the same place as on good ole' Bosworth. I can't believe this is a coincidence."

Brian's eyes narrowed. "I don't believe in coincidences."

Toby removed his glasses. "By the way, I have the drug's name listed on the back forensic sheet."

Brian flipped over to the last page of the file; on the left-hand side was the forensic report from the Calmine County Coroner's office. He had never heard of this medication and doubted if he could even pronounce it.

"What the hell is *this*?"

"Propaganician," Toby said.

"*Propaganician?*" Brian figured medical professionals would be the only ones to have a need to know what it was. *Until now,* he thought.

"Yes, very good, Daniel san," joked Toby in his best Mr. Miaggi voice. "Apparently, this kind of drug stops breathing within a few minutes of being administered. Before that happens, it first paralyzes the individual. They're still very much alive at this point. If they weren't hospitalized, the individual would die right after because the supply of oxygen is cut off from the brain."

"Nasty stuff," Brian critiqued.

"The way I understand it is the paralytic is only used

when a nurse or doctor places a patient on a respirator. This usage is for someone the medical staff would label as condition critical."

"So, pretty hard to get a hold of?" Brian asked, trying to pose a question more than a statement of fact.

"Anyone working in a hospital on a medical unit could get their hands on it, buddy. When I investigated this before, I checked for any reports of missing meds from local, county, or metro hospitals. I came up with a big zippo. Not one agency in this state reported a shortage."

"So whoever committed your murder and the ones I'm investigating may have a medical background and a stash of drugs that can paralyze a person within a few minutes?"

"Not your everyday case, is it?"

"That really doesn't make me feel any better." Brian sighed.

"Yep, and the killer is a very capable son-of-a-bitch, who knew how to remove the major organ from Bosworth without any difficulty. I can tell you the other injuries on Bosworth were not consistent with that level of expertise."

Brian rubbed his brow. "If our toxicology screen comes back with this paralytic drug, we might have ourselves a serial killer."

Toby cringed before answering. "Appears to be the case. First time for everything…and thank God for that. Maybe since this Lucifer didn't engrave his initials on Bosworth, he may have changed his style and method. I also think Bosworth might have been a starting point for this loon. If a serial killer did commit both of our murders, you're in for more victims."

Terrible news, indeed. "I just can't believe that with all the technology in modern day forensics, we don't have any physical evidence." Brian shook his head in denial, but it seemed to be accurate. He scoured the crime scene for a long time yesterday and was still amazed not even one fingerprint was left on any of the victims.

Toby ran his hand over the glossy photos." What scares me even more is this person understands how to cover his tracks."

" I pray we are wrong about more bodies, partner. Dead wrong."

After several hours and a twelve pack of imported beer, Toby and Brian completed the crime scene comparison. The two five-star investigators understood if the killer was the same, the metro area of Valentine may have more to fear than local gang bangers and drug dealers residing within their jurisdiction. Unless the forensic team was successful in identifying a suspect through the collection of evidence, it would just be a matter of time before the killer would strike again.

Chapter 11

Parallel Findings

Brian left the estate and headed back to Valentine, convinced a killer was living in his city. *This was fucking real.* Whoever Lucifer was, he was certain the man was after his next prey, lying in wait for the perfect time to strike. *Not a damn clue, anywhere.* The one useful piece of evidence was the killer's inscription. *Some clue*!

As he hit the edge of the city limits, his phone vibrated. Staring at the number, he realized it originated from county offices.

"Jeffers." He shook his head, hoping the caller was unable to ascertain he was under the influence.

"Detective, this is Alan Sanderson from the coroner's office."

Please be good news. "Since you're calling me, I can presume you have the toxicology screen back from our victims." *Sounded like I'm sober.*

The sound of shuffling papers filled the speaker. "Indeed I do, Detective. All of the puncture wounds I told you about earlier were consistent with all of the deceased."

Brian held his breath, despite what he already thought the outcome would be. *Fuck*!

"The wounds were all located under the right arm, midway down. Puncture marks were consistent with ones you would find in hypodermic needles. It also appears...all were made by separate needles—"

"The killer spent time using different needles on each victim? Why the hell would he do that?" Using individual needles would be pointless; it made no logical sense if the killer planned to kill them all anyway.

"That remains to be seen. I don't think any qualified person could even hint as to why your killer would waste the time. What is very interesting, is what I found in the lab results a few hours ago." Dr. Sanderson shuffled through more papers. "There was a large amount of the chemical compound found in all three victims. After testing the composition, the identification was proven conclusive to be Propaganician."

There was no escaping the truth. Ross Bosworth was the key. The paralytic drug was being used in Valentine. This was a nightmarish reality. The killer struck a few years ago with this same method of incapacitating his victim, and now, he was using it again. Brian spoke with calm and concern. "Doc, I need you to send me everything you have on this drug and how anyone would have access to or need access to it." Brian didn't share the information he and Toby had discussed. This way, a medical professional could give him insight he wouldn't have.

Dr. Sanderson continued his explanation. "Usually, this type of medicine would be obtained by the purchasing and order offices from medical facilities, and this would mean about eighty hospital and satellite clinics within two hundred miles of Dunlap County may have access to it."

Brian let the information sink in. *That was a lot of ground to cover, but if one person reported a loss, it could lead to something."* Okay, I think I know where to go from here. I'll contact the various hospitals, veterinary clinics, and pharmaceutical organizations. I'd think some accountability for this type of drug would almost be criminal not to require. I do have one burning question that has been bothering me since finding out about these puncture marks on the deceased."

"Yes?" The eager-to-please county coroner inquired.

"With your knowledge of how this killer utilized this medicine, do *you* think we might be looking for a physician gone awry?" *Gotta pin him down.*

"Son." His voice changed from informative to one expressing concern. "I believe we are dealing with someone possessing extensive knowledge of the human body. This person would also have completed some medical training in the usage of drug distribution."

"That doesn't sound very promising," Brian said.

"You could be looking for anyone that uses even a small amount of medical-based training in connection with these murders. The proverbial needle-in-a haystack analogy. I'm sorry for painting such a bleak picture."

It was an honest answer, and Brian respected it. "Thank you for your assistance, Doc. I appreciate everything you've done in the last couple of days." He left the fax number and point of contact information for his office and ended the conversation.

The digital display of the in-dash radio indicated it was almost time to meet the next of kin of Justin Paul. At least Dr. Sanderson had given him a direction to concentrate on; unfortunately, it wouldn't bring the Paul family back. He reached into the console and tossed a few breath mints into his mouth. A few turns later, he was outside the police department. Brain stared up at the sky in search of answers…hopeful but not certain more clarity would be visible after meeting with Mr. Paul. As he stepped onto the concrete pad, Brian felt sobriety flow back into his veins. *Thank God for small favors…*

Chapter 12

A Relative Mourns

As Brian Jeffers entered the foyer, he noticed the section had just a few law enforcement personnel present. The departmental offices had a different feel to them on the weekend. It lacked uniformed patrol officers booking suspects; the staple of local citizens complaining about their neighbor's unleashed animals were nonexistent and the sweet treats which made a daily presence in the breakroom appeared to be replaced by the scent of cleaning solvent. Brian stopped at the darkened corridor that led to his supervisor's office. The larger-than-life monstrosity was a direct reflection of the man. The oak door with three-layer tempered glass was a façade on the skill set of the man who sat within its confines.

Commander: A.H. BARNUM.

Brian laughed a little at the bold lettering. A.H. Barnum. *Asshole Barnum. This was a perfect way to describe the investigative authority.* Barnum was indeed skilled at the required administrative duties, but when it came to the interaction with human entities, not so much. *Well, maybe today he would personable.* Brian knocked on the door, waiting for the approval to enter the office. He looked own at his watch. *I'm even early.*

Barnum responded to the knock without too much hesitation. "Come in."

The interior of the office was much like his, except for the black leather couch sitting in the corner of the office. It was now occupied by a slim, pasty white man with thinning hair. Brian would have guessed he was much older than Justin Paul. He was outfitted in a dark blue pinstripe suit, way too large for him. Brian greeted the visitor with a warm smile. He was about to introduce himself when Barnum waved him off.

"Mr. Paul, this is Detective Brian Jeffers. He's handling the murder investigation at this time." Barnum said it in a way that would make someone think there were an endless amount of investigators ready to take the helm, in case Brian's tenure on this case was in question.

Mr. Paul's teeth were clenched; his face was red. He shook Brian's hand with a fierce, powerful grip. "I *want* the bastard that did this to my brother." Paul's accent sounded like he was from the east coast.

"We'll get him so he doesn't hurt anyone else." Brian spoke with confidence. It may have sounded cliché, but it was the honest truth.

Barnum cleared his throat. "Mr. Paul, we are vigilantly looking throughout the area for the suspect and have searched your brother's residence for any type of evidence that may help us identify the individual. I think Detective Jeffers has a few questions for you."

Nice speech. Brian pulled out a notebook, referring to his list of notes; hopefully, the answers would provide some insight. "Mr. Paul, when was the last time you spoke with your brother or his wife?"

Paul's eyebrows rose as he thought. He spoke in a much more subdued tone. "Last week. Just all small talk, though. Nothing too dramatic, just what the family has been doing…that type of thing."

Brian cringed as he asked the infamous, Murder 101 question that always appeared outdated and overused. "Did your brother or his wife have any enemies you know of that would wish the family harm?"

Paul's response was quick and to the point. "No, my brother was sort of like the life of the party. People enjoyed being around him. I can't think of anybody that would want to hurt him."

Brian was aware most people had at *least* one enemy and didn't think Justin Paul was the exception to the rule. He shook off the answer and proceeded. "Are there any relatives on your brother's wife's side needing to be contacted who we don't know about?" Brian tried to ask the question with empathy.

As soon as the question was asked, Paul's demeanor became very saddened. His eyes lowered to the floor, and he sobbed. The thin man was having a difficult time trying to respond. "Tammy didn't have any living family. She was an orphan. She kept in contact with her foster parents, but they passed away a few months ago."

"Do you know why they would've been in the park that evening?" Brian asked.

"No, I don't, Detective. I know Tammy had been trying to sell her artwork. After her foster parents died, my brother said she was working hard on some new paintings."

"Did she have regular employment, or was it strictly art?" Brian's pen was poised above a yellow pad.

"No. Tammy had been focusing the last few months mainly on the art, at least, according to my brother—"

Barnum disrupted Mr. Paul's answer. "There was an art show in the park the night your brother and his family were killed. Do you know if that's why maybe your brother was in the area with their daughter?" Barnum leaned so far back in the leather chair, the man almost toppled over.

What the hell? Brian perked up in his chair when

he heard this. Barnum didn't bother to share this information; no mention of the event was given by any of the uniformed officers, either. Brian glared into his supervisor's eyes, as Barnum looked away.

Paul's hands shook, as he struggled to wipe the dampness out of his eyes. He tried to answer the question. "My brother said Tammy was a very good artist, more than likely she had a few pieces of work at the show."

Brian did his best to piece together, what might have happened. He envisioned Tammy was at one of the booths where the artists often set up their paintings, sculptures, or anything else buyers would consider art. The killer was in attendance at the show, watching his future victim. There was a distinct possibility; the two other family members were there to support her. Originally, the killer keyed in on just his main target, and the other two were just in the wrong place at the wrong time. From the file on Bosworth in Calmine County, the killer *only* struck once there and moved on. Maybe when Lucifer saw the other two family members, it may have caught him off guard, giving him no choice but to kill all three. *No witnesses.* Barnum interrupted Brian's thought process and stated the obvious. The supervisor showed no emotion while delivering the message. "Mr. Paul, you're going to need to identify the remains of the family if you can. There are several personal effects that are in the back evidence room as well."

Brian was upset Barnum had circumvented him again when it came to procedure; he would address this issue later.

"Yes."

Brian watched as the determined supervisor retreated to the evidence room to retrieve all personal property of the victims for their family member. He offered Paul a glass of water, but the man waved off Barnum. Paul sat with his eyes closed in the chair, trying to remain as calm as he could. Brian remained quiet and let Paul come to terms with what happened to his loved ones.

Barnum returned with a large eight-by-twelve yellow envelope with a red identification seal. He turned over the envelope and signed his name in the block and released the property to Paul.

"Sign on line A for me, please." He handed him a ballpoint pen.

Paul gently opened the sealed envelope, trying not to damage any potential valuables, sentimental or monetary. Once it was unsecured, he reached in and pulled out the contents one by one. Making a quick mental inventory, his face reddened as a look of disbelief spread across it. He rummaged again and again through the contents.

Something's not right. There was a puzzled look on Paul's face, and Brian could sense the man was about to have a meltdown.

"It's not here! It's not here!" Paul slammed the envelope on the table, which, caused several of the items to drop off and land on the floor.

"What's the problem, Marcus?" Brian tried to console him.

"The expensive lighter I bought Justin for his birthday last year. It isn't here." Again, Paul sobbed.

Barnum did his usual departmental procedure response. "Mr. Paul, these were the only items on your family, nothing else—"

He slammed his hand on the desk. "The lighter I bought Justin last year…he always carried it with him.

Always."

Brian remembered the cigarettes found at the crime scene. *It was sort of odd that anyone would carry cigarettes without even a book of matches to light them with.*

"Marcus, what did the lighter look like? Maybe he left it at home by accident that night."

"He would never leave it at home. He promised to keep the lighter with him all the time." Paul continued. "It was a silver Zippo with the initials *J.P.* engraved on the exterior of the case."

Brian jotted down a few notes. *Maybe the item was indeed left at the deceased Paul's residence*. He would have to talk to the uniformed officers responsible for the post-death investigation inventory at the house and see if the lighter was there. "Mr. Paul, why do you believe he would have it with him?"

"I gave it to him last year…a few days before our mother passed away. It represented sort of our long-distance bond. Justin swore to me… it would *never* leave his sight."

Brian and Barnum exchanged looks; neither wanted to downplay the importance of the lighter. The promise his brother had made him, though, seemed a little *too* dramatic for Brian.

"Marcus, you said your brother always carried it with him. How do you know that? Brian tilted his head.

"I'm telling *you*, if it wasn't with him, someone stole it off his dead body. It was probably the son-of-a-bitch responsible for this. He made a promise…and he *never* disappointed mom or me."

Brian Jeffers couldn't deny the fact the contents found in Justin Paul's pockets lacked something. This might mean the killer would have the property, if it were indeed on Justin Paul at the time of the murder. Brian understood a little more about what kind of monster he was up against, as cold chills again swept throughout his body.

Chapter 13

The Necessary Purchase

Lucifer had been a shadow of his prey since his morning run. He parked his car on the opposite side of her street, waiting in anticipation for the succulent model to leave her house. He almost gave up until he saw the security gate lift up and the black sports utility leave the driveway. He was careful not to be noticed and kept the car a comfortable distance, so she wouldn't become suspicious. Her first errand was the video store, where she was inside for just a few minutes, dropping off several movies. The next stop was the mini-mall swimwear shop. Lucifer looked up at the pink sign and smirked. *Pleasurable Adventures. Sounds more like an adult hideaway than a swimwear shop.* Tamia was there for about an hour and left the store with a handful of small bags. She drove to another strip-mall in the downtown area and parked her sport's utility in the crowded lot.

He positioned his car close enough to see what the model wore on her defined neckline. She showed off a brilliant gold necklace with a single pearl attached to the chain. He figured her part-time lover; August Dellano had bought his mistress the expensive bobble. Lucifer was very excited; by tomorrow evening, she would be added to his collection of masterpieces. He loved the fine piece of jewelry. *It would be a nice piece to add to my growing collection.* This was perfect. His wait to resume his murderous hobby had taken a toll on his patience, but soon, he would strike at will and whenever the moment seized him. He hoped to be gone from Valentine in less than a week, leaving only human carnage in his wake.

The killer decided he wouldn't use the drug of his desire this time. He liked to change it up a little bit; besides, he didn't want it to be easy for the stumbling law enforcement community to track him. It's not like Lucifer believed they could catch him anyway, unless he made a critical mistake, which never happened. *That* was the beauty of it. He stared at the model as she paid for her purchases. I*t would be more pleasurable to have this victim fight for her survival and then be taken to the depths of hell by my hand*.

He felt exhilarated to watch Tamia walk across the crowded lot. Several pimple-faced teenagers riding skateboards ogled the beauty as she entered the tanning salon. *Young perverts*!

"Fake bake bitch." Lucifer laughed. That was exquisite and unfortunate, since it was sure to be a closed casket. Leaving his vehicle, he tried to blend in with the people scattered throughout the various stores. He eyed several young women, taking note of several potential targets. Lucifer's eyes lit up when he noticed a sporting goods store in close proximity to the salon. *Could have some tools of my trade*? Inside, several sales people rushed through the isles in response to the onslaught of weekend customers. *Just what the doctor ordered*.

He would be just another customer in the group of many, in search of a item, unimportant to the average person. Pushing through the aisles, he searched for something that attracted him. When he turned around, the gleam from a knife caught his attention. *It's calling out to me*. He stopped in front of the glass counter which housed the wonderful weapon.

Behind the see-through barrier sat many tactical

knives; Lucifer focused his attention. *That is it*. A teen-age sales clerk studied his customer, as the man stared through the glass, like he was in a drug-induced state.

"Hello, sir. May I help you find something?"

Lucifer looked up at the young man. *Just out of high school*. The clerk was ordinary but what stood out, was the bright green polo shirt with the store's stitched-on logo and a black nametag imprinted with white letters. The nameplate appeared to be crooked. *Brett.*

"Hello, Brett. I see you have several fine tactical knives on display. I have one in mind, but since this is your counter, you might have a better idea for me."

Brett eyes lit up. "Sir, we have the best line of knives money can buy. Can I ask what type you are looking for?"

Lucifer laughed. *Trying to pitch his product.* "Some-thing that would be good for camping in the woods but could also be used like an all-purpose knife." He placed his hands onto the glass case and peered through. The killer knew which knife to select, but he was going to see if the young clerk knew his trade as well as the store thought he did.

"I have just the thing." The clerk reached through the back of the glass counter and grabbed the large knife, which had enticed Lucifer. He was most impressed with the young man's taste for fine weapons. *Maybe a future prodigy*? Lucifer snickered as the clerk picked up *his* knife and handed it to him for approval. He nodded at the boy, well aware of the value for the piece of crafted steel. He tested the young man.

"How much is it, Brett?"

The clerk shifted his right eyebrow and spoke in a hushed manner. "Sir, the price listed on this Germanian blade is about seventy-five dollars, but this one was a rollback item, so the price is only fifty bucks."

Bravo. Lucifer liked this kid; the price was fair for this particular knife. The worth was greater than this simple clerk could ever imagine. Lucifer had used a few Germanian blades before; this appeared to be of the same quality. He reached in his pocket and pulled out three twenties, then handed them to him for payment. He wanted to reward the boy for a job well done.

"Keep the change."

Brett waved a hand at the offered tip. "I *can't* keep it. I'm paid hourly, and my supervisor would fire me for taking it. I *so* need this job to pay for my car." The worried clerk peeked up at the two-way mirror and realized his behavior was always being monitored.

Lucifer rubbed his chin. *This young man has much to learn about the real world.* He leaned over the display. "Well, I won't tell anyone, if you won't, okay?"

The clerk reached down under the counter and brought out a brown leather case. The proud salesman placed the new purchase in the case and handed it to his customer. "Thank you for your business, sir. I hope the knife works out well for you." The clerk grinned while he pocketed the leftover change.

He was very pleased, Brett decided to revisit the whole moral issue and accepted his token of appreciation. "You're welcome. I may come back and see you in the future for more of your expertise." The killer walked towards the entrance. Lucifer never would come back here. It was almost certain capture if one got too comfortable and ventured into the same water twice. This was how he conducted business.

Lucifer would spend valuable time with his new

blade, satisfied when the steel was at its finest and ready for its debut performance. Soon, it would be time to conduct some business. The newly-purchased weapon would be used to end the life of Tamia Stevens. He reached into his front right pocket and felt the worn edge of the fifty-cent piece. He took it out and ran it through his right thumb and forefinger. Lucifer anticipated the night and how soon he would add to his collection.

Chapter 14

Kendra & Maggie

Brian Jeffers drove Marcus Paul and Barnum to the Dunlap County Coroner's Office. There, Paul identified the remains of his brother and his family. Brian felt a deep sympathy as Marcus Paul broke down in the morgue. The investigator offered to drive Paul to the residence of his late brother, but he declined, preferring to stay in a local motel. Before Barnum drove Marcus to a quaint motel on the edge of town, he suggested Brian go home and spend some much-needed quality time with his family.

Brian couldn't argue with his boss. He dropped off paperwork at the police department and was halfway home, when he remembered there were still two witnesses to contact, and there was no time like the present. The investigator had stuffed the paper that contained the necessary information in the glove box and expected to follow up before now. Removing the crumpled paper, Brian glanced at the two names. *Kendra Ball and Maggie Earnst.*

The address listed was 610 Grande Avenue. *Not far away from the park at all.* Several minutes later, he was in front of the residence. It was an old-fashioned stucco home with a brown wooden fence that surrounded the property. Two stylish sport cars were parked in the driveway. *Someone has cash.* He tapped on the door. It was answered by a mid- twenties plain, young, dark-haired woman.

"Hello, I'm Homicide Detective Brian Jeffers with

the Valentine Police Department. I need to speak with Kendra and Maggie." Brian flashed his badge and credentials.

The woman squinted at the shiny metal. "I'm Kendra and Maggie is inside. Come in, Detective."

The interior was quite trendy. The living room area had a three-cushion couch; in each corner, beanbag chairs with pink and black designs voiced out the pair of roommates' flair for the unusual. There were several small clay designs of nude women in various poses sitting on three styles of glass pedestals. It also appeared to be absent any television or entertainment systems. *Not the norm.*

He followed Kendra Ball as she escorted him to the couch and motioned for him to sit. "Hold on. I'll get Maggie for you." She walked without a sound through a metallic door, which led into another area of the home. After a few minutes, Kendra returned with her roommate.

Except for her age, Maggie Earnst was the exact opposite of Kendra Ball. She was tall; long brown hair with streaks of blonde that gave her an exotic look. Her face was blemish-free, and her green eyes made her very sexy. *She could have been a contestant for beauty pageants.* Both women sat down in the beanbag chairs a few feet from Brian.

"Ladies, I didn't get a chance to talk to you the day you found the bodies. I apologize for that, but I just need a few minutes of your time, and I'll be on my way." He pulled out his green memo notebook.

"No problem, sir. It just sort of scared us, you know…seeing those poor dead people." Maggie reached over and touched her friend on her shoulder.

"About what time did you two discover the victims?" Brian asked.

"Well, we left our other girlfriends at the club around one-thirty in the morning; we usually walk, since it's not too far from our house here. We decided to cut through the park, and that's where we ended up finding them," Kendra said.

"Detective, it was closer to two o'clock by the time we made it to the park," Maggie said.

Brian wrote a few lines in the notepad. "Okay, did either of you see anyone else on your way back?"

"No, not that I can remember." Maggie said.

"Wait, Mags…don't you remember seeing that hot guy walking in the street, as we were…um…" Kendra said. Her face flushed in realization she had given too much information.

"Detective, I do remember seeing the guy she was talking about, but I'll be honest with you. Both of us were very drunk when we left the club, so I don't want to act like I could give you an accurate description." Maggie frowned.

Brian nodded. "Look, anything you could do to help is appreciated. You never know, your information may help us catch a killer."

Maggie tugged at her friend's shirt. "Kendra, honey, do you remember anything about this guy when he walked by?"

"Actually, *someone* was a lot drunker than I was." She pointed at Brian. "This guy was about your height and had long wavy hair. He was really built. I mean… like muscles everywhere. He looked like he could have been a body builder or football player of some sort. I don't think he said anything to either of us as we passed by though," Kendra said.

Something at least. "That's a start for us, though. Do you think if you saw this guy again you could recognize him?" Brian scribbled on the paper.

"Not really. He was all by himself just walking in the street." Kendra paused. "Plus I was drunk."

Shit, Brian thought. He hoped the girl would try a little harder to recall that night.

"Kendra, anything out of the ordinary about the man you remember?" Brian asked.

"No, I don't think so, Detective. He was just a big guy. Wait a minute, I do remember something." Her eyes lit up.

Brian leaned in further. "Take your time." *Please be something.*

"The muscle guy was flipping a silver coin in the air. But he said something when he caught it." She tapped at her head. "What was it again? Yeah, it was, heads, you lose, tails I win. That was it. I thought it was odd, and it slipped my mind until now."

Odd to say the least. Brian jotted down the passage. "Anything else?"

Kendra shook her head. "That's it. I'm sorry if that doesn't help much," Kendra said.

Brian closed the notebook. "You and Maggie have *both* been helpful. This may give us a little idea of a time line."

"Detective, I hope you catch this man. I don't think I'll ever forget seeing the mangled body of that little girl." Maggie's gaze was distant.

"It was horrific…it really was," Kendra said.

"I know, ladies. We have trauma counselors, if you need to talk to someone." Brian handed the girls his business card.

"Thank you." Kendra stood up and escorted him to the front door.

"I won't take up any more of your time. You girls take care; it was a pleasure to meet you,"

Opening his car door, he stared off in the direction of the park. The weird phrase uttered by the mystery man could be something…or with Brian's luck, it was just the apex of coherent conversation of another drunk who came from the same club. Regardless without a good description from Kendra, it was a dead end. The two girls indicated they had found the Paul family around two in the morning. *No telling how long the bodies were there prior to that.* Brian tried to clear his mind as he drove home. He hadn't seen Sarah or the girls since early and he wanted to spend a little time at home before further developments. He turned into the alley, which made it quick access to the back garage of his home.

He enjoyed the look of his house. A five-bedroom ranch, with room enough for a built-in pool and Jacuzzi. Brian gazed up at the residence, still sort of shocked that it was his. He and Sarah were so happy; the bank had let them have the loan to build this wonderful home for the children. Usually in law enforcement, this type of house was not affordable, but as fate would have it, everything worked out in his and Sarah's favor.

Sarah's minivan was parked in the garage; he was happy they were home. He pulled the unmarked vehicle into the garage and stumbled through the cluttered corridor. Brian heard the sound of shuffled feet, as the girls appeared at the top of the stairs and gazed down at their father.

"Daddy's home!" screamed Victoria.

"Yeah, Daddy!" Exclaimed Alyssa. She was always happy to see her father, even though she was a little upset yesterday when he dropped them off.

Brian laughed. *Already the drama queen teen.* His oldest daughter sat in a chair engaged with a gaming device which he was certain included her squad of online support. "What's up, Dad?" Melissa addressed her father as more of a courtesy than a heartfelt greeting. Brian knew she had gotten over yesterday, or she would've given him the silent treatment. Melissa was a lot like her mother in that way. He was glad to be home for a little while as he hugged and kissed all of them.

"Hey, how are my ladies doing today? Sorry, Daddy left too early to say goodbye."

Sarah approached him and gave him a quick peck on the lips. "We had a very busy day, didn't we?"

The girls smiled and nodded their heads to acknowledge their mother.

"Honey, guess what the girls and I did today after church?" Sarah smiled with a flirtatious grin. Brian didn't even have time to answer the question before the youngest Jeffers' girl blurted it out.

"We went to the park, Daddy and it was quite enjoyable." Victoria was better with her words than most her age. *My little Einstein.*

The other two chimed in as well. "We had lots of fun!"

Brian eyed the girls with jealously. "I wanted to go to the park, too, but Daddy got stuck doing grown up stuff all day."

The girls were intelligent for their ages, so he would always say things like that. It would get them off track, and they would find little interest in what he did at work.

"We made brownies for you while you were gone." Sarah pushed a flat pan in his direction.

The young Jeffers' girls' eyes widened. This enticed them in an instant. Anything to do with cookies, candy, or the combination of the two put them onto the concept of eating. Brian laughed and enjoyed the fact the girls were over yesterday's disappointment. His life had been stressed out enough in the last twenty-four hours; he didn't need his own family upset with him. He smiled at his offspring as he changed his voice to sound like a cartoon character they enjoyed. "Okay, girls, brownies sound very good, I'm starving anyway."

He had forgotten to eat anything since earlier that morning, so the Jeffers family had a meal together, ate some homemade brownies, and to cap off the evening, enjoyed a movie that made the girls laugh. They all drifted off to sleep on the couch, then Brian carried each to their individual rooms. He was tired from the long day, and the energy tank was almost on empty.

Time for much needed rest. Brian hoped the pager didn't go off for the rest of the night. Lucky for him, the night was silent. Unfortunately, miles away… death was about to strike another.

Chapter 15

Visit from Lucifer

Lucifer decided to move the timetable up on his next masterpiece. *Might as well strike while the creative juices are flowing*. The law enforcement community wouldn't expect him to strike this soon. There was joy in doing the unexpected; it was sort of his demented style. Grabbing the thin black leather gloves from his dresser drawer, he left the apartment. He *always* wore gloves when creating masterpieces. If the killer didn't leave any physical evidence, they would never catch him, and the work could continue *forever*.

He pulled his car into a sparsely filled lot. The twenty-four hour pharmacy always had several vehicles in front of the business; no one would even notice it. He opened the trunk and pulled out a black backpack and strapped it on. *Three blocks away*. He dodged between side streets until he located the alley that emptied out into the street adjacent to Tamia Stevens's house. The neighborhood was quiet; only a couple houses had their lights on. He edged along the tree line covered by the darkness. As he inched closer, the killer observed the security gate. *Keyless reader*! If this was the primary access point, the mission would have failed, but the hours he'd spent with his prey provided him with a much better option.

A chain link fence ran the entire length of her residence, which also split the property of another home owner. Lucifer was overjoyed the woman who lived on the other side made little or zero effort to upkeep the fence, and through years of weather, combined with natural erosion, this was perfect. *Quite a shame for Tamia*.

Lucifer removed his newest toy from the sport shop and cut through the chain link with little difficulty. A few steps after the breach, Lucifer spotted a cozy alcove tucked into the rear of the property. *Perfect hiding place*. He looked up; a soft glow was present behind the curtains in the next-door neighbor's house. If Lucifer was quiet, he should remain unseen. He crept along the fence line and to the back of the house. There was no sight of Tamia Stevens's vehicle in the driveway. *Good, no way for her to escape*. He crept his way back to the alcove to await his victim. Lucifer peeked at his watch; it was close to one in the morning and almost time.

He slid off his pack, relieved to be rid of the extra weight for the moment. It was not his accepted practice to carry this much, but tonight's masterpiece called for some special treatment. He opened it and inventoried the contents: a change of clothes, some sanitary wipes, and a small towel. After the completion of his masterpiece, there would be a need for more clothing. He would take the soiled ones and wash them. Lucifer didn't like to dispose of things that could be used again. Peering out from behind the foliage, Lucifer's eyes lit up. *The garage door was ajar*. When Tamia went out, she forgot to close it. *Lucky for me, not so much for her*. It wasn't attached to the house, so that made it even better, since she would have to walk by him to gain entry to the rear entrance. He laughed to himself. *I may want to try my hand at the lottery, as well*.

Zipping up the backpack, he set it down next to him. Excitement filled him as he methodically massaged the fifty-cent piece in his right pocket. *Selecting and collecting from his prey was too easy*. Lucifer placed the tool of his trade in his hand and studied the blade with envy. There was immense pleasure in the way it felt. Lucifer held it up to the night sky and watched the moonlight reflect off the stainless steel. He gazed into the metal and could see an almost perfect reflection of himself. He stared into his own distant eyes, almost like it was from another perspective. Lucifer tested the blade on a loose piece of fabric which hung from his trousers. A slight movement of his hand, and the fabric floated to the ground. *Ready and willing.* He picked up the severed clothing and shoved it inside his shirt. Proud of his work, he slid the killing instrument into the sheath from which it came. Then, he waited. After about thirty minutes, the sound of Tamia's Steven's Navigator approached. The brightness of the headlights beamed on the pavement. Lucifer's face became hot and flushed. *The time was almost at hand.* He was enthralled with the rhythm of his own heartbeat as it pounded with frenzied fever in anticipation of the event that was about to take place.

* * *

Tamia stopped the sports utility and waved the proximity card in front of the electronic reader to access the gate, then followed the pavement to the back of the house. She was exhausted and yearned for sleep before her trip to Chicago. *Borziana,* the up-and-coming designer, wanted her to do a commercial for the new swimwear line. They picked a select few models a year to represent their brand, so it was quite an honor. Tamia believed things were looking up, and her career was about to launch in the most wonderful fashion.

She knew Italian sugar daddy; August Dellano had told her he knew people who would help her move up in this business. He might be full of shit, but Tamia decided to trust him. He did talk to her agent, Serena Clarke, about a great photo shoot in Malibu next month. The gig was still on the backburner, but August had promised it would happen. She felt a little guilty about sleeping with a married man. It weighed heavy on her conscience, but once she secured enough of her own assets, she would kick August to the curb. Besides, Tamia needed to find someone her own age, and August was married. *Not a healthy combination.*

She laughed a little, thinking that most guys her age were still very adolescent in their behavior. Most of the men she met were after *one* thing, and she wouldn't just give it up to anyone. It was easier to stay with August and have some fun. *Plus, the man is rich,* she thought. He wasn't the best-looking she'd been with, but he wasn't the worst, either. *Enough deep insight for today.* It was time for a long, hot bubble bath.

* * *

Lucifer slid back further into the darkness, as Tamia Stevens exited her vehicle. When she passed the alcove, the strong, luxurious odor of her perfume filled his nostrils. She placed her house key into the door lock. *Take her now!* Before the model realized something was wrong, Lucifer shoved her farther into the residence. He kicked the door shut with his back foot and slammed it, ending any hope of escape. Tamia's purse flew to the floor and spilled her possessions onto the surface. The brute force propelled Tamia through the air head first, until the kitchen table stopped all momentum. Her skull bounced off the edge and sent her onto the ground. She tried to sit up, but Lucifer was relentless, and grasped her golden hair. His muscles flexed as he lifted her body and placed her off balance.

He maneuvered the blade so he had a death-like grip on it. Lucifer smiled as the knife plunged deep into Tamia Stevens's right side. He thrust upward, which caused blood to pour from the wound and stain the sharpened metal. Lucifer turned her body to face him. Her eyes widened with a look of sheer terror. Lucifer watched in delight as Tamia gasped for air. He had calculated where the blade penetrated, impressed with his skill. Drawing back the blood-drenched blade, he was ready to end the young model's existence. Tamia was close to the edge of death when the killer whispered. "Easy now, it will all be over soon. Do me a favor…say hello to my mother for me?" Lucifer let out a maniacal howl. Then, with decisive quickness, he placed the sharp edge across her small throat, as a flick of the wrist ended it all. Lucifer continued with the knife, which sprayed fluid in all directions. After the work was complete, the killer retreated from the carnage, and admired his "masterpiece."

He scanned the ground where her purse had fallen, locating a silver flip cell phone. *Must have fallen out*. He picked it up and smiled. Her lover might try to call her and maybe even leave a message. Lucifer fingered through the other belongings to see if the item he needed had landed on the ground. The item wasn't there, so he picked up the purse and inspected the contents. In a few minutes, he located the coveted article and shoved it in his right pocket. He grabbed a hold of the necklace from Tamia's bloody neck and ripped it from her lifeless form. Satisfied, the killer stuffed it in his backpack. He reached into his jacket and removed the fifty-cent piece.

"Another masterpiece in my collection," Lucifer mocked, in realization there wasn't anyone present to acknowledge him. He exited the house and stopped in front of her vehicle. Using the keys, he opened the sports utility in silence. He eyed the sunroof and climbed inside. A short time later, he completed the last of the work, making sure his signature was in the perfect place.

Lucifer walked unchallenged back to the parking lot. The night was *very* profitable for the killer. He had collected a trophy he would forever cherish. Soon, he would visit Tamia Steven's Italian lover and create another artistic piece to add to the ever-growing collection. Lucifer turned the ignition, but as he shifted the vehicle into drive, the voice of his long dead mother made a repeat performance.

"You're a damn fool, boy! You will never be any good for anything, and you're a pitiful loser."

Lucifer thought he had disposed of her post existence spirit, but it was only stronger and clearer. Opening the glove compartment, he grabbed the brown bottle of pills and popped several into his mouth, hoping this would rid him of the nuisance. Once the voice subsided, he maneuvered the car through low-rent neighborhoods, careful not to draw attention from the city police officers.

Once home, he headed for his bedroom, exhausted and exhilarated. Lucifer fell into the small bed, unaware he still had drops of Tamia Stevens's blood on him. The sanitary wipes did very little in the removal of evidence from his body. Lucifer would deal with that later as the dosage of medication had taken effect, and the killer soon drifted off into a deep, evil sleep.

Chapter 16

Miles Kagan

Brian Jeffers stirred before the alarm went off; just enough time so a family breakfast could be enjoyed before the day became too unbearable. He had barely taken a bite out of his second pancake when the cell phone attached to his belt started to chirp. *Sooner or later.*

"Jeffers, this is Barnum. I have some news about an art show held on Friday and Saturday. I've scheduled a meeting for us with the promoter of the event. You got like fifteen minutes to meet me at 2131 Washburn Street."

This could be a much-needed break. Maybe Justin Paul's wife had entered the show, and Brian's theory might just be right.

"See you there." He clicked the phone shut; still pissed Barnum hadn't been honest and was still more than likely holding onto valuable information.

* * *

Brian parked in front of the address on Washburn Street; Barnum's patrol vehicle was already in front of the five-story business complex. The building was covered in mirrored glass and was a new addition to a downtown area of dilapidated structures. The compound also appeared to be very well protected from unwanted visitors; two armed security personnel located at the front entrance appeared to inspect all those who entered. Brian flashed his credentials to the security personnel. The two young men waved him through. Barnum was waiting for him on the other side. "Good morning, Jeffers. Good thing we're cops, or we might have been beaten." Barnum tugged at Brian's arm.

"Right." Brian tried not to smile.

Barnum continued with his thought. "I'm sure you're wondering why we are here today?"

"Let me guess. You're looking for a new job in event planning?" Brian grinned.

Barnum didn't partake in the humor; he glared at Brian, slow to shake off the comment. "We are here to see Mr. Miles Kagan. He was in charge of the art show downtown last weekend. Tammy Paul had entered several pieces of artwork for the event."

Brian knew he was right about the artist being the main target of the deranged murderer. He inquired further. "So Mr. Paul was contacted by this Kagan guy?"

"Yes. Paul contacted me about six this morning. He said Kagan had a check for the deceased artist in regards to one of her pieces. Kagan, in fact, requires all of the artists to register for the shows he sponsors, and Tammy didn't stay for the completion of the show. By the way, this Kagan fellow is also a personal friend of the Pauls' so he took responsibility for anything sold after she left the show."

Interesting. Can't wait to meet him. "What floor is our guy on, Boss?"

"Suite 215."

When they arrived, there was a secretary positioned at an "L" shaped metallic desk. The woman eyed the two but returned to her multi-tasking duties. The ambience of the office held the stylistic attitude of new-age art design. The spacious room was covered with expensive furniture. The key feature was the giant crystal chandelier, which hung from the triangular ceiling.

Strange place for that, but then again, rich peo- ple were often bizarre. Brian's attention drifted to the bronzed naked sculptures in the most erotic of poses scattered throughout the office. One in particular was al- most a mini version of their female host. *Really?* The secretary, clad in a pantsuit which defined all of her nat- ural gifts, looked up and adjusted her glasses to inspect the police badges that hung from both men's belts. She appeared to be about twenty-five years old; her short, brown hair was the perfect style. Ignoring the older in- vestigator, she focused on Brian. "My name is Colette. How may I assist you today, Officers?"

Barnum, responded with authority. "Mr. Miles Ka- gan for official police business."

The receptionist kept her eyes on the junior detec- tive. "I will tell Mr. Kagan you are here." She pressed a button on the multiplex telephone system next to her.

Soon after, an older man stepped out from a steel door hidden behind the sculptures lined against the wall. He was thin with snow-white hair and a tan complexion, which would suggest most of his time away was spent in sun-drenched lands. He wore a chocolate-colored suit with a black long-sleeved shirt and a red tie. This man had movie star quality looks about him.

He extended his right hand. Barnum again, took charge and spoke on behalf of both investigators. "Mr. Kagan, I'm Commander Barnum and this is Detective Jeffers. I spoke with you earlier in regards to the Paul homicide investigation."

Kagan gripped each of the men's hands; the look on his face saddened as he spoke. "Ah, yes we did, Com- mander Barnum. My office would be a much more *pri- vate* place to discuss this further. I think I may have more information that may aid you in your ongoing investigation." Kagan paused. "I hope you electrocute the criminal who did this to poor Tammy and her family. Follow me this way, gentlemen."

The secretary noticed her boss walking away and called after him. "Sir, would you like me to hold all of your calls until you are done with these detectives?" She winked at Brian as her supervisor turned his head to lead the group to his office. Brian felt a little embarrassed, but smiled.

"Yes, Colette, that would be fine." He escorted the investigators through the iron door and into a large office. It was covered with the same style of the artwork as the waiting room. The brown leather furniture looked like it was brand new and matched the office to perfection. Brian was very impressed with the man's taste; quite sure *his* yearly salary didn't cover the expenses for the furnishings.

"Gentleman, I was a very close friend of Tammy's for the last five years, and anything I can do to help you with your investigation, I will gladly offer." He pulled out a small bottle of liquid from his top desk drawer.

Brian and Barnum exchanged quick glances at each other, while the man took a drink from the bottle. He realized both investigators were watching him and offered an explanation.

"Sorry about that. Damn medication I have to take twice a day." He tossed the remains back in the top drawer.

Brian sat erect in his chair; his gaze focused on Kagan. "Sir, *you* told Commander Barnum all the artists register their individual painting and sculptures with you before they sold anything. Is that standard industry protocol, or is it guidelines you alone have placed on the participants of every sponsored art show?"

"Detective, I have a very strict protocol when hosting an event such as this. All of the participating artists have to register their work for accountability, plus I receive compensation for each piece that is sold."

The officers again exchanged inquisitive glances. Barnum nodded. "So, your art show pretty much makes money for all artwork sold, not registered?"

"I receive compensation for just the paintings, sculptures or whatever sells at the events. Not everything does."

Brian thought about the check for the last painting sold of Tammy Paul's before her death. "I understand you contacted Commander Barnum in regards to compensation you received from one of Tammy' buyers—"

"I did," Kagan said. He shifted in his chair.

Guy's not comfortable. "I have two questions. First, when did she leave the show, and second, did all of her artwork sell at your event or were there pieces left?" Brian removed his notebook.

Kagan reached into another desk drawer. He pulled out an envelope and a piece of printer paper.

This old man is sort of like a pimp for struggling up and upcoming artists. These observations made him wonder if the relationship with Tammy Paul was because he cared for her or because she was another source of income.

"To answer your first question, Tammy left the show a couple hours early. And for your other, all of her artwork sold except for the one she took with her when she left." Kagan handed the envelope and printout to Barnum.

"Did you talk to her at all that evening?" Brian said, shooting a glance at Barnum.

"For a moment." Ignoring the younger investigator, the man turned and smiled at Barnum. "Here's the check I called you about, Commander. I've also included the printout that documents which artwork was registered and sold." He handed the information to the senior investigator, avoiding Brian's piercing stare. *Nice!*

Clearing his throat, Brian motioned for his supervisor to hand him the list, which Barnum did with reluctance. After a hasty scan, Brian folded the printout and placed it inside his notebook. Barnum took the white envclope and tucked it inside his suit coat pocket. The check would be the last amount of money Tammy Paul would ever earn. "I'll forward this to her brother-in-law, Mr. Kagan." Barnum frowned as he continued. "What about this artwork she left with? All the personal belongings were returned to her family. It didn't include this so-called painting you're talking about."

"Excuse me. I know she left with one mosaic painting."

"Mr. Kagan, We didn't find anything like that at the scene." Brian scribbled in the notebook.

"Are you two sure? This piece had quite a bit of promise. It was a wonderful work of originality I knew someday would make her a lot of money."

Not anymore. "We're positive."

"Someone must have stolen it then. It was a done in a unique style. A forgotten time period and very lovely. I would love to see it again."

Marcus Paul took the only personal belongings found at the crime scene and all of those were very inexpensive items. Brian was certain the officers whom responded to the murders would have made sure a valuable like that would be included in the inventory. If it wasn't at the house, maybe Kagan was right: someone may have stolen it from the crime scene. *Why would someone take it?*

Could it be possible this killer was involved in another hobby besides marking his victims with his signature? Was this executioner responsible for dismembering the Paul family also taking something from them? Marcus Paul did mention a missing lighter, and now, possibly, a piece of precious artwork was unaccounted for.

Kagan spoke up. "If you find the design, I'll pay a very fair price to her family."

"If *it's* located, we will mark it as evidence to evaluate, Mr. Kagan." Brian corrected him.

"Oh, I'm sorry. I didn't even think of that."

I'm sure you didn't, Brian thought. "It's understandable. You're focused on the monetary portion of your loss."

Shaking his head, Barnum stood up and tapped Brian on the shoulder. "Mr. Kagan, thanks for your time, and if we need to talk to you further, you *will* be available?"

The handsome promoter ignored Brian's comments. He turned, facing Barnum. "Find her killer, please. She was my friend…she really was." Tears welled in his eyes.

Brian looked at Kagan. *Probably not as true a friend to Tammy Paul as he claims he was. No one would ever know.* The investigators excused themselves and left the complex. Brian was afraid Lucifer was not only a killer but a collector as well…

Chapter 17

Tamia's Friend

Roseanne Tustin was the next-door neighbor of Tamia Stevens. After the loss of her husband, she had moved to the community. She was unable to work and retired from her executive secretary position at the local advertising agency, A.P. Lodfig. These days Roseanne was the epitome of a recluse.

Tamia Stevens had moved in to the vacant house next to hers just two years ago. The young woman made it a point to introduce herself within just a few days. Roseanne didn't like unexpected company, but she could see Tamia was a beautiful and pleasant young woman who possessed a charming personality. Roseanne tried to keep her distance from the new neighbor, but Tamia was very persistent with regular gifts of expensive chocolates and the occasional bubble bath. One morning, Roseanne saw the young girl on a morning jog through the neighborhood and decided being alone all the time wasn't in her nature, nor was it healthy. Roseanne invited Tamia inside her house, and they talked for what seemed like hours. She enjoyed having the girl around; sort of like the child Roseanne was never able to have.

She always thought the girl reminded her a little of herself when she was younger. The vibrant, young blonde always seemed very happy; this positive perspective rubbed off on Roseanne and changed her outlook on life.

Today she was doing the weekly baking ritual. This often kept her busy, and the woman often dropped off baked goods. She also knew Tamia didn't have relatives in the area, so Roseanne had taken on somewhat of paternal role. Roseanne's creation for the day was her famous homemade chocolate fudge; Tamia loved that best. She had just set the sheet pan on top of the stove and was waiting for it to cool. After a few minutes, she placed the fudge on a porcelain platter. *Hmm, time for final touch.* Opening the refrigerator, the woman pulled out a tinfoil plate and emptied its contents on top. She knew Tamia loved her oatmeal raisin soft-batter cookies. Roseanne hoped this would put a little meat on the thin girl's frame. Tamia was too skinny and ran almost every morning, rain or shine. Today, she didn't see her and became a little worried. Again, Tamia was single and she was a woman who had needs, Roseanne wasn't too naïve to believe that young women nowadays acted more forward. She had been brought up differently, but times change.

Earlier, around dawn, the woman was still awake, engrossed in the latest suspense novel, when she noticed the headlights of Tamia's SUV. Roseanne's window faced the rear door to Tamia's house, which gave her a perfect view. Roseanne decided she wouldn't yell out the window, but she would watch Tamia make it inside safe and sound. This would ease her mind. She knew there were crazy people in this world, so she sort of felt responsible for her friend's welfare. She was relieved when she witnessed the young woman at the back door. Roseanne felt this was the reaction of a worry-wart and focused her energy towards her novel.

After wrapping up the platter in foil, she was out the door to deliver her gifts to Tamia. Roseanne stopped at the gate and placed the key card in front the sensor.

Tamia had given her the extra key card a few months back when the fence was completed; she told Roseanne the widow was *always* welcome in her house.

As she walked alongside the pavement, Roseanne stopped at Tamia's SUV. The sunroof screen was open, which was odd. Poking her head around the rear of the vehicle, the door on the driver's side was ajar. As she approached, her nostrils were overwhelmed by an odor so horrendous, it made her nauseous and she almost fell to the ground. She eased it open but realized that was a mistake. Her face cringed with fear, as the platter loosened from her grip. The porcelain shattered against the paved driveway, which catapulted the fudge and cookies in various directions. The old woman's vocal cords erupted in a fury of anguish.

The young girl was covered in blood, with filthy, grotesque insects eating away at her lifeless form. Her neck and throat were slashed so severely, Tamia's head appeared to be connected by just a few inches of muscle and flesh. Roseanne backed away from the door, stumbled to the ground, and cried with uncontrollable pain. "Oh my God! Oh my God!" shrieked the widow, running towards the gate.

Roseanne made it to the front of the driveway before her legs gave out, and crashed against the cement with panic. She screamed at the top of her lungs, "My friend is dead! My friend is dead!" Roseanne wailed for what seemed like eternity until an older man stopped his vehicle to investigate.

What the woman didn't see because of the mutilation was the fear-provoking calling card Lucifer had left. *This* time, it was engraved on the upper back of Tamia, not visible to anyone not looking for it. The signature had now been changed to two words instead of the killer's initials. This time it said:

    LUCIFER'S CALLING.

Chapter 18

The Signature

Brian Jeffers had just turned into the law enforcement center when the police radio buzzed with broken static. The voice was panicked, which was very uncommon for a professional dispatcher.

"Dispatch to thirty-nine, two."

Brian's call sign or designation was 39-2. Most of the time, he received direct phone calls instead of radio traffic. The dispatch center would only use radio protocol if there was an emergency. Brian ripped the hand-held microphone from the cradle. "Dispatch, go ahead with your traffic."

The female's voice cracked on the return transmission. "Respond to 1147 Lockhart Lane. Meet with patrol officers McKenzie and Borello. Go Code Three."

Code Three was the numerical designation for Emergency response. Brian acknowledged the dispatcher and accelerated the vehicle with urgency. He hit the transmit button on the microphone. "En route to said location, dispatch."

The female responded, but the detective was fixated on something else. He didn't even want to consider what waited at 1147 Lockhart Lane, but Brian's thoughts got the best of him. *It could be a gang shooting, or possibly a domestic abuse case…more than likely, Lucifer killed again.*

Brian didn't realize his speed had increased to the point where it bordered on the verge of dangerous and reckless. Reaching down, he plucked the Nextel phone from his waist. He pushed the send key and tried to avoid several panicked drivers along the way. *Way to multi-task.*

"Detective Barnum," the supervisor said, sounding like he had something stuffed in his mouth.

"It's Jeffers. I'm on my way to 1147 Lockhart Lane to meet with uniforms... sounds like another homicide."

Barnum replied in a dry voice. "I'll meet you. If you get there before I do, make sure the damn press doesn't get anything to start a panic with the public."

"Gotcha," Brian said as he was almost sideswiped by a newspaper delivery truck.

Several minutes later, he was on Lockhart Lane. One patrol car was positioned at the corner, blocking off the street entrance. Brian parked next to it and flashed his detective badge to the younger officer. He motioned for Brian to roll down the window to engage him. Time was of the essence, and Brian didn't want unnecessary chitchat with this guy. The rookie must have observed the look of determination and thought better in the delay. *Let's go.* The officer backed away from the unmarked and waved him on. About a half a block away, two more patrol cars were parked in front of a fenced-in residence. The area was marked off by a stream of yellow plastic.

The house appeared to be a recent addition to the many older ones which bordered the property. Through the barrier, Brian scanned the brown outline of the residence. It was a two-story with diamond shaped windows on the front exterior. A few trees were present as white patio blocks led to the door. Brian closed his eyes, afraid of the horror that awaited him. He spotted one uniformed officer knelt down on the curb. He was engaged in conversation with an older woman who was currently on her hands and knees. She had a death-like grip on pavement like it was life itself. Brian leaned in to hear the exchange. "Now, Mrs. Tustin, how long ago did you find—"

"I can't believe she is gone. Why—"

"I'm sorry, I really am, but I just need a few minutes of your time." The officer glanced up when Jeffers entered the area.

Brian scanned the grounds, relieved to see local news media vans and their bloodhound reporters hadn't made it to the area. The neighborhood was very quiet, and none of the other home owners appeared to be interested in the commotion, Brian watched his steps, careful not to disturb any evidence that may be present. He kept a watch on the woman as she sobbed.

Brian turned to see another patrolman, exiting the fenced-in garage entry area. The middle-aged man shook his head in apparent disbelief. Glancing up, his gaze met with Brian's. He conveyed a somber look, one not found on the face of hardened police personnel. *Something terrible happened here.*

"Detective Jeffers?" A strained voice escaped the uniform-clad man.

"Yes, McKenzie." Brian stared at the gold nametag.

The man pointed to the woman who was still perched on the curb. "She is Roseanne Tustin; the one who found the body." He exhaled. "I'll take you to the area." Officer McKenzie's voice seemed to drift off.

Brian glanced behind him. The distraught woman pounded the pavement with her fists. *God help her.*

He followed McKenzie along the driveway, while he slipped on a pair of latex gloves. The two walked around the corner of the driveway; more of the yellow police tape was visible. It surrounded the perimeter of a black sports utility vehicle and extended all the way to the rear entrance of the residence. Brian didn't follow the tape, because the stench told him *this* is where the evil was. Visions of the Paul murder scene, flashed through his mind. *Now or never.* Pushing forward through the undergrowth, Brian's jaw dropped. Post-death insects were swarming around the SUV and its host. Glancing down, he noted there were several shards of white broken glass next to the vehicle. He inspected the driveway and grass. *What is that?* Brian bent down and sifted through the remains of the bug-infested, uneaten cookies and blocks of chocolate. *Baked goods.* He approached the driver's side door, and pushed up on the slick, black handle. Brian stepped back. *Something out of a slasher movie.*

The woman was almost decapitated from the numerous deep lacerations across the soft tissue and muscled remains of her throat. Her corpse was now a home for all sorts of creepy life forms, all in battle to taste the spoils of unearned victory. Tamia was naked from the waist and her torso was ripped open. The intestinal track was weaved throughout the steering wheel and its column. Blood still dripped from the mutilated appendage into a puddle on the black floor mats of the SUV. The back of her woman's light beige, short-sleeved polo shirt was ripped to expose something most sinister.

Brian reached behind the vestiges of her torn flesh and eased down her shirt. *Something on her.* The investigator was unable to see what lay underneath, so he motioned for the closest tech to snap a picture as he proceeded. Brian used caution as he tore the t-shirt further to investigate. *Fuck*! On the bruised and bloodied back of this once-beautiful girl were a series of letters that appeared to be carved into her flesh. He glared at the message; a sudden shudder once again surged through his body.

Chapter 19

Questioning a Witness

Brian Jeffers clenched his teeth as he stared at the rear of the residence. *Fucking animal*. The evidence techs were in full swing processing this scene. He climbed up the three concrete steps that led into the house. There, he was greeted by a multitude of blood splatters on most everything within a ten feet radius. The crimson stains were accompanied by dried, pooled blood throughout the surface of the wooden floor. *This is where the bastard did it*. Her belongings were scattered on the hardwood; in the center was a half-open pink purse. As he bent down to inspect the contents, the familiar, voice of Detective Barnum from somewhere behind him, almost caused Brian to lose balance and land in the grisly residue.

"A little jittery, are we, Jeffers? Anyway, I have the medical examiner and a few more forensic guys headed this way. Look at all this damn blood! Have you got anything so far?"

Brian shook his head, overwhelmed. "Nothing." He pointed in the direction of the garage. "Did you see what the psycho did to her? Look in the damn sports utility. He wants to outdo himself with each murder."

Barnum cocked his head. "Maybe we have more than *one* killer, huh?"

"No. One sick fuck and I'm sure of it. Check out his calling card *this* time."

The look on Barnum face told Brian he hadn't taken a first-hand visual inspection of the victim, so Brian led him to the devastation. Barnum stood there for several minutes, without a single utterance. By the time he turned to face the junior investigator, most of the sarcasm had vacated. "Okay, I will go with one killer on this." He wiped his brow. "Fourth attack in less than four days. Unbelievable. Seems like he's in a hurry to butcher these people…but why?"

"I couldn't tell you, but whatever the answer is, I can guarantee there's *more* coming."

Barnum scanned the room, focused on the crimson covered walls. "In all of my days, most sicko bastards get the hell out of town after just one murder. This guy has three times as many and could keep killing until God knows when?"

They returned to the rear entrance. "Remember when *you* mentioned the demonic cult thing? You can scratch that one off your list." Brian picked up the dead girl's belongings.

"Well, I'm glad you erased that thought. And by the way, fuck you. I never said anything of the sort. Not that I will admit to… we would have all the religious zealots declaring the end was near." Barnum wiped more sweat from his forehead.

"Boss, let's hope he made a mistake."

Barnum sighed. "Jeffers, he can't keep getting this lucky."

Spill it. "I think we have a serial killer on our hands. And if we don't get a break, fucking fast, the death count will continue to rise," Brian said.

"Do you think she was drugged like the Paul family?" Barnum's voice cracked as he accepted the statement— a serial killer was responsible.

"We will know more once Dr. Sanderson does his investigation. He should be here soon with his team."

Brian tapped at his watch. "Officer Borello is with a witness who might be able to help us. I will check on his progress."

"Okay, do your thing. I'll stay here and look through the house and see if I can find some more about her. I also had patrol run the vehicle registration. The owner's name was Tamia Stevens. Ever heard of her?"

"Heard she was a model. Other than that, not much."

"Talk to that witness and see what you can find out," Barnum commanded.

Brian nodded as he returned to the front of the house and slipped off the gloves. Patrol Officer Borello was still in consult with the woman, who appeared to be in her late fifties. She was short with light blonde hair and well dressed; adorned with an assortment of jewelry most would envy.

He approached with caution, as not to disrupt the information gathering. Brian knew Officer Nick Borello well. They worked together in Valentine for about five years. Supervisors often commended the man for his extraordinary service. Brian knew he was exceptional in the patrol division. In most situations, Borello was known to be quite personable and could interact with almost *anyone*.

Borello motioned for the detective. "Sir, this is Roseanne Tustin. She was the first one here at the scene."

Brian offered her a warm smile, even though it was almost a challenge to do so, given what he'd just witnessed. His voice was gentle as he spoke. "Hello, Roseanne. I understand you knew Tamia Stevens. I know this may be a difficult time right now, but I would appreciate any information you could give me."

"I'll try to help," The woman said in a somber tone.

"Roseanne, you may have to repeat some of the story for me, so I want to apologize in advance. But if you would please bear with me, and I'll have our trauma counselors with you soon as I can, okay?"

She clutched her palms and nodded. "I'll do my best."

Brian pulled out his notebook. "Roseanne, do you remember hearing anything out of the ordinary or strange last night? Go ahead…take all the time you need."

Her eyes were distant. "I heard Tamia pull into her driveway close to one thirty in the morning. I was doing some light reading when I heard the door slam. I looked out my window. I always try to look after that girl, Detective. I then remember seeing her walk to the back door of the house, and thought everything was fine. I went back to my bed to read. I didn't think to keep watching her. If I would have, I may have seen who did this to her. So, so… very sorry—" The older woman broke down again.

Reaching into his coat pocket, he pulled out a tissue, and offered it to the fragile woman. *She really cared about the girl.* By the way it sounded, the two were friends; Roseanne appeared to have spent a lot of time with her. Brian looked to his small pad of a paper and scribbled a few lines, purposely waiting a few minutes before she composed herself. He peered into her sad eyes. "Roseanne, I know you feel you should have seen something, but you had no control over what happened. You're still alive. Chances are, if you had seen the person responsible, you may have been a victim yourself." Brian let that sink in before he continued. "Do you know of anyone who would want to hurt Tamia for any reason at all? Maybe someone she talked about? A lover, a romance gone bad, or anyone she was having problems with?"

"I don't know who would want to hurt that poor girl. I can't believe this is happening here. She was a sweetheart, Detective. Tamia never talked like she had major problems with anyone that I can remember. Tamia told me many men would call her, but she never brought any of them *here*. At least…not that I saw."

"Sounds like you did spend a lot of time with her," Brian said.

"I'm an older woman. I don't have much to do around here, so I looked out for her. Roseanne hesitated. Well… there is one thing she told me once about seeing a married man."

"Did she ever mention his name?" Brian asked.

"No… just told me small things."

"Like what, Roseanne?" Brian leaned in and touched her on the shoulder. "Anything would help."

Roseanne closed her eyes. "She said the two of them would meet a few times during the week, but that was about *all* I can remember."

"Are you sure there wasn't anything mentioned about who the man was?"

The woman wrung her hands. "She kept that kind of information quiet, unless she wanted me to know something. I can't really tell you anymore. I'm so, so sorry."

Brian closed his notebook. More questions might cause her to have a complete breakdown, so he backed off and switched gears to uncover a time line.

"Tell me a little about the events this morning. You don't have to rush…just do the best you can," Brian said.

Roseanne smiled. "I made some chocolate fudge and cookies for Tamia."

That explains the broken platter and why it was

there, Brian thought.

She continued. "I have a key card the young dear gave me to get in the security gate. I was walking to the back entrance when I saw the door of her truck was open a little bit. I smelled something horrible, and I opened the…that's when I found her." Roseanne was unable to finish the sentence; she crumpled to the ground once again.

Roseanne had given him everything she could, as he watched this sweet woman; heartbroken at the loss of her young friend and exhausted. Brian stood up and motioned for Officer Borello. "Hey, do me a solid and make arrangements to have trauma counselor, Annette Denning, meet with her later."

Officer Borello nodded. "She's lucky, more than she knows."

"Yeah, but she doesn't see it that way. Take care of her for me, Nick."

Brian returned to where Tamia Stevens's sports utility was parked. He glanced up. The all-too-familiar county coroner's office van pulled into the driveway. He opened the door to the SUV and gazed into the face of the woman. *Heaven help us…*

Chapter 20

The Collection

Lucifer awoke around mid-afternoon with remnants of dried blood on his body. Sleep was peaceful, which it usually was after that kind of artistic performance. Easing out of bed, he felt rejuvenated as he positioned himself in front of his workstation. This was one of the only other pieces of furniture in the tidy apartment. Lucifer reached down to the lone drawer and opened it. His face lit up when he spotted the gold key. It was taped to the bottom floor of the drawer, the perfect hiding place. *Nobody will find my treasures*.

He grabbed it and rushed into the main living area. Next to the cramped kitchen was an indentation in the wallpaper, which appeared to be hiding *something*. Reaching into the fold of the tan paper, Lucifer peeled it back and revealed a door, secured by a gold rusty padlock. *Secrets to keep*. Carefully, he placed the key into the antique lock. Lucifer heard the tumbler in the security device click open; within a few seconds, he had access to the hide-away.

Inside the closet on the right side of the wall, he flipped a switch. This created an amber glow from a series of low-wattage light bulbs. They were affixed in areas that focused on the shelved of the interior, which created a spotlight. He stared; fascinated by his collections, except for the special fifty-cent piece that accompanied him on all of his conquests. Each of his victims held a special place in his blackened heart; there was honor in death. Lucifer stood for a few minutes in recollection and the ritual of counting the trophies. He admired all of the masterpieces. This was Lucifer's usual routine. He would count and admire.

There were fifty-seven as of right now; more valuables would find a home here as well. He reached into his right cargo pocket and pulled out the beautiful gold necklace. It was lightly stained with Tamia Stevens's blood, which excited him to no end. He admired his new keepsake as a young boy would be in awe of a brand-new bike on his birthday. Lucifer wiped off the blood with a hand towel and placed the newest part of his collection in one of the empty spaces. *Almost time to expand.*

The killer stood with his eyes closed for several minutes, before he flipped off the switch and relocked the door. He retreated to his bedroom and hid the key away.

Lucifer reached for his backpack. He unzipped it and removed the bloodstained clothes. He balled them up and retrieved a black garbage bag from underneath the sink. Placing the ruined garments inside, he tied it in a knot, making sure nobody would be able to open it unless they damaged the plastic. Lucifer anticipated he would have the time to wash the articles but decided just to dispose of them and concentrate on his next victim. He thrust a hand into his right pocket and removed the item. His fingers ran across the cold plastic texture as he turned it over and analyzed the magnetic strip. This wonderful object would assist him in the creation of the next masterpiece and the expansion of his collection.

Chapter 21

A Serial Killer?

The scene at 1147 Lockhart Lane was chaotic, at best. At least this was the opinion of Brian Jeffers. The local presses had finally arrived and were now littered throughout the adjacent streets, cornering anyone *they* deemed to know the slightest of gossip. Brian worried about this since his arrival, and understood it was just a matter of time before it would come to fruition. Many other residents had begun to pour out onto the sidewalks in front of their homes. Some of the gathered onlookers were still dressed in their pajamas, as they eagerly approached several of the uniformed officers. They were less than cooperative, and demanded to know what happened in their wealthy Utopia. Brian distanced himself and sought out the patrol supervisor. The two decided it would be essential to have several extra uniformed patrol officers provide crowd control. Brian, having fixed the problem, returned to inspect the manmade hole in the chain link fence. He noted several unkempt trees and bushes which concealed pieces of the fence. *This is where that bastard hid.* The evidence technicians were still in the collection process and were almost finished with the last of the photographs.

The coroner's office was ready to transport the victim to the county morgue when all of the necessary photos were completed. The techs *even* picked up the smashed fudge and cookies. Brian returned to his work and moved several of the bushes aside. He inspected the jagged edges around the hole, quick to notice the ground was covered in the metal shavings of the ripped-open barrier. From his evidence kit, he removed several brown bags. He unfolded them and filled them with the metal scraps. It was possible these held the killer's fingerprints, but he wasn't holding his breath. Brian heard the heavy steps of Commander Barnum plod up behind him. "Bad news. Some dirt bag has leaked information a serial killer is loose in Valentine."

"*What*? That's just great! Is that why—"

"You got it, youngster. More press here than normal. These dumbasses are parked all over the place. It's going to be a madhouse around here now that the word is out... some maniac is responsible for all the murders in the last few days." Barnum ripped off his tie and shoved it inside his pants pocket.

Brian's face was flushed as he placed his finger inside his shirt collar and loosened the stranglehold it had on him. "Who the fuck is the leak? The departmental press officer hasn't said a word which would lead anyone in that direction."

"I would guess it was the scanner freaks who intercepted a transmission from an unsecured radio channel. I'm sure the idiots posted it to social media...networks love that shit," Barnum said.

"We need to get on top of this, before we lose control to mass hysteria—"

"It's too late. Panic is setting in anyway because of whoever disclosed the information. I'll get with the chief and let him work damage control."

Brian knew there wasn't much to say after the politics started to show itself in any investigation. He bowed his head in defeat. "Well, guess it's his place to address the media. I'll direct any reporters to that effect." He returned to his task and finished with the last of the metal shavings. The media would help the madman; once Lucifer knew the information was out about a serial killer, he might try to hide until the dust settled on these homicides. It was most likely the killer would leave here and set up shop somewhere else, where any law enforcement unfortunate to deal with Lucifer's handiwork would almost be starting over from square one. Brian didn't want that to happen; he *couldn't* let it happen. With the last of the metal in the paper bag, he was ready to face the Blitzkrieg of faceless reporters.

The urgency of the medical examiner's voice told him the man had found something. "Detective Jeffers, Detective Jeffers!" Dr. Sanderson ran up to the investigator.

Maybe some good news? Brian got up from his bent position, and met the man halfway.

"Whatcha got, Doc?"

"I took a quick look-see at our victim and the location where the killer used the Propaganician on the previous murders. The area underneath each arm appears to have none of the hypodermic needle marks the Paul family had."

"That doesn't make any sense, Doc. If the killer uses the Propaganician for his victims as torture, why would he not use it this time? Do you think he may have injected her somewhere else?"

Dr. Sanderson's face formed a quizzical look as he spoke. "It seems the killer determines *this* location as his preferred place to inject all of his victims."

"Maybe this Lucifer thinks it's time for a change." Brian shrugged.

"I wouldn't think he was going to alter the entry

point for the drug on a whim like that."

"Unless he feels using it too often might cause him to get caught, Doc."

"I'll do a thorough autopsy of her and let you know if he decided to invent a new target area."

"I just have this gut feeling the son-of-a-bitch didn't use the drug this time," Brian said.

"Detective, give me until late tonight to get back with you on it."

Brian applauded Dr. Sanderson for working around the clock helping the investigation, but he didn't want to stress him out further. He touched Sanderson on the arm. "Do the best you can. It's been hell the last several days for all of us. I don't think it's about to get any better either." Brian sighed.

"I'll try to hurry with the results."

"Just let me know when you can. If this guy didn't use his drug of preference on this girl, you can damn well bet there is a reason." Brian's cell phone vibrated; he glanced down and noted the number.

"I'll let you get that. I'll be in contact with you later." Sanderson turned, and walked away.

"Doc, one more thing. If Lucifer is willing to change his pattern like this, it may say something for how he adapts. That does worry me…"

Dr. Sanderson nodded and stepped onto the ramp of the coroner's van. Brian picked up the filled evidence bags. Barnum stumbled over to him, clearly disturbed. He spoke in a rehearsed tone. "While you were talking with Sanderson, I was on the phone with Chief Anderson. Said he tried to call you, but apparently you didn't hear it?" The condescending tone made Brian cringe.

"Uh, oh, I don't think he likes you. Probably, why he

called me first?" Brian grinned at his supervisor.

"Very funny, asshole. Now shut up and listen. The word is this, young man. Later today, the police spokesman, Troy Doyle will address all local media. He'll announce all the recent killings are being investigated, and the *killers* are still at large."

Killers? I don't like this. "Anyone with some common sense could figure out one man is responsible for these deaths." Brian threw up his arms.

"You and I know that, but hopefully, this little smokescreen with the public will work," Barnum said.

"Boss, I think most people are more intelligent than you think. What about the inscriptions on these victim's bodies? How is that being kept from the public?"

"Well, here is the deal. Not a fucking word is being released about the engravings or the lettering on the bodies as of yet."

"I see." *Not a great fucking plan at all.*

"Jeffers, the Chief wants to leave that detail out for right now. He did say if any more occur with the same method, he would have no choice but to add the information on the cryptic marks to the future press conferences."

Asinine. "*If* any more people are killed? There will be more." Brian kicked at the grass.

"Why do say that? Shit! Keep your damn tingling spidey sense to yourself! Let's hope your senses are short-circuited." Barnum's face was beet red.

"I hope you're right."

"Hey, the last thing the Chief told me was that if there were any more related types of murders, he would address the serial killer idea himself." Barnum flipped open his notebook and jotted something down.

At least they had bought some time before mass panic spread throughout the community. "Well, that gives us breathing room. I hope it's enough to stop him before he kills again." Brian turned his back on the man, leaving his supervisor by himself. Brian was unable to avoid the onslaught of story-seekers as he pushed through, in order to get to his vehicle. He stared at the mob. *Time is not on our side and Lucifer was very much aware of that.*

Chapter 22

A Message Received

August Dellano had been hard at work at his prosperous and posh restaurant, since before dawn. *Augustino's* was a high-class Italian eatery in the most expensive part of Valentine. The people who dined here were some of the wealthiest in the state. He enjoyed how much the restaurant looked like a seamless replica of the many his father had built and run thirty years ago on the west coast. The building was unique among the other featureless businesses littering the community. It was an authentic recreation of Italian history. He considered many factors before he unveiled it to the small Midwestern city.

August figured with all the Italian chain restaurants in the city, the public might find it nice to have something original. It was truly one-of-a-kind. The establishment was large, by restaurant standards. The two-story was built with beige brick. Oval shaped windows lined the front of the structure as the exterior walls were homage to picturesque settings of Old Italy. The front glass double doors had a dual purpose. One was the obvious entryway into the place. The second was to be a glass *carte du jour* where the specials were written at eye level in dry-erase marker.

The first floor was home to the vintage eatery, while the next level was a larger area constructed for various types of parties and events. The back of the restaurant was home to a medium sized man-made lake encircled by a marble exterior patio. August had decided to scatter several tables along the piazza. The restaurant owner knew the weather in the Midwest was sometimes severe and often unpredictable, but he enjoyed the realistic look, and most of his customers liked it as well. He had made it mobile; all the tables could be taken down whenever climate became an issue.

He adored the interior of the restaurant; it was dimly lit on purpose to create a wonderful ambience. The walls and bar were finished in redwood, and the floor was of the same marble that lined the ceiling. There were several pieces of original artwork that lined the corridors of the lobby and entrance. August had been busy behind the bar in deep thought of the liquor count and paid little attention to the LCD television, affixed above the bar by steel rods on both sides.

Bending over the bar counter, he noticed a report from *Eye-Spot5 News* flash across the screen. The reporter was a young man in his mid-twenties, who he recognized as Bradley Walker. The newsman was one of the regular patrons at the restaurant; he was speaking into a small microphone attached to his brown suit jacket. August stared at the screen and thought the houses in the background where Bradley stood, appeared to look quite familiar. He continued with his tedious task but neglected to turn up the volume to hear what the young man was saying. If he had, August would've heard Bradley's special report on the most recent homicide…one which would change his life forever.

* * *

"This is Bradley Walker, from Eyespot 5 News, with a special report. Local police are reporting a homicide at this hour. The residence behind me is the scene where the police say the body was discovered. The victim appears to be a woman in her early twenties. They are not releasing her name until family members are contacted. Police report around eleven-thirty this morning; a neighbor had come over to visit the woman, when she found the body. The police further state the female had been in this location for quite a while before being found. As you can see, there are about ten police units at the scene still investigating.

Police continue to say there are no known suspects in this case at this time. The city has seen a rash of murders in the last few days, and I spoke with police spokesman, Troy Doyle in regards to the recent outbreak. He indicated police are stepping up patrols to have more officers on the street. I'll have more on this story as it develops. This is Bradley Walker, sending you back to regular programming."

* * *

The picture on the screen returned to the talk show, as August looked up and noticed his good customer had completed the report. After he finished with the bar stock, he decided to give his Thursday to Saturday lover a call on her cell. He was anxious to see if Tamia was back from her modeling shoot. If Tamia ever decided she wanted to commit, August would leave his wife without hesitation.

August dialed the number from the bar phone, knowing never to call her from his personal cell. His wife would check the phone bill; he didn't need any evidence of his adultery on paper. August waited several rings, and then was transferred to Tamia Stevens' voice mail. "Hey, you. It's August. I can't wait until I see you again. If you can't make it Thursday, let me know. You won't need to renew the keycard for another month, so just show up at our room, and I'll be waiting. Love you, babe."

He hung up and headed back to his office, fantasizing about the night of pleasure Tamia and he would soon have.

* * *

Lucifer sat at a picnic bench in the Valentine City Park, enjoying a late lunch, which consisted of turkey and provolone cheese on rye bread with a side salad. He purchased the quick meal from a quaint deli a few blocks away from his apartment. He had taken along the cell phone of Tamia Stevens, in hope that the Italian slob would call. Lucifer sat by himself, watching the park's assortment of daily visitors, when his cargo pocket began to vibrate.

Hmm, I wonder who's calling? He took his time and finished his side salad, then flipped out the device. The new voicemail dialog envelope flashed across the L.E.D. display. He pushed the center call button to see if the voicemail would dial. If it didn't, he wouldn't spend much time with this phone. He would throw it in the lake and be done with it. Fortunately for him, the voicemail initiated; within a few seconds, he listened to the message left by part-time lover August Dellano. Lucifer hit the delete key; any trace of the message was gone forever. He placed it back into his pocket and finished off the rest of his turkey on rye.

Lucifer picked up his trash and stopped short of the garbage can. Two adolescent boys wearing baggy blue jeans were next to the canister engaged in the act of smoking. *Future Fortune 500 members.*

Ignoring them, he shoved the refuse through the slot. One of the boys flicked the butt of his cigarette in the killer's direction. *Really? You must be kidding.*

"Hey! You can't put that stuff in *our* garbage can."

Lucifer turned to walk away. *Just keep going, No time for deviating.*

"Did you hear me, asshole? *I* said you can't throw that crap in our garbage can."

Guess not? Lucifer whirled around and approached the loudmouth teenager. "I'm sorry, did you say something to me?"

"No shit! I said something to your dumb ass!" The punk kid rolled up his long-sleeved shirt exposing a tattoo of a red skull and crossbones on his right forearm. "I'll say it again so you can *fucking* understand me!" The other teenager slid alongside his partner to express solidarity.

Not the best move, my friend. Lucifer waved a hand at him. "I don't think that will be necessary." Lucifer smiled, standing face to face with both juveniles. "I will go this way—"

"I don't give a shit what you think is necessary. You're lucky I don't cut that Ken doll smile off your damn face. Do you know who you're messing with?" The other boy watched the two in silence.

"Look, I'm sure you think you're a tough guy, but I'm busy and don't have time for this bullshit." Lucifer clenched his teeth; his body started to tighten. *Just a little closer.*

"Bullshit? You think disrespecting me is smart? You need to take a look at the tattoo again. I'm…what do you smart people call it? Oh yeah, *affiliated.*" The overzealous teen reached down the front of his pants and yanked out a large hunting knife.

You're fucked now! Lucifer was quicker than the future prison inmate and delivered a forceful blow with the palm of his hand to the neck of the young man. He toppled over as the knife clattered to the pavement. Lucifer moved in and grabbed the knife and placed it against the throat of the downed juvenile.

"Let's see, what was that again? I think you meant to say *you* don't know who you're messing with." Lucifer smiled at the juvenile, who displayed spasms from Lucifer's well-placed strike.

"Please, I was just trying to scare ya," the young man whimpered.

Lucifer locked eyes with the other boy; he stood with his hands up in the air.

"Sir, we're sorry!"

Lucifer chuckled, stood up, and discarded the knife into the garbage can. "See, gentlemen, maybe the thug life style isn't for the two of you. I would suggest a career change." Walking away from the misguided juveniles, he left the city park with a smile on his face; satisfied in more ways than one.

Chapter 23

A Pattern Emerges

Brian Jeffers' drive to the police station was quiet, except for the occasional radio traffic from patrol officers in communication with the dispatch center. He pulled into the station garage and entered through the back. The department's administrative assistant, Cynthia Cornerstone met him as he stepped into the hallway. She looked him up and down. "Brian, when was the last time you slept? You look like shit."

He flashed a weary smile. "Well, my dear Cynthia, it has been a long day and probably won't slow down any time soon."

"You're not going to do anybody much good if you don't get some rest." She patted him on the back.

"You're right. I could use some. How did the press release go with *Eyespot 5 News?* I hope we didn't sound too bad."

Cynthia returned his smile and consoled him. "I think all things considered, we came out the best we could. Commander Barnum stormed in here a short time ago, and Chief demanded to see him. It didn't sound like it was going to be a friendly discussion."

Everybody gets what they deserve. Chief Ralph Anderson didn't like Barnum any more than Brian did. He knew the directive Anderson gave Barnum to release information within the circle of media was more to show Barnum who was in charge than anything else. Barnum hated when he was made aware he wasn't the highest on the food chain. They didn't have a good relationship because of the countless number of conflicts between them and neither would give an inch when it came to power. Brian reminisced as he stood and shuffled through the paperwork.

Chief Ralph Anderson had been a fan of his since an earlier investigation. It was about a year ago to the day when Brian found the mayor's kidnapped daughter. Two of the local drug dealers wanted several million dollars in exchange for her life. Mayor Boston Stone wasn't a rich man, and asked Chief Anderson to have his best investigator assigned to the case. Brian was asked to head up the search, and after paying some informants, it led to a few targeted warehouses downtown. He searched all the abandoned buildings until Brian got lucky. When he found the kidnapper's sanctuary, a gun battle ensued. Brian was wounded, but the two hostage-takers were killed.

He found the bound and beaten girl locked in small room, barely alive. This was the day Brian earned the detective shield. Cynthia waved a hand in front of his face. "Earth calling Brian? Did you hear what I said?"

"Um, no. I was thinking of something. Sorry."

"Well, I said your boss went into the chief's office and has been there ever since." Cynthia placed her hands on her hips.

"Well, good for him. Maybe a good ass-chewing will do him justice. He's been trying like hell to take over most of this investigation. Now, maybe he'll be happy to let me do my job so he can sit behind his desk with his high-dollar salary and read policies."

Cynthia smirked and attempted to stifle a laugh. She reached down on her desk and handed him a dark brown folder. "This is the information on Justin Paul's vehicle registrations you asked for a few days ago."

"Thanks. I hope this will help us."

"I also included the inventory from the residence. Officer Kelly documented all belongings at the house, and it looks like all appropriate valuables are listed."

Brian opened the file and skimmed through it and looked for one particular item that was of extreme interest to him. The silver Zippo lighter Marcus Paul had given his brother wasn't on the inventory list. It was unlikely it would be found there anyway, but he was happy Cynthia procured the inventory for him. He wasn't sure, but he had a strong sense Justin Paul's expensive lighter was taken from the scene, as well as his wife's artwork. *Lucifer has to be the person responsible for the missing items.* "Thanks for the information. I know I can always count on you." Brian closed the folder.

"No problem. That's why you pay me the big bucks." Cynthia shot him a playful wink.

Brian had the strong hunch that if Lucifer had taken those items from the Paul family, he may have taken something from the Ross Bosworth murder, as well. He picked up the phone and dialed the number for Toby Wall.

"Hey, dude, what's up? How is the investigation coming?"

"Question for you. Do you have the case file with Ross Bosworth still handy?"

Toby stepped away from the phone for a short time, and then returned. "Right in front of me, dude. What are you looking for?"

"Do you know if Ross Bosworth was missing anything other than the obvious removed body part?"

"I didn't think anything of it till you just mentioned

it, but yeah, man."

"*Really?* What was it?"

"Brother, somebody ripped off some crazy little animal statue."

"I didn't see that anywhere in your files."

"Partner, it wouldn't be. It was a separate complaint filled out after the family packed up all of Bosworth's stuff. According to the complaint, it was like a family heirloom."

"Family heirloom? Do you know what it was *exactly?*" Brian asked.

"Hold on, I'll check." Toby put Brian on hold. The sound of late 80s pop rock filled the background. He soon came back on the line. "The item missing is identified as a tiny ivory elephant figurine. The report indicated it was supposed to be at the dead guy's house."

"So it was stolen?"

"Bri-my-man, that thing could have been sold by Bosworth himself."

"I don't think so. I think our killer took it from the victim. I believe Lucifer has a secondary hobby, *besides* murder."

"That's some crazy thinking. So are you telling me psycho killer is like stealing stuff from these dead folks? What in the hell would he do with the junk anyway?"

"It looks pretty much like he is taking things from the deceased. The answer to the second part of your question is… maybe he keeps the personal items for memorabilia purposes," Brian said.

"Huh? Dude, this guy is no doubt a whack job. I would think if he was stealing from his victims would sooner or later get him caught."

"You would think so. Maybe that's how we can

catch him."

"Well, if I can find anything more to help, I'll let you know."

"Thanks. I'll keep you posted on what's going on," Brian replied.

"I'm sorry about not calling about this statue thing. I didn't think about it," Toby apologized.

"No worries. You had no idea what the deal was."

Brian sat a few more minutes, thinking about the conversation and in search of any evidence that would lead him to the murderer. He knew sooner or later Lucifer would have to make a mistake, and he would be there.

Chapter 24

Preparation of a Masterpiece

Lucifer stopped in front of the Motor Transportation Office of Dunlap County. It was a fresh and modern structure, which sat just a few blocks from the Law Enforcement Center. The building was gray and the front was lined with various sizes of windows. It also had small reflecting pools along the figure-eight sidewalk. Lucifer had written down the information from the minivan on a yellow notepad and stuck the paper inside his right cargo pocket. He was in a good mood, especially after the incident where he scared the hell out of those wannabes.   Checking his left cargo pocket, he was glad he remembered to bring actual cash for the vehicle registration information fee. He wasn't about to use a credit card or write a check that would leave an imprint he'd been there. It would also make Lucifer forgettable to the administration clerk who collected his money. He wanted to make it as difficult as possible for the police to catch him. Lucifer had spent about an hour on his computer to create the phony driver's license. Its' sole purpose was to purchase the vehicle information. He believed most of the transportation employees would have difficulty to identify whether the license was real or fake.

Most of the chairs were filled with people eager to see a service representative. He approached the automated number dispenser and ripped a ticket from the bottom. *813*. He looked at the various numbers on the displays above the service windows; the current number was 700. *I don't have time for this*. Lucifer perused the room. He pretended to read the various brochures on the numerous racks throughout the area. This would be an effective way to search for what he wanted. Lucifer made small talk to several people just to peek at their ticket numbers. He was in search of the perfect someone to help him. After about five minutes, he came across a middle-aged Hispanic woman with several children. He glanced down at the ticket number she clutched in her dark, wrinkled hand and was very pleased when he saw the number. He glanced up at the service windows and noticed it scroll to 709.

Lucifer needed to act fast because her number, 711, was up soon. The woman's face appeared a little drained, as the children were involved with the standard arguments little people have at their age. Many of the patrons close to the small group glared in obvious disdain. *This is my chance*. He put on a sinister smile and reached into his pocket and grabbed a fifty-dollar bill. Drawing very close to the woman, he spoke with calculated charm. "Hello, my name is Patrick. I see you have your hands full with the children, so I have a deal that may interest you."

The woman turned to smile at the devious killer. "Hello, Mr. Patrick. Yes, my hands are full here, but what can *you* do for me?"

Lucifer liked how the woman got right to the point. "I'll give you fifty dollars and my ticket number for the one in your hand."

"I don't know, sir," the woman said.

"I have to get home and watch my poor, sick mother, so it would be great if you could help me," Lucifer said. He thought ad-libbing about his mother was the perfect way to hook her.

"Sir, that is a very nice offer, but I've been here for two hours. The little ones are kind of hungry. I really didn't want to do this today, anyway, but I'll need a little more than fifty," the woman said.

Lucifer winked; impressed she had the courage to ask for more. It was worth it to get out of here with minimal time spent in the open. He handed seventy dollars and his ticket to her.

"All I have is this extra twenty besides what I need to renew my license," coaxed Lucifer. He knew she wouldn't turn down the extra cash.

The woman stared at Lucifer, smiled, and took the money and ticket. She handed him hers and stood. "Take care of your momma, you seem like a nice son." She motioned for the children to follow.

"I will. She'll be grateful." *Oh, that's right. She's dead.* Lucifer was pleased with himself as he waited. Within a few minutes, the number he had acquired came up on window twelve. He noticed the clerk and thought since this homely young woman appeared bored and disinterested in her job, it would be easy to trick her so quality assurance wouldn't be her number one priority.

She possessed a fair complexion, with long, braided jet-black hair and wore a black polo shirt with the motor transport emblem on the right side. The woman sort of reminded Lucifer of a Gothic girl he murdered a few years earlier. She didn't seem to be focused on the customers at the window. Lucifer laughed to himself as he approached. He smiled and stopped at the glass enclosure.

The girl returned the gesture. She was wearing a white lanyard around her neck that held a nametag in the plastic sleeve, which identified her as Lydia Jordan.

"Good afternoon, Lydia. Looks like this place is pretty busy?"

The clerk seemed to be caught off guard with this greeting. She straightened up and bit her bottom lip; Lucifer knew the woman found him attractive. "Hello, sir. Yes, it has been very busy. What may I assist you with today?"

Lucifer presented the false identification. "Lydia. I need to purchase an owner registration printout for a vehicle I was thinking of buying."

"Sir, we don't normally give out that information." Lydia tapped the counter with her fingernails.

"I was driving my old, beat up Honda down the street when I saw this great-looking van sitting on the grass next to an empty parking lot. I went to look at it but the owner must have forgotten to put a contact number on the cardboard sign in the window." Lucifer shot her a boyish grin.

"Well, doesn't sound like you've had very good luck." She sounded interested.

"Yeah, if you only knew." *I've reeled her in.* "I was thinking I could get the information and approach the owner with an offer."

"Well, he should have left a number on it." Lydia sympathized with the killer.

"I know, Right? Plus the guy left it in a parking lot. There wasn't any other way I could think of to track him down." Lucifer shrugged his shoulders.

"Okay, I'm a sucker for a story like that." She inspected the identification without too much scrutiny. "The printout will cost you a few dollars." Lydia batted her eyelashes at Lucifer. Valentine's killer realized he had accomplished his little scam.

"How much do I owe you?"

Lydia punched several numbers into her computer. "Six dollars for a complete vehicle history. Do you have the make, model, and plate number for me?"

"Six dollars sounds good to me. Thank you." Lucifer pulled out the scrap of yellow paper that held the information.

"All you had to write on, huh?"

He laughed. "I told you it was a parking lot and I was in a hurry," he lied.

The clerk took it and typed all the data into the computer screen. In a few minutes, she placed the printout in an envelope and slid it across the counter to Lucifer.

"Here you are, Patrick. I hope everything works out for you."

"Thank you, Lydia, I appreciate your help. Hey, do you have a pen? I think you should call me sometime. I would love to go to a movie or something." Lucifer slid a crisp twenty-dollar bill to her.

Lydia made change for him and started to giggle like a high school girl on her first date. She handed him a pen; he wrote down a number on one of the dollar bills she returned as change. He slid it back over in front of her. Her pale face began to redden as Lucifer shot her a wink and exited the office. On the bill he had given Lydia, he had written the phone number to Tamia Steven's cell phone. He never discounted the need for another victim; this would work out perfectly. Lydia would be a nice addition to his collection. Lucifer put the unopened envelope in his right cargo pocket and would save it until later. He knew it held the name of his ultimate masterpiece. *A creation of epic proportions*. Lucifer pulled the fifty-cent piece out of his pocket and ran it through his thumb and forefinger. He became exhilarated. *Just a few hours left until another victim would be added to my collection.*

Chapter 25

The Autopsy

Brian Jeffers parked the unmarked in the lower garage of Dunlap County Hospital. This isolated entrance was reserved for the medical examiner and various funeral home employees throughout the state. The hospital administration didn't want covered dead bodies pushed through the main halls of the medical facility, as it didn't fit the "community friendly" image they tried to project.

Brian was here to meet with Dr. Sanderson in regards to the autopsy of Tamia Stevens. The medical examiner's other facility was still filled with Lucifer's other victims, so the hospital was the next available place to conduct an autopsy. Brian passed through the lower entrance of the hospital and accessed the elevator, which led to the morgue and autopsy examination room. He stopped at the security desk. One of the officers, dressed in the hospital's gray duty uniform, asked for identification, while another sat at a small wooden desk and protected the large metallic door that led to the morgue. The detective pulled out his badge and credentials.

Brian entered a cramped, fluorescent filled corridor which led to a set of metal doors. Pushing them open, he moved into the autopsy examination room. He had been down here many times before, but would still get chills whenever he stepped foot inside. The room had plastered white walls adorned with various medical posters. A black chalkboard was on the far wall behind two examination tables centered in the middle of the sterile space. One of the two tables was home to a recent addition. *Tamia's body*.

The corpse was covered with a drab green, blood-stained hospital sheet; the smell of decomposing flesh surrounded it. The majority of the space was full of medical equipment; two ancient gray metal desks were pushed against the near wall. Dr. Sanderson had his back to the door and turned around to face Brian as soon as the doors swung shut. "I don't have very good news for you." Dr. Sanderson led the investigator to the covered body of Tamia Stevens.

Brian knew before Sanderson continued something wasn't right. "Propaganician isn't in her system, is it, Doc?" Brian rubbed the top of his forehead.

"No. It isn't. I'm sorry; your killer didn't use it on this particular victim. I wanted to show you something on Tamia Stevens' body I think you will find strange… indeed." Sanderson raised up the bloody sheet.

Brian found it difficult to swallow, as the coroner's work on her almost made the former model *ugly*. "She doesn't even look human."

"I know. The body decomposes so fast." Dr. Sanderson moved the sheet aside for more visibility. Tamia's ripped-open intestines were placed back inside the body cavity. This was necessary for the medical examiner to determine how the killer attacked the young woman. The corpse had a story to tell, and Brian Jeffers was more than ready to listen. Dr. Sanderson took out a scalpel and pointed to a location on Tamia's right side. The flesh was peeled away, but Brian could see a visible perforation where some type of weapon entered her.

Dr. Sanderson spoke with great intensity. "Take a look. She was struck from her right side by a blunt instrument, maybe a large knife of some kind. When the object penetrated her, it was thrust upward, which punctured her lungs." Sanderson pushed on the lower part of her lung with the medical instrument. Brian noticed a laceration; it appeared to be extremely deep.

Dr. Sanderson continued his observation. "Five inches in depth. Do you see the blood pockets surrounding the tissue?"

"Yes." Brian peered at the wound.

"She wasn't dead until the gash on her jugular vein was inflicted." Sanderson pointed to the shredded throat of the dead girl.

That doesn't make any sense. "Repeat that?" Brian asked in amazement.

"It was hard to tell at first because she was almost decapitated, but I checked the wound pattern; it's consistent with my theory," Sanderson said.

"Doc, the whole damn body looks like one giant wound pattern…"

"Your killer watched as he punctured Tamia's lung and waited until she was close to drowning in her own blood… then he sliced her throat."

"This son-of-a-bitch wanted to torture her when she was about to die anyway?" Brian asked. He stared into the model's empty eyes.

Sanderson's head dropped. "The other mutilation occurred after she died, more than likely, in the vehicle. This killer is an expert in inflicting pain."

The inscriptions on her back! "Doc, he marked the dead girl's body with what I consider his signature. Was the engraving done with the same blunt instrument that killed her?"

Dr. Sanderson was gentle with her as he flipped over her body, and showed Brian the wound pattern. He spoke with pronounced wisdom. "This so-called signature was completed with such precision. The killer could only use one item that would accomplish these cutting edges." Sanderson hesitated for a few seconds and raised the thin steel. "Your killer used a scalpel, similar to this one."

Of course. "Like you said before, it still could be anybody with a little medical training, right?" Brian hoped to pin down the doctor to a definite answer.

"After his, I think we can narrow our search," Sanderson said,

"Narrow it to what?" *Say it.*

"I believe your killer is a surgeon."

"Well, this is a better lead than we've had so far."

"Yes. I hope it will identify who is responsible." Sanderson yanked on the sheet and covered Tamia's remains.

That was the verification Brian needed. A physician of some type had gone berserk and was practicing his *own* style of surgical procedures. Brian thanked the doctor and spoke to him for a few more minutes before he left the hospital. He knew a madman with specialized training who displayed little remorse was on the loose in Valentine. Brian didn't know how, or if, he was ever going to be able to stop him.

Chapter 26

Waiting for August

Lucifer drove to the Daltry Hotel instead of his daily walk. He rarely liked to get behind the wheel, but today was special. The extra room was needed for what he had planned. He left his Honda at the apartment and rented a vehicle at the airport. The hotel staff would be suspicious of his beat-up car parked in the upscale parking garage. They would not, however, have any suspicions of the rental, a newer black SUV. He would return it tomorrow, after his latest masterpiece was completed and another token was added to his collection.

The rear lot of the Daltry was almost empty; his rental wouldn't get any extra attention from the occasional police patrol. He knew the officers routinely drove through the hotel grounds once a night, in search of thieves or the occasional reckless vandal. Lucifer pulled the truck into the cobbled driveway and parked next to the sidewalk. He opened the rear hatch to retrieve a few items. One was an overnight suitcase filled with various goodies he couldn't wait to use. The other was an old, rusted-out wheelchair. Lucifer stacked both against the back- row seats of the sports utility. The killer liked to keep all his tools in neat fashion. He placed the suit-case in the seat of the wheelchair, and then wheeled both along the sidewalk adjacent to the back entrance.

It was still daylight, and the killer was cognizant the Daltry's internal security required guests to use their access key cards at night to enter. The hotel's security protocol was reserved to the overnight hours and once daylight broke, the standard loosened. Lucifer reached into his right cargo pocket and pulled out one of the items he had taken that glorious night of Tamia Stevens' death.

He wanted to make sure it at least worked here first. If it didn't, this would be a short-lived trip, and he would have to rearrange his schedule. He inserted the white plastic rectangular card into the access key slot; within five seconds, a bright green access light illuminated the keypad. The back door opened, making the killer smile. Lucifer wheeled the belongings to the first room on the right. *This is working out just as I intended.* The last time he was here, he was hidden from his future masterpieces. They were so caught up in their devious behavior; the restaurant owner hadn't seen him when he walked by to get some ice.

Inserting the key card into the lock, his heart pounded through his head. The green light activated the lock. As Lucifer grasped the handle of the door, his breath became hastened; his hands started to perspire. This was the first time he had been this nervous, and it was not optimal for his plans. *Get it together*!

Entering the room, he flipped on the light switch, which exposed the interior. This place was a major disappointment. Lucifer figured the rich Italian would splurge a little more than *this* on his top-model mistress. It was a featureless hotel, which housed the customary double bed, a medium-sized closet, and a sink with a mirror. The sink adjacent to the bathroom was almost *too* small for the overweight cheater and his lover. The room was completed by a brown entertainment center that contained a standard-sized television set.

"August, you're a cheap bastard. Couldn't even spring for a hot tub for your girl," he muttered in disgust.

The killer circled the room, immediately spotting the best place to carry out his agenda. After removing the suitcase from the seat, he folded the wheelchair and shoved it into the corner of the room's closet. Cradling the suitcase, he placed it on the maroon comforter of the double bed. He unlocked it; his eyes opened wide, a baby witnessing light for the first time. Lucifer removed the necessary equipment needed for the implementation to create the desired masterpiece. The first object was a small, clear syringe, filled with a regular dose of his prized paralytic. He had come to like this drug; it was his signature trademark. There was a supply available at the storage space he rented just outside the city limits.

His hands grasped the next item, a black plastic hand-held stun-gun. *This* was one of Lucifer's favorite tools. He had picked up this little gem at an army surplus store a few years ago and enjoyed its convenient portability. This particular model would deliver 250,000 volts to the intended prey. *Quite a jolt*. He hadn't used it in a while and was eager to revisit the kind of pain it would deliver. Next on the list was a wonderful apparatus that would pierce through the Italian's flesh and bone without any trouble. The fourth and final item was a black teddy that was stolen from one of the local lingerie shops. He knew *someday* the provocative outfit would come in handy,. Lucifer threw the lingerie onto the bed, ready to initiate the second stage of the devious plot.

He removed the prepaid flip cell phone of Tamia Stevens. He opened it and a blue light display illuminated the area. Lucifer scrolled through the phone's bothersome options in search of the text message menu. *Nice. Ready to send message*. He punched several letters, and each appeared on the vibrant color screen. Scrolling through the various options, he located the address book symbol. This would aid him to locate his target. A devilish look filled his face as the name of his prey appeared on screen. Lucifer pressed the *send now* key button. The message displayed the text information sent to August Dellano.

I'm here at the hotel. Make an excuse to your wife. Bring champagne. We'll make love all night. No photo shoot tomorrow.

He shoved the cell in his pocket; it would be disposed of when it had served his calculated purpose. All Lucifer needed to do now was wait for the next addition to his collection to follow the message and find him.

Chapter 27

A Carried-Out Attack

August Dellano was elated; he'd just received a text message from Tamia. He hadn't planned to see her until their scheduled time, but the man would always welcome her, no matter *what* day it was. August would make sure to call Janice later to make up an excuse. His wife almost never questioned his whereabouts anymore; ever since the day he made the choice to get physical with her. *The bruises were always hidden.*

August smiled at the small pink box on his passenger's seat. He bought Tamia this little token of affection last week and had forgotten to give it to her at their last encounter. She would love the diamond and ruby necklace; maybe she would finally agree to be his exclusive girlfriend. Even though he was married, August could envision himself leaving his wife for the seductive Tamia. *It's worth a try,* he thought.

The hotel staff had recently started to be more enthralled with the eye candy on his arm; it even seemed like some of the employees would spy on the two any time a chance presented itself. August enjoyed his privacy, and didn't appreciate the unwanted attention. He would make sure to speak with the overpaid hotel manager, Stanley White, about future relocation and increased privacy. *Kill the onlookers' curiosity.* He parked his car next to a newer model black Tahoe, admiring the particular style of sports utility. It was on his to-do list and soon, one of these beauties would be his. He popped the trunk and gathered his brown overnight bag, along with a medium-sized maroon paper bag. His restaurant's logo was on both sides. *Can't play on an empty stomach.* The colorful bag contained the requested champagne, two crystal goblets, and a fresh chocolate raspberry torte for dessert. He grabbed the pink box off the front seat and entered the hotel. August handpicked the room, even though it wasn't the most exquisite, or as of late, the most private. It did, however, have easy access. It was right inside the rear entrance of the hotel; he figured it was the best place to partake in the couple's lustful activities. August used his access key card and opened the door to the pre-paid room. As he stepped through, he observed it was dimmer than normal. *Ah, a little tease, she is.* There were two pillowcases thrown over the set of bedside lamps. This created a soft, romantic atmosphere. *Nice touch.* His attention was drawn to the dark-colored nightgown placed on the bed next to a suitcase. August spotted a thin strip of light from underneath the bathroom door. He pressed his ear to the door; a mischievous grin crept from his lips. The muffled sound of bath water, being sloshed back and forth in the tiny tub, told the cheater that the festivities were about to take off. *Tamia is getting nice and clean, so she can get dirty.* He was ecstatic about the necklace, and was in a hurry to present it to her. August wanted to add to the already seductive ambience of the room, so he removed out all the items and set them on the bedside table. Testing the champagne, it was a bit too warm and would need to be chilled. He glanced around the room, but noticed the ice bucket wasn't on the surface of the sink, like it usually was. "Damn, worthless hotel employees!" August stormed over to the main light switch.

He flipped the button, but nothing happened. August

glimpsed up; the light fixture on the ceiling had a few deep cracks in it. *Oh great, now the hotel will probably charge me for breaking it.*

August crouched down next to the sink and opened the cabinet. He reached in and found the needed ice bucket, a few paper towels and a light bulb that no doubt belonged in the cracked fixture. He snatched up the bulb and screwed it in where it belonged. A flip of the switch this time, resulted in success. The room was filled with a yellow glow. August approached the bathroom door and knocked. "Tamia, I'm here. I like what you did to the room."

A return knock told him his lover was ready and waiting. He grasped the doorknob, and turned, but stopped when he remembered he still lacked ice for the bubbly. Snatching the bucket, he exited the hotel room and scurried towards the vending area, and whistled as he went. August completed his task; a couple of hotel maintenance employees waved to him from further down the hallway. August sneered in disgust, as he headed to the room. He stepped through the door and observed the bath water had stopped.

August was also aware the light underneath the door was no longer there. *Kinky little games.* He decided to join his lover, as he picked up the champagne and filled two glasses. He placed the goblets on the table and undressed. Grabbing the glasses, he pushed open the door to the bathroom. It was muggy, as clouds of steam rolled out into the open. The lack of any movement, human or mechanical both, aroused and made him nervous at the same time.

August called to his lover. "Tamia, baby, open the curtain. I have something for you." Before the Italian could react, the curtain flew open and the now-exposed Lucifer sent 250,000 volts into the restaurant owner's bare upper chest. The odor of burning skin filled the air as Lucifer struck again and again. August lost control and dropped both glasses, which caused them to shatter as they hit the white tile floor. The liquid splashed in all directions; he fell backwards, and bounced off the towel rack, which propelled him forward. Lucifer struck him over and over with the vicious device. This time, the killer showed no mercy as he lowered the torture device to the naked man's most vulnerable area. The volts rippled through his flesh. August cried in tremendous pain. He slumped to the ground but Lucifer was on top of him, and within seconds the weapon's wrath seared every layer of August's most private region. The restaurant owner tried to call out for help, but the pain from the attack ended his subdued whimper. The constant barrage of electric shock treatment sent him into trauma-driven unconsciousness.

    * * *

Lucifer dragged the unclothed cheater's limp figure to the hotel bed. He forced open the closet and ripped out the wheelchair. He flipped it open, grabbed a hold of August, and slammed him upright into the device. He snatched a hand towel from the water-stained sink and tied it over his newest victim's mouth.

Is that…? Lucifer smelled an invitation from inside the maroon bag. He looked over at August and then stole a quick glance at his watch. He knew the Italian would be unconscious for a while, so he opened up the bag and was delighted to see the torte. He figured he might as well help himself; after all, there would be plenty of time.

    * * *

August awakened to find himself upright in a wheel-

chair. His hands and feet were tied to the medical acces-
sory by what appeared to be torn sheets. He felt a strong
pressure through the front and sides of his mouth, which
forced his jaws to be crammed open.

Groggy from the onslaught of pain to his body, he
discovered the gag. A sudden panic struck him and tears
flowed down his face. *What's going on?*

His pain was so intense; the memory of what had
transpired prior to his current situation was vague to say
the least. *Tamia.* He became more aware by the minute,
as he peered down at the floor. The white silk sheets from
the bed were sprawled out all around the wheel chair. His
vision was focused straight ahead. There, he observed
a very muscular man sitting on the now-stripped bed.
This unknown intruder smiled at him and engaged in the
consumption of, *August's* special dessert, to top it off,
the asshole also appeared to have a plastic cup of champagne. *Son of a bitch.* He wasn't sure if this man was
some stalker of Tamia's or worse yet, a former boyfriend
who had followed the promiscuous couple and was determined to scare the shit out of him. *Well, so far, it had
worked.* The man laughed when he noticed August stir.

* * *

Lucifer had removed all the sheets from the bed to
prepare the stage for his masterpiece. He plugged in the
powerful drill and attached the specially-made industrial
bit. Lucifer hid the potent tool underneath the bed, so it
would be sort of a surprise to the Italian. *The look on the
cheater's face will be captivating.* He discarded the torte,
empty plastic cup and utensils into a white plastic garbage bag. Lucifer wiped off his mouth and bent over, and
gave a complimentary bow. "That was excellent!" The
Italian struggled to free himself from his linen prison,

but was still too weak and the effort was almost comical. August watched as Lucifer sat on edge of the bed and removed all of his clothing.

"Oh my God, please don't hurt me! I will do anything," August whimpered. The cloth strangled his words. Lucifer smiled. He was amused by the man's plea for mercy. The killer knew the drill would make a gory mess, so the lack of clothing would be essential in disposal of the expected carnage. Lucifer opened the entertainment center and turned on the TV. He adjusted the volume so it would mask the sound of the whirring drill. He grabbed the syringe of Propaganician and watched as August started to thrash within his confines.

"No! Please, no." August garbled. Lucifer positioned himself behind the chair; in one movement, he plunged the syringe deep into the right side of August Dellano's neck. Stepping back, the killer watched the lethal medication do his will. He removed the empty syringe and returned it to the suitcase. He glanced back at his prey, snickered, and clapped while the man gasped for air. Lucifer undid the straps and pushed the naked Italian out of the wheelchair. August Dellano landed facedown onto sheets.

Lucifer picked up the drill and flashed it in front of the slob. He pushed the orange power button on the tool and aimed the device over the man's flesh. *Time to get to work on the next masterpiece.*

Lucifer was impressed with how quick he finished his work and retreated to the bathroom to shower off the blood spatter. Once clean enough to get dressed, he inspected the pink box the dead man left on the table. He would take this for an addition to his collection. He was inquisitive to know what lay inside the wrapped container; he opened it as though it was for him. He had a sinful smile on his face. The diamond and ruby necklace shimmered y back at him. Lucifer closed the box and placed it in his suitcase along with all of his necessities.

He studied the table and spotted the cell phone of August Dellano. He scrolled through to the text message he sent Dellano and deleted it. Lucifer wiped down the phone, placed it back on the table and turned off the television. He made sure to pick up the white plastic garbage bag as he walked to the door. He flipped off the light switch, took one last look at his new masterpiece and closed the door on August forever. Lucifer smiled all the way to the lot, as the killer reached into his pocket and felt for the fifty-cent piece. He ran the silver through his right thumb and forefinger. Lucifer couldn't wait to get home and prepare for his next victim. He was very pleased the voice of his mother was silent. *Maybe she was finally gone?* He eased into the rental vehicle and drove away from his latest piece of art with temporary fulfillment, and the focus to move onward to the next installment.

Chapter 28

Serena's Information

Brian Jeffers spent the majority of the next day perched at his desk. He was quite certain Tamia Stevens owned a cell phone, but the search of her residence turned up zero. Aware the killer was a collector; Brian was concerned if the late model was in possession of a cell at the time of her death. He was also curious to know who would have been the provider for the service. He had spent time in her house in search of phone bills, unable to fathom, how a modern era girl would be able to reach out to the world without a device. *One person might know.* He located the phone number to Tamia's next-door neighbor, Roseanne Tustin. "Hello," Roseanne answered.

"Hello, Ms. Tustin. This is Detective Jeffers."

"Oh, hello. How can I help you?"

"Roseanne, I'm sorry to bother you again, but…"

"Anything I can do to help, young man, just ask," Roseanne urged.

"I just had a few quick follow-up questions for you. I was going over some of the notes and noticed Tamia didn't have a phone anywhere in her residence—" Brian hinted.

"Detective, Tamia never had a phone installed in her house, but was constantly on her cell. She lived her life by that blasted thing."

"Cell phone? So she did have one?" Brian asked, as he wrote in the notebook.

"Of course. She always had a phone with her. I used

to tease her about how much the darn thing rang."

"We didn't find it at her house, Roseanne. You wouldn't happen to remember what the phone looked like would you?"

"Yes, I know what the phone looks like. It's one of those silver camera flip phone types, if I'm not mistaken; her agent provided it to her."

Already on my list. "Roseanne, you don't know what help you have been to me with this information. I need to find out a few more things, but I appreciate your help in this."

"Detective, do me a favor: just catch the evil man that killed this poor girl. That is all I ask*.*"

"I'm trying, Roseanne. Believe me, I'm trying." Brian hung up. He thought about the Justin Paul family and the artwork, Zippo lighter and now Tamia Stevens' cell phone. *One piece of this puzzle hopefully figured out.* He shuffled through his daily notes, still in limbo for Tamia's personal agent, to return his call. Her name was Serena Clarke; one of the only agents in the Valentine metro area, best known for her discovery of the talented artist Bell Willows. Serena used to be a model herself, before she realized the industry had a shelf life. To embark on a career in the representation portion of the business was lucrative and didn't require the figure where a size 6 was considered overweight for business standards. Bell Willows was Serena's first client and to this date, the most successful. She found the young artist several years ago employed at a second-rate video store. Two sculptures in the store were on display, which tempted Serena to approach Bell, and address her skill. Almost overnight, this catapulted the former store clerk's career. The partnership led to great fame and fortune.

Brian reviewed the stapled ten-page inventory list of personal effects found in Tamia Stevens' house, when he received a buzz on the speakerphone. The smooth voice of Cynthia Cornerstone filled the room. "Brian, I have Serena Clarke on line two for you. She says it's urgent and needs to speak with you."

"Put her through, Cynthia." Brian took a breath. "Serena, Detective Jeffers, here."

"Detective, I can't believe this has happened. I just talked to her on the phone two days ago. Tamia was getting ready to do a calendar shoot next month in Malibu."

A bright future indeed. "I'm very sorry about what has taken place. I'm doing everything I can to find the man responsible. I need some help from you, if you're up to it."

"Yes, I will try to tell you anything I know," Serena said shaken.

Brian wanted to get what information he could without undue pressure. "Serena, you spoke with her just a couple of days ago?"

"Yes, to give her the good news about the Malibu shoot."

"Did she call you on a cell phone by chance?" Brian asked.

"Sure, Detective, that's the only way she ever calls me. Why?"

"We couldn't find a phone or any bills at the crime scene," Brian said.

"Detective, the cell phone was issued by us."

"It was? Great, does the agency take care of the expense, or how does it work?"

"The agency takes care of the cell phone bill for her. Contract perks. It's through our provider *F-Zone*. The phone isn't registered to her; I have it registered in my name. It's easier."

Brian realized he might have caught a break. The phone bill would have all the incoming and outgoing calls recorded. He also knew in this techno-savvy world, there would be data transfers such as text messages. *She probably uses a lot of texting*, Brian thought.

"Serena, How about text messages? A lot of those?"

"Well, who doesn't nowadays, Detective? Yes, she would text me at least twice a day."

Brian was positive the phone bill would contain clues, which could lead them to Lucifer. So far, the killer had been getting all the luck. It was about time for the good guys to have some.

"It would be helpful to get those phone records. Is there a way you could do that for me?"

Serena started to cry. It was important to give any information she could to help find Tamia's killer. She regained a little composure. "I can get the records for you in the next few days."

"Serena, I really need it quicker if possible," Brian pleaded.

"Let me see what I can do," Serena said. "Hold on, I think we set Tamia's phone up for online account information."

Brian heard her fingers on the keyboard. "That would be a big help for us."

"Hey, I will still request a paper copy for you anyway. I'm sure you will need it."

Brian was amazed at the kindness of this talent agent. In most situations, he would have to get a subpoena just to look at the records. Serena, in obvious sorrow for her client, had circumvented the normal difficulties in cases like these. Brian looked up. Cynthia Cornerstone stood in the doorway, a sense of, urgency and a wave of a green folder told him, this couldn't wait. "Brian, I have something you *need* to see," Cynthia said in a hushed voice. Brian motioned for the administrative assistant.

"Serena, I have an issue. You okay on hold for just a few minutes?"

"Yes. The account information is taking longer than we expected," Serena was still at work on the keyboard, when Brian stuck her on hold and turned to his assistant.

"Cynthia, what's in the folder?"

"Open it up, it will explain itself," Cynthia pointed. He flipped it open and scanned through the pages. The file listed all of the lost/stolen medications from various medical facilities for the entire state. "Wow! I bet this took some ass-kissing to get." Brian smiled. "*I* was supposed to compile this inventory."

"Of course you were, dear, but I did it for you. A few calls here—a few calls there."

"Man, we need to hire you as a detective," Brian joked.

She ignored the comment. "Turn to page fifteen, before you get *too* excited about the results."

He turned to the page and reviewed the medications listed. His heart jumped, as his eyes scanned the Xeroxed paper. He searched for the paralytic drug. "Damn!" Brian closed the folder and shoved it in the metal inbox on his desk. "I thought for a minute we had found our link."

"I'm sorry, but the list is current as of last week, Brian. Not one facility reported your drug," Cynthia said.

"Well, that tells us the psycho didn't steal it here at least. Hey, thanks, for this." *Another goddamn dead end*! Brian pounded his fist on the desk.

She tapped him on the shoulder. I will let you get back to Serena." Cynthia exited the office.

Brian took the phone off hold and was sure the talent agent had hung up. "Serena, you still there?"

"I'm here. I just got logged in a few seconds ago."

"Did you find her call registry yet?"

"Give me a second." Serena again tapped at the keyboard. "I think maybe I found some usage error," Serena said, worry in her voice.

"What's the matter?"

"The automated system call log shows text messaging was used yesterday."

"Yesterday?" Brian was now more troubled than ever. When?" Brian grabbed a pen and scribbled in his notebook.

"It was sent late afternoon. Detective, that doesn't make any sense if she was killed the day before."

"In a way it *all* makes sense." Brian felt his stomach churn. He understood his fears were now being realized. The killer of Tamia Stevens and the Justin Paul family had taken personal belongings from his victims. Brian was confident Tamia Steven's cell, was now in the killer's hands. It all made perfect sense. Lucifer was responsible for Justin Paul's lighter and his wife's artwork, as well as the forgotten case in Calmine County. It all started with the elephant statue at Ross Bosworth's residence. Brian knew the killer must have planned this for some time, before actually he could implement it so it wouldn't draw suspicion. *Until now*! He figured Lucifer would have the stolen items and enshrined them to mark his conquests. It was the most logical explanation in these homicides, if logic had anything to do with it? He was ever more concerned Tamia's cell phone was used to send a text message to someone who believed the model was still alive.

"Detective, what did you say?" Serena awakened Brian from his daydreaming.

"I was talking to myself, Serena. Sorry about that," Brian lied. "Do you know if Tamia was involved with anyone at the time of her death?" There was a brief silence. Brian could tell the woman was in conflict if she should reveal the details of Tamia's relationships.

"I would guess you would mean… her, um, romance life?" Serena said, caution in her voice.

"Yes, in a way. If she was seeing someone, it very well may have been the killer."

"She didn't mention her boyfriends very often. I do know at her last shoot someone sent her three dozen red roses,"

"Really? Do you know from whom?" Brian asked.

"The only person I ever heard her talk about was someone named August, or Augustine. The guy's name was along that line."

"That's a start at least," Brian jotted down the name. He wanted to review the phone call list as soon as possible. "Serena, can you print the information onscreen of the phone calls and text messages and fax it over to me?"

"Yes, right away. Just give me your number."

Brian recited the department's fax number. He was anxious to find out if the killer had made a mistake which involved the dead girl's cell phone. "You have been a great help. I'm sorry about Tamia's death, but maybe this will be the link we need to catch that son-of-a-bitch."

"I will send the information when I get the phone bill in the next couple days. I'm glad I could help."

"I think you have done more than you know," Brian

complimented her.

"Detective, if you need anything else, I will be at home preparing the arrangements with the funeral home. She was family, not just another client. Good luck catching this fucking guy."

"Serena, take care." Brian hung up the phone and sat for a few more minutes He was tired; he needed a refill of coffee. He picked up the blue and white cup from his desk and walked out of the office. Administrative assistant Cynthia Cornerstone met him in the corridor, in hand was a fax transmittal document.

"Brian, dear, this just came from Serena Clarke." Brian took the paperwork and returned to his office. He scoured the paper for the information he needed, until he located the number on the text message. *Hell yes, it was yesterday afternoon.* The number listed was, 999-933-9445. He knew this numeral combination identified it as another cell phone in the Valentine area. He dialed. After the third ring, the voicemail system was activated. A muffled recording of a man's voice filled the speakerphone as Brian heard these words:

"You have reached the phone of August Dellano. I'm unable to take your call right now. If you leave your name and number and the time you called, I will get back to you as quick as I can. Thank you, and ciao."

Brian waited for the beep. "Mr. August Dellano, this is Detective Brian Jeffers of the Valentine Police Department. I'm calling in regards to a case in which you may know the party involved. Please call me at 997-633-7218 as soon as possible." Brian heard the options to deliver the message as priority and pushed the button to do so. Hopefully, August Dellano would get the message. Brian felt a cold tingle run up his spine. He decided it would make sense to run a background on Dellano. He knew Cynthia had left for the day, so he called her voice-mail and left her Dellano's name and explained what he needed. *Maybe August Dellano didn't know Tamia was dead and Lucifer used the text message to lure Dellano to him.* The killer seemed to have one agenda, to continue his reign of terror. Brian picked up a few files and walked out of the office. The detective was only sure of one thing. He needed to find August Dellano…

* * *

Lucifer had finished his daily run and grabbed a drink from the water fountain, where a few days earlier, he was fortunate to have met the Jeffers' family's girls. He stopped in the middle of the bridge and looked down at the thin waterway known as Points River. He reached into his pants pocket and pulled out Tamia's phone. Scanning the recreational area for nosy onlookers, he determined, his actions would go unnoticed. He hated to discard the phone,–it helped him create his last piece of art. Lucifer was curious to see if the motor transportation clerk Lydia Jordan would contact him. *A most promising masterpiece*, he thought. He was out of time and it was not conducive to believe the unattractive Lydia would fit into his schedule, since she had waited so long to contact him. O*h, well, another will take her place*.

He looked around once more before he removed the battery and catapulted the shell of the device into the river. The killer walked a few more feet, and spotted a moldy trashcan. Insects were in flight around the staple of, ripped-open pizza boxes, fast food wrappers and other waste which overflowed the top. Lucifer reached down through the garbage and stuffed the battery in as far as possible. He pulled his arm out of the refuse and peered at the various substances, which dripped from it. *The price I pay*. He strode away from the area and sported a very deep and evil smile. It was *almost* time to create the ultimate masterpiece.

Chapter 29

The Link

Brian Jeffers stopped by Barnum's office to update him of what Serena Clarke had sent him via fax. He knocked. The gruff authoritative voice of Alex Barnum greeted him.

"Come in!" yelled Alex Barnum.

Brian eased open the door and witnessed the distaste in Barnum's eyes. No doubt, he had gotten the word from the Chief of Police, to let Brian investigate without the micro-management from Barnum. *Thank God*. Brian ignored the thousand-yard stare and divulged the new information received from the helpful talent agent. Barnum was in pretend not to give- a shit mode, as he stared at the compilation of pens and pencils atop his desk. "Boss, the cell phone of Tamia Stevens was stolen."

"Are you even sure the dead girl owns a one?" Barnum didn't bother to look at him.

"It was issued by the talent agency," Brian folded his arms. *Suck it*.

"Who was the agent who gave you the information?" Barnum asked.

"Serena Clarke," Brian said.

"Serena fucking Clarke? You gotta be kidding me, Jeffers," Barnum's face flashed another shade of ugly.

"What's the deal with Clarke? You just don't like her, isn't that it?"

"I caught that little bitch in the back of a nightclub smoking dope." Barnum waved off Brian with a flick of his wrist.

"When was that?" Brian raised his hands to the sky.

"Mr. Detective doesn't know everything does he? I busted her years back, when she was still modeling," Barnum mocked.

"What, like ten years ago, when *you* were on the street?" Brian placed his hands on his hips.

"Yeah, something like that." Barnum shifted in his chair. "Well, anyway, what did she tell you, hotshot?"

"Your former dope smoker said she issued a phone to Tamia through the agency's provider *F-zone*," Brian said.

"We're gonna need a subpoena for the records, Jeffers," Barnum tapped the desk with his fingers.

"I'm already on it. She faxed me the information for the last few calls. She will also be requesting a printout for us to review,"

"Hmm, well I imagine that's the printout in your hand there?" Barnum pointed to the files.

"Yes, it is," Brian said. *Did I say suck it?*

"Give it to me then, youngster," Barnum motioned for the folders.

Brian was reluctant to hand over the information, more concerned it might end up in the trash can, but thought better of it and handed it over anyway. "I think Tamia was seeing this August Dellano; somehow the killer was well aware of that, boss."

"Okay, hit me with it. I can't wait to hear *this,*" Barnum said.

"Turn to page seven. The data transfers are on that page. Do you see what time the last one was sent?"

"I'm looking, but that doesn't mean shit, young man. Tamia Stevens could have pre-dated a message to this number," Barnum scoffed.

"I don't think so. Look, it was sent a day after her death."

"Jeffers, technology can do amazing shit these days. What makes you think *this* is something else?"

"The stolen cell phone would be the obvious answer." *Duh*?

"Okay, someone stole the cell phone. That happens all the time—what else you got?" Barnum placed the file flat on his desk.

Losing my patience. "Listen, Serena Clarke mentioned Tamia was sent some roses by this guy named August, or Augustine," Brian said.

"I take it the number on this record is none other than Mr. August, or Augustine?"

"That is correct. Next, the killer steals the cell phone from the scene and sends a text message to this August person," Brian said.

"Okay, I'm sure you have more. You always do."

"August thinks his "*lover*" is contacting him for a hot night of sex, when it's actually the killer?" Brian suggested.

"Let me guess, you called the number on the text message and it was this August individual?"

"I also left him a message to call me," Brian said.

"You don't think he's gonna call you back, do you?" Barnum asked.

"I'm hoping he does. We might be able to save his life." Barnum rubbed his double chin with the palm of his right hand.

"That would mean this possible lover of Stevens would think she was still alive. I can't buy it—the story has been all over *Eyespot 5 News* non-stop. Plus, the other media channels have reported on the murder as well."

"Yes, her death was on all the networks. Somehow, though, I don't think August Dellano knows she's dead," Brian said.

"Do you really believe that? If those two were involved in any type of relationship, wouldn't you think he would have been calling her more than those records indicate?" Barnum leaned all the way back in his chair.

Brian understood his supervisor made sense, but just because it made sense didn't mean it was the right answer. "You would be right to think along those lines, but here is my point…" Brian said.

"I figured my logic wasn't good enough for *you,* Jeffers." Barnum rolled his eyes at the younger investigator.

What an ass. "Let me finish, *Bossman*. If August wasn't in the area at the time of the murder, or didn't have any need to watch the news, he wouldn't have any idea something had happened to her."

"He would be living in a fucking shell if he didn't, young man," Barnum laughed.

"Maybe for all intent purposes he was. What if those two meet on a regular basis, and they do so by texting messages or quick phone calls?"

"Possible, but not very likely, Jeffers."

"When I spoke with Roseanne Tustin, she indicated Tamia dated several men, but noticed the girl never brought them home. She also said a man Tamia was seeing, may have been married."

"Hold on, is this August guy married?" Barnum asked.

"I will let you know when he calls me back." Brian smiled. "So here's the kicker to tie this together. Tamia and August probably have a place they meet for their encounters and I think Lucifer has seen them there."

Barnum shook his head. "That is a lot of speculation on your part, too much… if you ask me."

"I have a gut feeling about this. I think Lucifer is ready to kill again."

Barnum's eyes widened; small beads of perspiration formed on his thick brow. Brian watched the man, as he contemplated what the junior investigator shoved down his throat. It was a theory, but it was all Brian and Barnum had. Legitimate or not, wasn't the question. Now, it just seemed to be all a matter of time, before something else bad happened and they all would be second guessing themselves.

"All right, let's get everything we can on Dellano, vehicle registration, parking tickets, criminal records, all of it. Once we find this guy safe and sound, you're buying me a big fat steak dinner," Barnum challenged.

Brian managed a faint smile. He didn't need to tell Barnum he had Cynthia Cornerstone collect all the information they required. "Okay, it's a deal, and if I'm right—"

Barnum pointed at him. "Jeffers, if you're right, God help us all." Barnum handed the files back to Brian.

He exited the office and headed to Cynthia Cornerstone's cubicle. He didn't think she was still at work, but there she was, perched at her desk involved in the middle of a phone conversation. She motioned to him with her index finger to wait while she finished. After a few minutes, she rushed towards the fax machine and returned with a stack of papers.

"I thought you left for the day. I left you a voicemail." Brian said.

She waved her arms. "I'm still here. This is the information on August Dellano. It was pretty easy to get, since there aren't too many people named Dellano in the metro area," Cynthia smiled.

"Well, there had to be at least one." Brian winked.

"Make sure and pay close attention to the third page. *That* is his criminal record."

Brian picked out the third page and noticed August Dellano was arrested a year ago for domestic abuse of his wife Janice. He scanned the address listed as current on the paperwork. *3411 Park Vista Estates*. "The rich guy likes to beat his wife." Brian shook his head in disgust, placing the page back into the stack of papers.

"Not the ideal guy I want to marry," Cynthia said.

"Hey, I need to use your phone." Brian reached for the desk phone.

She saluted him. "Yes, sir." Cynthia said as she left the desk and disappeared down the hall. Brian was well aware of Park Vista Estates. He knew these homes were only affordable by a select few. He picked up and dialed Barnum's extension.

"Yes, Cynthia, what is it?" Barnum answered in his usual gruff tone.

"Well, it's not Cynthia," Brian jested with him a little as he continued. "Boss, I think we should take a little trip to the Park Vista Estates and see if Mr. Dellano is home."

"That damn guy lives there? You *know* I hate those rich asshole types."

"Well, I'm sure a lot of them don't like you either," Brian teased.

"Hey, youngster, you already have all of his information?"

"Yep, in my hands as we speak."

"Okay, meet you in back of the station in two minutes."

Brian exited the back door; paperwork tucked under his arm. He slipped into the driver's seat of the unmarked. He sat motionless and was hopeful August Dellano was safe and sound at home enjoying dinner with his wife. Somehow, he didn't believe there was a chance in hell this was the case, not even for one second.

Chapter 30

Janice Dellano

The two investigators talked very little on the drive. Brian maneuvered through a series of streets lined with multi-million-dollar townhouses. He came to a four-way intersection and turned onto a newly paved road. This led to the private paradise called, *Park Vista Estates*. There were just a handful of residences, but a majority of them appeared to be mansions of one sort or another. Each structure had a monstrous gate which encompassed the property and a select few, possessed security booths, as they were manned with a uniformed security official. Both Brian and Barnum gave each other a quick glance to acknowledge their disbelief at these architectural wonders.

"That's it over there," Barnum pointed to a house on the right side of the street. Brian pulled up to a booth. The white featureless structure appeared to be mirrored and impossible to see the shielded guard, but *he* had unobstructed view of all who tried to enter the surroundings. *Probably paid more than police too.* Brian flashed his badge at the enclosure. "Hello, we're with the Valentine Police Department. Detectives Jeffers and Barnum to see August Dellano, please." Brian tried to sound cordial even given the urgent circumstances.

The security guard slid aside a panel which exposed an open area to the booth. He verified Brian's badge and credentials. "Gentleman, Mr. Dellano isn't here. He left early yesterday on business and hasn't returned as of yet. I think Mrs. Dellano was worried about him as well. He always returns from business within the day, unless she is with him."

Spidey sense is tingling. "Is Mrs. Dellano here? It's important we speak with her." Brian readied the unmarked.

"I don't see anything on the pre-scheduled meeting list which mentions a visit from Law Enforcement today."

"*We* don't have an appointment, for Christ's sake!" Barnum leaned over and berated the guard.

"I will call her and let her know." He picked up the phone.

For shit's sake. "Open the gate! This is urgent business involving her husband!" Brian shoved his badge back inside his jacket pocket. The security employee seemed to understand the urgency in the detective's voice. He opened the gate and paged the residence to inform Mrs. Dellano.

"That guy was getting on my nerves, Jeffers. Do we have an appointment? What the hell has the world come to?" Barnum shook his head in disapproval.

Brian nodded as he drove through the gate and up a long circular driveway. The estate consisted of a white four-story residence with a large front yard. The yard was host to a giant rose garden, similar to the one behind the President's home in Washington, D.C. There was a large white canopy which extended from the front entrance over the driveway. *Almost resembles a five-star hotel.* The estate also possessed cathedral-style windows with various designs scattered on the facing and sides. It had a spacious garage, about one hundred feet from the house. Brian parked the unmarked under the canopy and watched as a woman about fifty years old exit the front door at a hurried pace. She fashioned very dark hair which appeared to match her European complexion. She was a petite woman, who wore a one-piece yellow spring dress that accentuated her hourglass figure. The two investigators met her at the end of the sidewalk.

"Mrs. Dellano, we are—" Both flashed their badges, while the woman scanned over them.

"Officers, did you find my August?" The woman rushed towards them; her hands shook with definite worry. She was aware of who they were. Even if the security guard hadn't phoned her, it wasn't too difficult to tell. The entire neighborhood was full of socialites; it was obvious the two weren't from around here.

"We're hoping you can give us an idea where he might be, Mrs. Dellano," Brian said.

"I haven't seen him since yesterday; I was very upset, thinking he might have been involved in an accident or worse." Dellano looked away.

"I left a message on his phone, but I haven't heard anything back as of yet." Brian consoled her.

"I tried to call him too, Detective. He never stays gone this long without contact."

Brian saw the fear in her eyes. "Mrs. Dellano, we think August might be hurt or injured and can't get in touch with the police or anyone else."

Her hand went to her face. "Oh, God! I hope he wasn't drinking and driving again," Dellano said, with a scratchy and worn voice.

"No, I don't think that's the case. We have reason to believe someone may be trying to hurt your husband." Brian glanced in the direction of his supervisor.

"I know my August has his share of enemies, but I wouldn't think to that extent," Dellano said.

"It's not for certain, but it could be possible." Barnum interjected his opinion.

Let me do the talking. "When did he call you yesterday, Mrs. Dellano?" Brian glared at Barnum.

She looked up and to the right. "Early…I think, while he was working at our restaurant."

"What is the name of it?" Brian pulled out his notepad.

"Augustino's. It's on the other side of town. Auggie did say he might be late because he would have to complete a food inventory."

Auggie… nice. "We will check the restaurant to see if he may still be there." Brian jotted down a few notes. "Does he usually work there by himself overnight?"

"Sometimes he does. More in the last few months," Dellano crossed her arms.

"Does your husband have any friends he may stay with, if he did drink?" Brian didn't want to complicate the situation with the mention of Tamia Stevens, but a man's life might be in jeopardy. He noticed Dellano's facial expression change from worry to disappointment. Janice Dellano cried.

"My husband and I… have been having marriage difficulties… for the last few months. He has been late almost every night and I'm afraid he may have been with… another woman."

"We're not sure of that either, Mrs. Dellano, but given the circumstances that is possible," Barnum said.

Mr. smooth in action. Brian tried to show empathy with the woman, even as he tried to get all the information he needed to find her husband.

"I haven't found any evidence of him cheating. It's just a feeling a woman has, when things aren't—"

"Mrs. Dellano, I can put out an all-points bulletin on your husband and the vehicle he's driving. Maybe he's still here in the city." Brian tried to avoid the issue of infidelity.

"He took his precious blue sports car." Dellano spat out the words.

"I'll give the dispatcher a call and tell them." Brian closed his notebook. "Excuse me a minute." Brian turned. He removed his cell phone and advised the dispatcher of the vehicle information. He rejoined the two, as Janice Dellano touched his arm. "Do you think August was sleeping with someone else?"

"I don't know, Mrs. Dellano," Brian lied; he didn't want to tell the woman anything that would further upset her. "Mrs. Dellano, if you have a picture of your husband that would help us."

"The only recent photo I have of Auggie is about three months old, but I can provide you that one... if you want."

Brian could sense the strong mix of emotions, which ranged from worry to anger, but he tried to make it as easy as possible. "We appreciate your cooperation. That should be good enough for what we need. I will get that information out to the patrol units and hopefully August is still in the area."

"Please find him for me." Dellano clasped her hands together.

"I will also have a unit drive by your husband's restaurant. Maybe he's there," Brian nodded. He tried to convince the woman of hope even if none was on the forefront.

Barnum remained quiet but did offer his sympathy before the two returned to their vehicle. The police radio crackled. "Thirty-nine, two, from dispatch." A faint female's voice sounded over the receiver. Brian picked up the handset. "Go ahead, dispatch."

"The all points-bulletin on your subject, Dellano: August's vehicle has been located in the rear lot of the Daltry hotel."

"Ten-four, dispatch. Is there an officer on scene with the vehicle?" Brian asked.

"Sir, he is waiting for a backup unit to assist," the dispatcher said.

Pretty good luck. They needed a break and since the bulletin was issued less than ten minutes ago, this was a definite improvement in the odds to find Dellano. *Still not good, but a chance.* Brian pushed the button. "Dispatch, show myself and Commander Barnum en route to that location. Our estimated time of arrival should be in about ten minutes."

The voice on the handset cracked with static. "I have you responding. Let me know when you make the scene."

Brian activated the emergency lights and siren, dodging between traffic to get to the Daltry. The closer he came, the less confident he felt they would find August Dellano alive and well. The likelihood Lucifer had struck again appeared to be more certain and any expectation the killer would remain in the area was a fool's hope.

Chapter 31

Krista, Krista, Krista...

Lucifer was deskbound at his work station. All of his unique instruments utilized in the creation of his masterpieces, were scattered on the surface of the table. He picked up one at a time, and marveled in the beauty each displayed, as one in particular seemed to beckon him. Lucifer gazed wild-eyed at the stainless-steel scalpel; this was the perfect weapon to use on his next victim. Today, he had decided who would be bestowed that honor. It wasn't a secret; Krista Meade was next in line to feel his blade. He knew it was destiny to rid himself of the flirtatious slut, since their first encounter. He realized her usefulness had run out, and it was now time for her to be added to his collection. Even though Krista was more than eager to please him sexually, Lucifer realized he couldn't have any distractions to interfere with his mission. His sole devotion was to create exceptional masterpieces, and the girl kept just enough of his focus to become a nuisance. *No time for those*. It was foolish to have been involved with her, and it wasn't all her fault, she was to be killed; his greed for earthly desires was part to blame. The killer had gotten way too involved with his carnal urges, and lost his emphasis on what was important.

Lucifer knew his destiny was to create pain and promote death to the special selection of his choice, but there was also more. Like most people pushed over the edge, a series of misfortune was a scapegoat for the blame... but for him, it was different. All he cared for had been taken, and now he was determined to regain his special status. The Valentine masterpieces were just stepping stones on the journey to his true purpose. One man was responsible; when that individual's broken body was at his mercy, his world would be set right.

He needed to take care of the Krista mistake, and it needed to be taken care of tonight. The August Dellano's death was less than a day old, so he needed to be careful. If luck was with him, the inept Valentine Police hadn't found his latest masterpiece as of yet. Lucifer planned to meet Krista at her apartment within the hour. He grabbed the pre-paid cell phone. "Hello," Krista said.

"Hey, sexy. How was your day?"

"I'm better now you called. Today was shit. The boss jumped me because some files were misplaced. *FYI,* not my fault," Krista said.

"Well, did he get over it?" Lucifer asked, not at all interested in the answer.

"He did. Are you coming over soon?"

"In a little while. I have to pick up a few things first."

"What are you buying me, Mr. Hottie?" Krista purred.

"You will just have to wait and be a good girl."

"You know I'm a bad girl, and I don't like to wait."

"Well, my dear Krista, you are this time. I promise it will be um—special*."*

"Well, hurry and get your sexy ass over here and give it to me,"

"I will be there soon, and believe me I will give you a present you will never forget." A sinister grin spread across his face.

"Oh, I will be waiting for that! Bye, I gotta go." Krista laughed.

"Bye, see you in a while." Lucifer flipped off the device. He grabbed a few items from the laundry basket and stuffed the items in his backpack. He searched through several compartments and located the items needed for the success in the creation of his next masterpiece. Lucifer picked up the scalpel from the desk and tucked it inside the front pocket of the backpack. He was vigilant to ensure the blade was placed down, so it wouldn't penetrate the material. He didn't need to be sliced open due to his own stupidity.

He left the apartment and slipped into the alley where the rental vehicle was parked. The killer had the inclination to return it to the airport right after the fat Italian's murder, but decided against it. *Not until.* The Tahoe would be ideal to transport Krista's body mostly, because his car was too small and this was beyond doubt the best choice. He made the trip to Krista's apartment in a short time. The lot behind her apartment complex was almost bare. He parked in an empty slot, away from the majority of the other cars. If the girl did get a scream out, no one would be able to tell where it originated. Lucifer's luck had been very good as of late. He was well aware that same luck would soon run out. He climbed the back stairs which led to Krista's apartment and knocked on the door, whistling. *One… two… three… come and die for me…*

Krista Meade answered the door in a tight black silk top, tan miniskirt and leather boots. Krista looked happy to see him as she gave him a quick kiss on the cheek.

"Patrick, where is my present?" Krista asked; she ran her hand down the front of Lucifer's shirt.

"It's out in the car, it's a surprise." Lucifer kissed her neck.

"You're bad for making me wait." Krista unbuttoned the top button on his shirt.

"I know. But it will be worth it." Lucifer raised his eyebrows.

"Well, let's go then, I'm fucking starved." Krista was forceful, as she escorted him out the door.

"Okay, let's go. We might have time for some dessert before our meal." Lucifer ran his hand up her miniskirt.

"I like the sound of that." Krista caressed his chest with one hand, the other focused further south. "Patrick, I'm dying to know where you are taking me tonight!"

"It's a secret. I will tell you one thing though… I promise you. Even in your *wildest* of dreams; you could never *imagine* what I have planned."

"Oh, I can imagine some nasty kinky shit, Patrick; I think you know by now." She teased.

He just smiled; the two hurried to the rental vehicle. Lucifer opened the passenger door of the SUV and buckled her in. Krista was impressed with his courtesy. "Thank you, Patrick, not only are you one hot and sexy lay, you also have some manners. I've never found any guy that has both." Krista beamed with excitement as she continued to tease her undiscovered killer.

"Well, thanks, I think," Lucifer said.

"Hey, I'm waiting for the surprise you promised me!" Krista held out her hand.

"I will give it to you when we get to the special place I have reserved." Lucifer bowed.

"A special place, huh?" Krista, cocked her head to the side.

"Indeed, the most special place." Lucifer reached behind the front seat and grabbed the backpack, just out of Krista's sight. With his other hand, he stroked Krista's hair and licked her neck. Lucifer eased the syringe out of the zippered pocket. He used caution not to stick himself with the needle, as he continued to caress her face and neck.

Krista moaned with pleasure from the foreplay and was lost in the moment as the killer climbed on top of her. He caressed her hair with one hand, but with the other, he now had a firm grip on the syringe. Lucifer gazed into her eyes, plunging the needle through her black silk shirt. The thin steel invaded her soft flesh and penetrated her chest cavity. He pushed with such force the syringe became stuck in place, as the Propaganician was emptied into her body, with not a drop to spare. Krista tried to scream, but he placed his hand over her mouth to stifle the sound. He watched; her eyes fixated on him with pure terror. She became frozen without movement within thirty seconds of the syringe piercing her flesh.

He always enjoyed the color of her eyes and loved how they accentuated her features. Lucifer was filled with excitement; in a short time his memory of Krista Meade would be as a conqueror and collector. He placed a hand on her chest and felt her lungs struggle to expel oxygen. Her breath slowed and within seconds she was gone. Lucifer ripped out the empty syringe and placed it into the backpack. He turned the ignition key and headed in the direction of the secluded place that would be home for another one of his masterpieces.

* * *

The drive to Dunlap County's conservation center was just long enough for the killer to calculate the majority of his plan. Lucifer knew the officers whom patrolled the area were done by six o'clock p.m. The con-

servation center was locked after this and a large gated
chain link fence would keep unwanted trespassers out. It
was a quite old and broken-down piece of mixed metal,
which the county conservation board really didn't want
or have the money to spend on necessary repairs. *This
will be perfect*, he thought. He was familiar with a special way into the park most people didn't know. His one
worry was to make sure a county deputy with keys to the
gate didn't stumble upon him while he was busy with his
masterpiece. Lucifer knew the ideal spot to complete the
work. He drove along the gravel road, until he located
the thickest wooded area. The killer parked between two
partially-covered trees. *Can't get any better than this*,
Lucifer thought.

Lucifer donned the heavy work gloves from his
backpack and covered the SUV in shrubbery. He left
enough of the sports utility exposed as necessary to take
out Krista Meade's corpse. Once she was removed, the
killer added more branches and leaves, until it was difficult for even him to locate. Lucifer strapped on the
backpack and picked up Krista's limp body, slung the
woman over his shoulder and pressed through the foliage. The extra weight didn't faze him. He hiked through
the wooded area until stopping in front of an old rusted-out support pole. *Beautiful*. He gaped at the massive
elm trees whose branches engulfed the area, hiding the
pole from view. He tore them aside; his eyes brightened
as it came into his path. Leaning into the corroded metal,
the chain link loosened. Lucifer grasped the fence and
forced it down with his weight. It lowered enough so he
could walk on it. Stepping over, he continued onward
until the familiar gravel road became visible.

Five minutes later, he scurried into an open area

which housed several brown wooden picnic tables. Playing a mimed version of eenie meenie, miny, moe, the killer hurled the carcass spread-eagle on the surface of the middle table. He removed all of her clothing and folded each piece until there was a tidy pile. Removing his backpack, the killer yanked out four medium-sized ropes. He tied Krista's arms and legs to the bolts underneath the bench, just in case the park's wildlife tried to carry away their new meal. *Can't have that*. Lucifer stepped back and admired her beauty and helplessness all at once. He opened the front pocket of the backpack and removed the scalpel and blue hospital gown.

He placed the gown over his head and tied the drawstrings, as a wave of adrenalin surged throughout his body. Placing the scalpel in his right hand, the madman sliced through the woman's supple flesh, like a seasoned fisherman would clean his latest catch from the salty sea. Lucifer carved his signature into Krista Meade's stomach and lower abdomen, ensuring that whoever found her knew *who* was responsible. After the killer signed his masterpiece, he reached back into the pack and grabbed a pint-sized container full of murky liquid. Lucifer took a deep breath and slid his newest collections inside the container.

Once the work was completed, he shed the gown and placed it in a separate pocket of the backpack. Lucifer took care as he positioned the newly-filled container. He stepped back to appreciate his masterpiece. *Nice, so nice*! Reaching into his front cargo pocket, Valentine's relentless killer caressed the fifty-cent piece. His time here was almost at an end, as this was all in preparation for a most-precious kill. *Not long now*! One final salute to bid his lady a fond farewell, and Lucifer was off into the woods.

He was excited about the unopened envelope on the computer desk at home. Again, the killer reached into his right pocket and clasped the fifty-cent piece. The simple touch of it always made him feel at ease. Several minutes later, Lucifer shifted into drive and pulled out into the road, impressed all was working out just as planned. *Upward and onward.*

Chapter 32

Death at the Daltry

Brian Jeffers parked at the rear of the Daltry Hotel. The lot was sparse but August Dellano's blue sports coupe *was* one of them. There were two marked units positioned behind the coupe. According to the dispatcher, officer Troy Beck located Dellano's car. The patrolman was doing a check of the garage when he spotted the vehicle. A quick scan through a tinted side window resulted in several Styrofoam cups, but not much else. Brian Jeffers touched the hood of the sports coupe. *Cold... been here a while.*

The young officer extended his hand in Brian's direction. "I'm Troy Beck. I radioed as soon as I realized this fit the description from the all-points bulletin."

"Pretty good timing, Beck," Brian congratulated him.

"Sir, I just happened to stumble onto it."

"Are there any officers with the hotel manager yet?" Brian asked.

"10-4, Detective. Got another inside interviewing the shift manger, so we can find our driver."

Barnum suspiciously eyed man. "Son, did you inventory the car?"

"Commander, it's pretty clear; nothing out of the ordinary."

Barnum rubbed his chin and grumbled. "Sure, not to you…"

Brian winked. "Good work, Troy. Do me a favor?"

"Sure, sir," Beck said, eager to please the detective.

"Go ahead and wait here until you hear from dispatch for any other instructions. We want eyes and ears on the ground… in case he comes back." Brian pointed to the car.

"10-4, sir."

"Commander Barnum and I will check with the other officer inside." Brian gazed at the personalized license plate of the sports coupe, and almost laughed when he realized the plate displayed *294EVER*.

"Gimme a break." Barnum shook his head.

The two surveyed the entrance. The door was propped open by wooden boxes to facilitate easy access to the hotel. They stepped inside and followed the corridor which led to the check-in desk.

When they arrived to the lobby, both investigators noticed a uniformed police officer, engaged in a discussion with an older, distinguished-looking man. The officer had a scowl on his face; his voice raised a few octaves. A boyish look filled his face, as he spotted them and motioned in their direction. "I'm Officer Peters, and *this* is the hotel general manager, Stanley White."

Brian eyed the manager, but didn't address him. "Peters, do we have a room number yet for our subject?"

Officer Peters shook his head with aggression. "Nope. I explained to Mr. White we were looking for August Dellano and it was urgent we get in touch with his guest." The officer put down his notebook and continued. "He says Dellano is a regular customer and has a room on the property. So far... he is reluctant to share that with me, sir."

Not very forthcoming. Brian stepped in closer to the hotel manager. "Look, Mr. White, I don't think you're getting the picture here. August Dellano *may* be in danger, and time could be very critical." He glared at the man.

"Gentlemen, our client's privacy is very important. I told him we would honor his wishes," White said.

"Mr. White, his wife is very worried about him. I wouldn't want to tell her the prestigious hotel manager delayed us in finding her husband. I understand you have rules, but his welfare is a lot more important *than* his privacy."

"Detectives, I assure you—".

Brian held up a finger. "I'm sure if we should find August Dellano injured in one of your rooms it wouldn't put your fine hotel in a positive spotlight." Brian folded his arms.

"I obviously don't want this, gentlemen but my… our *guest* has given us a strict order."

Brian raised his voice. "Do you understand what I'm saying? If it's too difficult, I can and *will* go room to room until we find him. Is that what you want?" Brian could tell White was more worried about the wealthy Dellano and his status than common sense. He was amazed at the man's self-preservation versus the safety of one of his best clients. The man stood for several seconds before he digested the detective's inference.

"Ah, Mr. Dellano is most our best customer… I wouldn't want to be responsible for putting him in harm's way, detectives—"

"What room, Mr. White?" Brian pointed to the ceiling.

Stanley White didn't want Brian to force his hand, because the presence of law enforcement rampaging through hotel guest rooms would with great certainty cost the man some business. Stanley shrugged his shoulders. "August Dellano's room is 101. I usually attend to it myself. Officers, I do know a young lady accompanies him to the room. I can direct you there if you wish?"

The three Law Enforcement personnel followed Mr. White down the hallway to August Dellano's registered room. Brian remembered he passed this area when the two detectives entered the hotel. *Don't like this at all.* Stanley White stopped in front of room 101, and removed a hotel key card from his vest pocket. He hesitated for a few seconds, glancing at the three police department members. Beads of perspiration rolled down his cheeks, as the man inserted the key. Both investigators drew their department-issued duty firearms as the door eased open. The room was black and cold. The odor of the dead leaped out from its confines and confronted all the new arrivals. Brian pushed the hotel manager away and forced his way through.

The green illumination of their weapons' night sights was the only light source. Brian removed his support hand on his firearm and groped for the switch on the wall. He flipped it and saw the wheelchair against a brown polished table close to the entrance. Staring at the center of the floor, Brian noticed the sheets from the lone bed were sprawled throughout this area. *What the fuck?* The linen was soaked in a bright reddish tint and sheets were arranged to provide a fitted shroud around the lifeless form of Lucifer's latest victim. Brian approached the deceased and ripped off the covers. The obese restaurant owner was naked, face down and a multitude of puncture marks riddled his upper back. The blood had seeped through the wounds and spilled onto the sheets, to create what seemed to be, a river surrounding the body.

Brian scanned the room; sporadic patterns of blood

filled the surfaces. *Holy Shit!*

"Oh, God, I can't believe this!" Stanley White ran from the room, clutching at his mouth.

Brian moved closer to the body and placed his weapon back in its holster. *Fucker is long gone.* His jaw dropped, when he saw the engraved words, *Lucifer's Calling* on the back of Dellano.

"Damn Son of a Bitch, we will get your ass!" Barnum lost his temper; the supervisor spat obscenities at no one in particular. Brian motioned for his supervisor to holster his firearm. Brian pointed to the air unit and instructed the uniformed patrol officer to shut it off. He *knew* Lucifer turned on the appliance, well aware that the body wouldn't decompose as fast, making the time of death would be difficult to decipher. *Lucifer didn't want to ruin his signature. Plus, he could be planning another kill*, Brian thought. A faint glimmer of silver caught his eye. *Cell phone?* The mobile device was laid on the stripped bed. "Barnum, you see that?" Brian tapped on the edge of the bed, as he kept his eyes on the victim.

"Yes, our model's?"

"We can only hope. There should be some juicy fingerprints on it." Brian motioned for Officer Peters to secure it.

"Well, junior, I guess you were right," Barnum agreed.

"Yeah, unfortunately for Dellano." Brian stepped next to the wheelchair. "I don't remember Dellano's wife telling us he used a wheelchair or was handicapped?"

"She didn't. The coupe isn't big enough to hold an old piece of shit like this."

No shit. "It isn't." Brian shook his head in the direction of his Supervisor, and did a quick once-over of the chair. "Peters, do me a favor… find Stanley White and ask him to meet me outside in a few minutes,"

"Sure, detective." Officer Peters left the hotel room.

"What are you thinking? Barnum asked.

"I don't believe Dellano used a wheelchair. I think this belongs to someone else…maybe our killer."

Barum rolled his eyes. "Okay, say Dellano is a perfectly healthy middle-aged man, why does the killer leave this evidence here?" He ran a hand through his thinning hair.

"Convenience is all I can think of." Brian knelt down to look at the underside of the blue plastic seat.

"Personally, I think this bastard is playing with us," Barnum said. "He hasn't left any evidence so far."

"Maybe I found something here. Take a look underneath the seat." Brian pointed to a spot.

"What is it?"

"Just take a look," Brian eased to his feet. "I'm going to check the bathroom, maybe there is something in there as well." He tip-toed past the body and opened the door to the bathroom. He scanned the interior; several bunched-up towels were in the middle of the red tiled floor and the shiny steel towel rack arm was broken and dangled close to the ground. Brian's gaze was drawn to the corner of the floor. He tilted his head; shards of broken glass were swept in a neat pile. *Took time to clean up.* Brian opened the shower curtain and ran his hand down the wall.

Still damp. Brian noticed a dark clump which stuck out of the hole of the drain. He reached into his suit coat and pulled out a pen. Leaning over, Brian used the utensil to reel in the foreign substance. He reached out and unwound a fair amount of toilet paper from the roll against the wall. The detective placed the matted material into the toilet paper to preserve its condition. Brian took out his cell phone. *Please, be something.* He spoke a few words into the handset and returned to the room. Brian cleared his throat. "Did you see what I was talking about?" Brian asked.

"I saw it." Barnum loosened his tie. "I have never heard of that place, though."

"Neither have I. Guess what else I found?" Brian held up the toilet paper for his supervisor to see.

"Do I want to even guess what's in your hand?" Barnum asked.

"I think it might be our killer's hair fibers," Brian said.

"Huh?" Barnum shook his head. "The guy took a shower*?"*

"I think he may have."

"Oh, I've seen everything now."

"I just got in touch with the boys at the lab; they will be out to help us soon," Brian said.

"Great, the more the merrier." Barnum removed the loosened tie. "About the wheelchair, you know there is a phone number to call."

"After we scour this room for prints, we will hit up the hospital it came from." Brian frowned.

"*Bourne Hospital Administration.* Probably a private medical facility somewhere?" Barnum said.

"That's what it sounds like to me, too." Brian hoped the cell phone, hair fibers, or even the wheelchair could tell him something useful in the hunt for the killer. He studied the puncture-riddled body of August Dellano, glaring at the executioner's signature as he waited for this nightmare to be over.

Chapter 33

Finally a Clue

The scene at the Daltry was now more of a venue for a media conference than a homicide investigation. The story-hungry reporters had monitored the police scanners in wait for the next homicide and now several television and radio stations arrived to conduct their interviews. The hotel room was now filled to the brim, with a combination of law enforcement and forensic team members. Brian Jeffers was still busy with the crime scene team, as they photographed and collected all available evidence. Brian was pleased to see the forensic team supervisor, Steve Bledsoe show up in person.

"Hey, Stevie, thanks for coming."

"No problem, Brian. This is a big case for all of us."

"Like I told you on the phone, I found these hair fibers in the shower drain. I need the stuff examined quick."

"Okay, I will get on it myself. I can't promise you a time frame but I will do my best," Steve said.

Brian handed him the wrapped-up hair. "Thanks, I appreciate it. I have to meet with the hotel manager, so I will give you a call." Brian watched, as his friend bagged the evidence. If there was anyone he could count on, it was Steve. The man would examine the fibers, until proof of positive identification was made. Brian exited and trudged up the corridor which led to the hotel manager's office. He was surprised to see officer Peters outside the manager's door.

"Peters, is White okay?" Brian peeked inside the entryway.

"Sir, he threw up like three times since I told him you wanted to talk." Officer Peters had a smirk on his face.

"Head outside. The media is a circus…more than usual. See if you can help a little with that." Brian tapped on the door frame.

"Come in."

Stepping through, the investigator was drawn by the ambience of the spacious room. The walls were adorned with movie posters, from the late fifties to the early seventies. Pieces of red leather furniture were positioned in a haphazard fashion, which tipped the balance where fashion was concerned. The final touch was a fifty-gallon aquarium centerpiece housed on a medium-sized wooden stand. It was filled with scores of colorful and Brain assumed to be, very expensive fish. Stanley White's ghostly figure sat behind the desk adjacent the aquarium. He held onto a box of tissues, like they were a haven for all he had seen. A tall glass of milky white liquid was positioned on a black square coaster.

Brian shot him a sympathetic look. "Mr. White, I just have a few quick questions. Are you going to be okay?"

"I have never seen anything that horrible…ever." The man took a sip from the glass.

"I understand, sir." Brian nodded.

"It was something I will never forget." White gulped downed the milky beverage, until just a frothy residue remained.

"Let's hope you do." Brian removed his notepad and pen from his coat. After several of the basic interview questions, he concentrated on the concerns at hand. "Sir, there is a wheelchair in August Dellano's hotel room. Did you know if that belonged to your guest?"

"I wouldn't know why he would need one, Detective. I have never seen him use one."

"Is it safe to say the wheelchair in the room doesn't belong to the hotel?"

"Of course not. The hotel has a few aid devices such as that, but they would be kept down at the front desk," Mr. White gripped the glass even tighter.

"That's what I thought. But you're sure August Dellano never needed those types of aids, or maybe even a cane?" Brian again pried.

"No, he didn't. Mr. Dellano has been a regular here for the last year. What kind of concierge would I be, if I noticed the man had any difficulty and didn't give him a suite with those types of amenities?"

Good point, ass kisser. "Well, that answers the questions I have. The department will be confiscating the device as evidence. If you think of anything, here's my card."

"Detective Jeffers, is it? I want to apologize for my rudeness earlier about the issue of hotel protocol—"

Brian raised a hand. "No need to apologize. I think we both understand each other." Brian closed the notepad. "Also, Mr. White, if you need any counseling, Officer Peters will refer you to our people." Brian walked out without another word. He hurried back to August Dellano's hotel room. The cramped space had cleared quite a bit and the county coroner had arrived. He prodded at the corpse, as thin streams of liquid seeped from the flesh.

Brian cringed. *Now, that's gross.*

Doctor Alan Sanderson waved him over to the body. "I have a couple of things to show you. I think you will find them *very* interesting."

"Like that wasn't?" Brian slid into the chair next to him.

"First, take a look at this. Every single puncture mark you see on the victim's back follows the same consistent pattern. Detective, the wounds are also excessive in depth."

"How much?" Brian strained his neck to look over the coroner's shoulder.

"I thought this was a series of surface punctures at first, but then I saw how the blood collected—just take a look how large each wound actually is." Doc Sanderson grabbed a yellow wooden pencil from his shirt pocket; it was about eight inches in length. Placing it in the first rounded hole, the pencil disappeared into the opening, leaving just the eraser tip visible. Sanderson repeated the procedure with every puncture wound. Each time he inserted the instrument into a wound, the results were the same. The tip of the eraser was the only part not swallowed up by the gap.

Brian's jaw dropped with amazement. "Doc, the length of each and its pattern is exactly the same. Looks like this was some sort of tool."

"Detective, I think it's probably a specially-made apparatus."

"Maybe a drill? Sure looks too perfect to be anything but."

The man adjusted his glasses. "I think you might be on to something. I'm not a mechanical expert but most standard drills only have bits under a few inches in length." Dr. Sanderson wiped off the bloodstained pencil. "This was done by a very sturdy piece of metal."

Tools of a deadly trade. "Do you think there would be enough metal particles left in one of the wounds to help us identify what type of drill he used?"

"There is significant physical evidence to help." Sanderson took off his brown wire-rimmed glasses and wiped the moisture from them. "Because of the depth of these perforations, any one of the wounds could be responsible for your victim's death."

"I wonder if these marks were done postmortem?" Brian cocked his head.

"I'm sure we'll find that to be the case. This seems to be your killer's preferred method," Dr. Sanderson observed.

"I'm betting Dellano is full of that damn paralytic. I didn't see any defense wounds on his hands, arms, or anywhere else."

"I have one more thing to show you." Dr. Sanderson slipped his glasses back on.

"Like this isn't enough?" Brian wiped his gloved hand against his brow.

"I wasn't sure at first what I was looking at, but this man also had several burn marks on his body."

"Burn marks?" Had he heard the doctor, right?

"Yes, they are small to the eye, but they are located in only two areas, his upper chest and *both* testicles," Dr. Sanderson said.

Holy shit. "Let's take a look."

The medical examiner turned over the body. The marks were difficult to make out, but were still visible. There were several red spots which resembled pimples about one half inch apart from each other. There were two separate groups located on the upper chest of Dellano. Brian had seen marks like this before, but wasn't sure what they were or what produced them. The surface of the right and left testicle were the recipients to the second wave of terror. The amount of marks was so great, the man's reproductive organs appeared to be swollen and stripped of all its protective skin. Brian could imagine what unbearable pain August Dellano had gone through as those marks were created. He stared into the medical examiner's eyes. "So, this bastard finds ways to inflict the most pain possible and when he thinks they have had enough, he promptly kills them?"

"It appears to be that way."

"Doc, let me know ASAP if the chemical compound is in his system. I have a couple more leads with the hair fibers found in the shower and the wheelchair over there." Brian pointed to the antique model.

"That does look a little prehistoric. It belongs to the deceased?"

"I wish. Wait—" Doc. Have you ever heard of The Bourne Hospital Administration?" Brian asked.

"I can't say that I have. Is that where the chair is from?"

"That's what is stenciled on the bottom of the seat. I think it belongs to the killer," Brian said.

"He left it here?"

"He did. Probably stole it a long time ago."

"Detective, it's more than likely an out-of-state private institution." Dr. Sanderson inspected the chair.

"That makes sense. It sort of sounds like it might be. There is a contact number to call as well." Brian showed him the number in his notebook.

"I wish you luck with that. I will be taking the body back to the morgue when the photographs are completed."

"I should be wishing you luck." Brian didn't envy Dr. Sanderson's autopsy schedule.

"I'll do my best to complete the examination and the toxicology report for Propaganician. You should have it no later than tomorrow morning."

"Thanks for your help. I would be interested in finding out what was responsible for making those burn marks."

"I will do my best." Dr. Sanderson edged closer to Brian and in a hushed voice, said. "I pray you find this killer, for the sake of everyone in this community. God knows…if this crazy is targeting any of us." The medical examiner stepped back and left Brian's side and returned to his duties. The medical examiner was more right than even Brian wanted to admit. It was clear this killer stalked all of his prey, and struck at will. Lucifer had evaded the police since the first murder and so far, he had created several *perfect* murders.

Brian waved at Dr. Sanderson as he walked out of the hotel room. He needed a breath of fresh night air, and he knew Barnum had vanished soon after the entourage of reporters flooded the area. The investigator acknowledged a couple of nervous uniformed officers on the way outside. The two men had the deer in the headlights look plastered on their faces; having no idea, their civil duties would result in combat with a serial killer. *Harsh reality*.

He stood by the rear entrance of the hotel and gazed out at the makeshift podium in the middle of the Daltry's back lot. A cluster of well-dressed reporters had surrounded the wooden stand. Each correspondent pushed or shoved his or her way to the front, jockeying for the best position to have their questions answered. A large number of microphones were staged in front of the round, red-faced Barnum.

Brian listened to the shaky voice of his supervisor as

he began his well-prepared statement to the media. *Better him than me*, Brian thought. His mind began to wander and he didn't hear one word Barnum uttered. He was in deep thought about Lucifer's latest barbaric attack and the use of the paralytic drug Barnum continued to speak as the crowd of media watched with persecution in their eyes. Several of the cameramen snapped pictures of the lead investigator; the white flashes from their intrusive devices filled the night sky.

* * *

"Ladies and gentlemen, I'm Commander Alex Barnum of the Valentine Police Department. I have been asked by Chief Anderson to give you this statement on a recent outbreak of homicides that have been occurring since approximately six days ago. We have had five murders that appear to have some similarity. A single killer, or multiple killers with the same method of operation, is operating in the city. All the deaths have been within the Valentine city jurisdiction and to this point… haven't spread to the outlying areas as of this time. The killer or killers have been leaving their calling card on each victim. I'm not going to explain the details on this, but will say this person or these people have a definite agenda.

The chief wants to urge everyone to be vigilant in his or her daily business, but not to panic. The Valentine Police Department, along with the Dunlap County Sheriff's Office will work in joint cooperation to bring this killer or killers to justice. Chief Anderson wants every citizen to know Law Enforcement will be stepping up the number of patrols and officers per patrol unit throughout the city. We will do everything we can to limit this killer's or these killers' chances to strike again. The chief has also informed me he will address the local news himself tomorrow morning for his press conference on the current events of these tragic homicides. He is very confident the Law Enforcement in this community is more than capable to stop these senseless murders. He also wanted me to express his deepest sympathies to the families of the victims. I also want to personally convey my condolences. If any of the news media wants to address questions to the press secretary, they may do so tomorrow.

I will not be able to field any questions on the subject matter right now. If media personnel contact the press secretary tomorrow, the chief will be able to address any of your individual concerns at that time. No questions will be answered until then. This will conclude all official statements from the Valentine Police Department regarding this matter. Thank you for your cooperation."

* * *

That was horrible, to say the least, and I only caught the ending. Brian heard several of the news media personnel grumble like they always would after a police news conference. He also noticed several of the panicked hotel employees tried to get answers from the senior investigator as he pushed through and hastened to vacate the area. Brian poked his head out to see his boss on a beeline to him. Large trails of sweat poured from the supervisor's forehead as Barnum reached into his suit pocket and pulled out a tissue. He dabbed at his face and collected all the unwanted wetness.

"Oh, shit. I'm sure you're going to add *your* two fucking cents." Barnum threw the soaked tissue on the ground. Brian ignored Barnum's inappropriate display.

"No, you will get enough attention out of this without me critiquing your skills."

"Fuck you, Jeffers," Barnum spat.

"Easy, Bossman. I'm sure this announcement will start a mess at city hall for us tomorrow."

If the look on his face could kill, Brian would be six feet under. "Just do your damn job and find this psycho and I will do mine, young man." Barnum said. "The chief will have to control this shit tomorrow. I'm just the messenger for him and it's only for today. That's why the man has a press officer."

"Maybe he will want you to do these public speaking events more often," Brian teased.

Barnum ignored the comment. "Anyway, Jeffers, what do you think about my television debut? Do you think the media caught my good side?"

Brian laughed a little, more to relieve stress than to give Barnum a hard time. "No, I don't think they did, Boss. You know they say the camera adds ten pounds."

Barnum appeared more than a little agitated the comment. He pointed to the unmarked patrol car as he spoke. "You got everything you need here? If you do, it's been a long day. Let's get the hell out!"

"Okay, I agree—it has been one to forget," Brian said. He completed all the necessary crime scene investigation needed. He would pick up the photos from the forensic team tomorrow, but that would be after checking on the killer's forgotten wheelchair. He looked past Barnum; the media's news vans had stowed their equipment and were now in quick retreat from the parking lot. The two detectives entered the unmarked patrol car, exhausted from the frequent long days. Brian couldn't help but visualize the last few minutes of August Dellano's life and the extraordinary pain he suffered. He stared at the dark outline of the Daltry Hotel, and wondered if Lucifer was done with *his* city.

Chapter 34

An Unplanned Target

Lucifer turned up the volume on the flat screen television. He liked to watch his favorite science fiction program while he conducted a strict routine of pushups and stomach crunches. It was late at night and the exercises would help with sleep, especially after creating the latest "masterpiece." He just finished the last set of pushups, when a news bulletin flashed along the bottom of the screen. He hated it when crap like this interrupted a beloved program. The killer glanced up. *Eyespot 5 News* was carrying a recorded statement from the Valentine Police Department. Excited, to say the least; this might have something to do with his latest creation. He waited to see if the clumsy police community was talking about his *"work."* It always interested him to hear the press conferences that followed. Lucifer sat in front of the screen, ready to soak up all the information. He watched as a rotund policeman talked about the recent outbreak of homicides in the local area. *What the hell?* Lucifer's ears perked up.

According to the written caption, the man in the cheap fucking suit was Detective Alex Barnum. He listened to the completion of the press conference, as each word gnawed at him. The investigator made it sound like there was more than one person responsible for the rash of murders. *Never!*

"Un-fucking-believable!" Lucifer punched the wall above the screen, which caused a picture frame to fall to the ground. The sound of shattered glass overshadowed the volume of the television. "Shit!" Lucifer surveyed the damage as he retreated to the kitchen to retrieve a broom and dustpan. The killer couldn't believe the stupidity of the sloppy investigator. He wasn't given the credit he deserved for these wonderful masterpieces. An example would be made, out of this overweight pig, and then there would be no question as to who was responsible. Lucifer jettisoned the broken glass into the trashcan next to the computer desk. *Calm down.* He sat at the desk, and picked up the white envelope received from the motor transport employee. Opening the seal, Lucifer smiled.

Brian and Sarah Jeffers
220 Palmer Court
Valentine, NE 66601

He expelled a little laugh when he saw the zip code of the Jeffers family residence. *Very poetic for the last of my victims.* The killer held the paper in his hands and studied it. He thought the name seemed rather familiar, but couldn't quite place where. He remembered the four females at the park and savored the thought of ending their lives in a most unique fashion. Lucifer would leave the father alive on purpose, to mourn them forever. After all, he wanted the man to find the remains of his family. It would be the ultimate tragedy and the killer would consider this to be an excellent dénouement to his vested time here in Valentine. Lucifer recomposed himself concerned with a new priority. *The loud-mouth policeman.* He would first have to deal with this Detective Barnum person, then would he be able to move on to create his final work. His face turned up in devilish grin. *Very ironic.* The detective who investigated Lucifer's masterpieces would now become one. He reached over and opened the bottom drawer of the desk and pulled out the phone book. He rummaged through a few old spiral notebooks and found the seldom-used prepaid cell phone. Lucifer flipped through the white pages, which listed the city directory of emergency phone numbers. He continued until he found the needed information. He checked the battery on the device. *Time to play.* He dialed the number and waited. *It's late.* After three rings, a woman's recorded voice answered.

"*You have reached the Valentine Police Department's Administrative Division. The office is now closed and will reopen tomorrow at eight o'clock a.m. If this is an emergency, please call Valentine Police Department Dispatch at—*"

Lucifer hung up. This office was the place where the detective worked. Valentine wasn't that large of a metropolis; more than likely the investigator's home address should be in the phone book. He turned to the page that listed the man's last name, and within just a handful of entries rejoiced in success. Flipping back to the yellow business section of the directory that listed local attorneys, he spent just a few minutes in search through various names and picked one. *This should work.* He grabbed a pink Post-it note and wrote down the information. The killer stuck it to the computer monitor, just in case he may need it again. He flashed the wicked grin, in strategic fashion. It would be foolish to think a city the size of Valentine would have two people named Alex Barnum, but it never hurt to check, and a positive location on the individual was needed anyway. Lucifer wouldn't waste time until he knew for sure this was his intended prey. Besides, 1222 Spruce Street was a lengthy drive. He typed the phone number into his prepaid cell and saved it under N for *next*. Lucifer hit the send key and after the fourth ring a tired female voice came on the line.

"Hello?"

Lucifer disguised his voice to make it even deeper than it was. *"I'm very sorry to be calling this late, Mrs. Barnum. My name is Timothy Miller; I'm a city attorney here in Valentine. I'm looking for Detective Alex Barnum. I apologize for calling his home, but I seem to have lost his work number. This is in regards to an ongoing case that is extremely important."* Lucifer paused to see how the woman would respond.

"Sir, what's your name again?" the woman said.

"Timothy Miller, ma'am," Lucifer said.

"Just a minute."

"Thank you," This must be it.

"Mr. Miller, I couldn't hear you. Is something wrong with your phone?"

"Sorry, ma'am. I'm on my cell phone. Sort of difficult to hear you." Well it was a piece of junk.

"Hold on, Mr. Miller, and I will try to wake him, okay? He just went to sleep a short time ago. It was a very long and tiring day for my Alex."

"I understand." Lucifer listened as the woman set the phone down. In the background, the woman called out her husband's name. Smiling, the killer ended the call. *Excellent*. He turned off the phone and threw it inside the drawer. *Time to do some work*. Lucifer reached over his head and pushed the power button on the tower of the pc. He waited a few minutes, until it booted up. Lucifer scrolled to his favorite web pages and located the correct website. He clicked on it; within seconds, the search engine popped up on the screen. He typed in the address of his apartment complex, along with his intended prey on Spruce Street. A few minutes later, he had a printed the specific directions that would aid him to surprise the know-it-all investigator. Lucifer spent a considerable amount of time to research his quarry before he struck, but this was different, and soon he would make a point nobody would soon forget. After he finished with this Barnum individual, everyone would know *he* was responsible. There would be no more talk about multiple killers involved with these deaths; just him and his body of work. There was ample time before the next planned masterpiece and the death of this detective would be a little warm up before the big finale. Lucifer would demand the respect he deserved. *No one was going to take the spotlight from him. No one, whatsoever.*

Chapter 35

The Blackbirds' Feast

The morning had a slight chill to it as Conservation Officer Alicia Strand checked the ridge for accidents. Satisfied the topography wasn't responsible for another fatality, she reached into a paper bag and plucked out a cold cinnamon roll. Alicia also brought along a bridal magazine, which she glanced at when time afforded the opportunity. *Not like Ethan will ever pop the damn question anyway.* Alicia popped the gate lock and entered the deserted Dunlap County Conservation Center. She turned the jeep onto the dusty road and followed until she was along the highest peak. The park consisted of one hundred and eighty acres; many recreational activities were available to the large number of tourists. It was known for its dangerously tall bluffs. Many climbers had attempted to ascend the mountainous terrain, but most were unsuccessful. That meant Alicia and the other patrol officers would spend a lot of time to conduct rescue attempts for the misguided. She passed one of the bluffs and was careful to maneuver the tan patrol jeep up through a series of turns on fresh paved road. *One turn too many and that could be it.* The overused vehicle bounced along the path; she felt every deformity the road had to offer.

"Damn Jeep! I told Renni to fix these shocks," Alicia said. She remembered the report she had given to the park's mechanic about the needed repairs. Alicia drove for a few minutes longer and then decided it was time for a break. *This will work.* Alicia had driven to the most secluded part of the park known as Parma Point. Not too many campers knew it even existed; most of the time the park's maintenance employees were the only people ever to spend time here. She turned into the gravel lot and noticed unwanted weeds had grown wild between various parts of the broken pavement. She would make a note of it and have the park engineer come out and throw some weed killer on the nuisance.

She turned into a haphazard parking spot, made of green treated two by fours. As she grabbed her magazine, the police radio came to life.

"Dispatch, to four-ten." The sound of a male voice filled the interior. *Great*!   "Four-ten, go ahead, dispatch."

"I need you to respond to a high angle rescue at Sutterman's Bluff *ASAP*!"

"Affirmative, dispatch, I'm about ten minutes from there now," Alicia said.

"I will show you en route to the location. Be advised I have already called fire rescue as well."

"I will let you know when I'm on scene." Alicia shifted the vehicle into drive and activated the emergency equipment. She turned the vehicle around to leave, but instinct directed her to look right. The conservation officer did a quick double take. *That's sort of weird.* She stopped the jeep and stared out at three picnic tables. The middle appeared to be covered in a dark mass.

She squinted to see what was on top but couldn't tell from the distance. She decided this may be just as important as the rescue and figured it wouldn't hurt to investigate. Alicia would need to call dispatch back and let them know. *The fire department will be expecting me.* She pushed the transmit button. "Four-ten, to dispatch."

"Dispatch to four-ten, are you at Sutterman's Bluff already?"

"Negative, I think I have discovered something else here at Parma Point."

"I already informed fire rescue you were on your way to their location. You're the only one on duty. You copy that?"

"I need to check this out. I will advise."

"Ten-four," the dispatcher said; the radio went silent.

Alicia exited her vehicle, and flipped on her portable radio. She walked toward the picnic area. When she was about twenty feet away, she noticed the massive dark object were a swarm of crows. They weren't the usual loud, obnoxious birds she was used to; *these* creatures appeared to be content. *Very eerie*. Alicia edged closer to see what they were drawn to, but couldn't tell what lay beneath the flock. She figured some careless campers might have left out their trash or spoiled food and forgot to throw it away when they departed.

When she got within eyeshot, Alicia looked down, and almost tripped over a folded pile of clothes. The garments were within arm's distance of the picnic table; she bent in closer. *Why would someone leave these here?* She took a few more steps in effort to scare them. They appeared to be oblivious to her presence; only a few made any noise at all. Most of them continued to shove another aside, as they flapped their wings in violence to include themselves in the feast.

Alicia waved her arms to shoo them off; they were deliberate to fly away but with her persistence they left and exposed what was underneath. Prone on the tabletop was a mutilated figure of what appeared to be a young female. She was naked; spread eagle and was tied to the underside of the bench, by thin ropes. They were secured to what remained of both her swollen hands and ankles. Alicia approached, choking on her saliva. The repulsive odor of defecation and torn flesh made her eyes water. She gasped at the sight of the woman's face. The skin around her cheeks was ripped away from the bone. Her eyes were now empty sockets that held a gateway to her brain tissue. The sight was so mesmeric; she was unable to look away. Alicia glanced down; the woman's fleshy midsection appeared to have a carving engraved into it.

Not him…not here. Those words, and that monster were enough to scare anyone in law enforcement the last several days, and she was no exception. Alicia out-of-breath yelled into the radio. "Four-ten, to dispatch. I need assistance from a county supervisor and a detective ASAP!"

"What have you got up there?" The dispatcher said.

Alicia lost all radio etiquette. "A fucking homicide here at Parma Point! Homicide and it's the guy… you will also need to call the coroner as well. I will secure the crime scene until they arrive." Alicia peered at the corpse.

The dispatcher's voice cracked. "I will get the detective on duty from the county! Also be advised more units are on the way."

"Ten-four." Alicia bolted to the patrol car. She pulled out a roll of yellow police tape and a plastic body bag. The cover would prevent the deceased from being eaten further by the wildlife. *It was going to be a very long day…*

　　　* * *

Brian Jeffers sat at the table with his wife and three

daughters, when the cell phone ended his family time. "Detective Jeffers."

"This is Investigator Pete Walters from Dunlap County Sheriff's Office. I need you to meet me here at Parma Point, in the Dunlap County Conservation Center."

"Walters, what's happened at Parma Point?" Brian asked.

"Sir, one of our conservation officers has discovered a body," Inspector Walters said. "I think your killer has struck again."

Brian remained silent. "Has anyone from your office contacted Commander Alex Barnum about this?"

"Just a few minutes before you. He's been briefed."

"I haven't heard from him. Did he say he would meet us there?"

"Sir, he indicated he was on the way," Inspector Walters said.

"Fifteen minutes." Brian stuffed the phone into his coat. *Another day, another death.* He gave the wife and girls a hug and kiss and a short time later, he was in front of the rusted-out gate of the conservation center entrance. He couldn't believe Lucifer would dare strike again this soon. Brian was greeted by an inexperienced Dunlap County deputy sheriff who stood at parade rest in the roadway. Brian flashed his badge.

" Detective Jeffers, here to meet Investigator Pete Walters."

He pointed to the roadway. "Follow along here until you get to a four way gravel intersection. Take a left there and Parma Point will be down a little ways," he said.

"Thanks, I've never been up here before." Brian

said.

"No problem sir. It's a real bloody scene there, sir, just so you know."

Brian shook his head. He followed the road for ten minutes and made the turn he needed to find the most out-of-the-way location in the conservation center. When he arrived, the lot was adorned with several gray and white deputy sheriff patrol vehicles. Brian stepped out and stared into the onslaught of uniforms, until, a slim, middle-aged man in a blue pin-striped suit got his attention. He gave Brian an awkward wave, as he rushed over; his hand extended. "Detective Jeffers, I presume?" "I'm Pete Walters from the Sheriff's office."

"I wish I could say it was a pleasure to meet you Pete, but under these circumstances..." Brian returned the friendly gesture.

"Ditto on that, Detective," Pete said.

Brian scanned for Commander Barnum's car. "Didn't you say Commander Barnum was on his way here?" Brian asked.

"He called a few minutes ago. He isn't gonna make it. Figured he would have called to let you know."

"He didn't." Brian shook his head. 'It's par for the course."

"Well, it seems he was tasked to help your chief pre-pare for the scheduled news conference," Pete said.

"Perfect." Brian's eyes narrowed. He was relieved Barnum wasn't here to critique every step of his investi-gation. "Well, I guess you and I can stumble through this without micromanagement onward."

The investigator led him to the crime scene. Several deputies filled the area, as yellow police tape was tied around trees. On top of the worn brown-stained table, a dark-colored plastic body bag covered what was the latest victim. Pete Walters lifted the blanket; Brian saw the horror in its entirety. It was very difficult to tell how old she was because the shredded flesh throughout her face almost made her unidentifiable. Brian shuddered as he looked into what remained. *Fuck this shit*!

He knew from the various styles of bite marks that the park's wildlife had gorged themselves on the woman's flesh. Her eyes were removed from their sockets, leaving a dark abyss in their place. Leaning in closer, it was obvious: these were exact wound patterns. Lucifer had used his skills to steal them and add to his demented prizes. The woman was planted here, and it was no coincidence, the speech at the Daltry played a part in where Lucifer dumped her. He examined the girl; she was still tied to the picnic table by thin ropes. He kneeled down to investigate where they were attached, careful not to contaminate the scene.

"Pete, take a look at this." Brian pointed to the thick rope. "Why do you think he even bothered?"

"I don't have any good explanation I would consider helpful; maybe he did this to show off for us."

"You know, that sort of makes sense. I guess my question would be; why did he bring the girl all the way out here to kill her?" Brian brushed away several large insects, which had invaded the picnic table and wanted their share of the human delicacy.

"I don't have a clue, Pete said.

"This doesn't make any sense at all." Brian stood upright. "I have a theory."

"I'm new to this case." Pete shrugged his shoulders.

"Lucifer identifies all of his victims with the signature like the one on her stomach there." Brian pointed to the words engraved in the woman's body. "The way he kills these people with different weapons and different styles shows he's trying to create a piece of sadistic art."

"I think this guy's just crazy."

"More than that. The Lucifer signature might denote the highest form of evil. I think he has a twisted goal but what the fuck could it be?"

"Fucking insanity and he's reached that." Pete bent down and picked up a brown paper bag. He withdrew a 35mm camera.

"Yeah, I know."

"For what purpose?" Pete snapped a picture of the engraving.

"Like I mentioned before, I think it has a relevance to this damn signature."

"Ritualistic killings in Valentine, sounds like a movie that *Hollywood* would make." Pete managed a nervous smile.

"Some movie," Brian said.

Pete re-loaded his camera. "Have you shared this satanic ritual thing with Commander Barnum and the chief?" Pete snapped several more pictures.

"I tried that already. Let's just say, he almost had a heart attack when I gave him my gut feeling," Brian said.

"I can imagine that would be the general consensus for most of the pencil pusher types." Valentine has never experienced this before, and that's probably scaring our elected officials."

"Probably, but we still gotta catch this madman."

"Why do you think he's stepping up the pace all of a sudden?" Pete shoved the camera back into the bag and zipped it. Brian remembered the graphic pictures of Ross Bosworth's homicide.

"This killer has done this before." Brian's eyes focused in the direction of one fearless crow, as it dove towards the corpse to have one last taste of fleshy tissue. Several uniformed deputies waved their arms, which drove the bird back into the atmosphere.

"When? I never heard anything about this." Pete cocked his head.

Too much information. "A few years back there was an unsolved murder in Calmine County, where the victim's heart was removed."

"I definitely don't remember hearing about that!" Pete raised his eyebrows.

"There wasn't any signature on the deceased body, like we have here. But I think this killer was just testing his sinful craft. Now he strikes on his own calendar, and with little mercy." Brian watched as a few media trucks rolled into the lot. "I believe Lucifer is setting a time table for himself and will try to disappear once he's done in this area."

Pete Walters' eyes widened with eagerness. "So, why is this nut job removing body parts from your victims?"

"It's not just body parts, Pete. This guy appears to be collecting things from each victim."

"What the fuck?"

"For example, the case in Calmine County, he took the heart but he also took a personal item of the victim as a possible token—

"Token?" Pete stopped what he was doing. "What kind of token?"

"In these recent murders…it could be anything."

"Fuck you and me… I have only seen a few quick paragraphs in the daily investigative reports that come out from the intelligence unit. Since Valentine Police was handling it, we didn't get a lot of the insight on much."

"I would have thought the department would have been forthright in giving out that information." Brian sighed.

"Ha, not so. Other than the last ten minutes you spent telling me about this psycho, I didn't know much about him."

Brian knew the relationship between both the city and the county was sort of strained; each agency was responsible for their own cases. That was a moot point now. If this murderer was to be caught, *everyone* would have to work together. Brian filled his new comrade in on other important details, to include the paralytic drug Propaganician. He explained how Lucifer would use it with most of his victims. Brian finished up; the fact Lucifer had stolen a cell phone and used it in the commission of one of the murders. Brian hovered over the girl's bruised and bloodied body. Staring at her chest, he figured Lucifer had used the drug of his desire on this woman as well. *There it is*! He summoned the senior investigator. "Take a look at the large red circle on her chest." Brian unclipped a mini flashlight from his belt.

"Is that what you were talking about?" Pete peered at the large red mark.

"It is."

"Looks sort of like a booster shot mark."

"I have never seen it this size on a victim before. Anyway, I'm not the resident expert with these kinds of things," Brian said.

"It's pretty noticeable."

"I remember the other puncture marks were a lot smaller and almost undetectable unless someone knew they were there." Brian inspected the mark. " W h y do you think this one is larger than the others you described?"

He shook his head. "I don't know for sure. It might be an allergic reaction to the drug or the needle itself. Dr. Sanderson will be able to tell us when he gets here."

"I called dispatch and told them to page out the coroner on call. Is he the head medical examiner?" Pete asked.

"He's helped on every one of these murders so far." The two worked in tireless effort to ensure this victim was spared any evidence collection errors.

 Dr. Sanderson arrived a short time later, as the two investigators finished up the scene. Brian pointed out the mark to Sanderson.

He leaned over the body and inspected the remains. "The puncture on the victim's chest was made by a large needle."

"Safe to say, Propaganician is in her system?" Brian rubbed his reddened eyes.

"I think, by the preliminary evidence, it was utilized," Dr. Sanderson said.

"It just looked a little different."

"The syringe was probably forced into the girl at a high velocity, which is why it's more visible than on our other victims. Someone with a very powerful upper body did this."

Investigator Pete Walters had overhead the two, and made himself known. "Brian, almost done with prelim stuff."

"Doc Sanderson, meet Pete Walters. He is the lead investigator for the Sheriff's Office."

"Hello," Sanderson shook the slender man's hand.

"Call me Pete, doc. Brian has told me you have been a big help in the case."

The older man smiled and nodded, acknowledging the compliment. "Just what I do gents. I will take the body back to the morgue, and get to work on the autopsy. Brian, can I speak with you for a minute?"

Never calls me by my first name. "Sure, you okay?" Brian asked. He tapped Pete on the shoulder. "I'll be back in a few."

"Sure, keep me in the loop, okay*?*" Brian gave Pete the thumbs up and escorted Dr. Sanderson to the van.

"I wanted to talk to you about another issue." He opened the back and pulled out a stretcher from the tight compartment.

"This is about our Italian friend, isn't it?"

"Indeed."

"You found something else when you did the autopsy of Dellano, didn't you?" Brian shook his head.

"I did. An electrical device, like we thought, tortured August Dellano," Dr. Sanderson said.

"I thought so."

"It appears to be a stun gun of some type. I inspected the burn wounds more carefully and cross-referenced the injury marks with other types of marks on the web."

"Modern technology at its best." Brian half-joked.

"You're correct. I showed the information to the forensic team downtown. They agreed that it was consistent with my findings of being a high voltage weapon of some kind—"

"Are they gonna be able to tell us what? Maybe I can send a couple uniforms out to the army-surplus stores; they sometimes carry those kinds of things," Brian said, with excitement.

"The supervisor of the team said he would let me know when he found out. It might be a good idea, though, to check those surplus stores." Doctor Sanderson nodded.

"I'll call Barnum later and tell him what's going on,"

"Detective, there's one other thing I need to mention."

"What, Doc?"

"August Dellano was positive for the Propaganician as well. There was a heavy concentrated dose showing in the lab results." Dr. Sanderson wheeled the hospital cart over the bumpy lot.

"I figured as much." He followed the medical examiner to the picnic table, where the evidence techs had finished their portion of the investigation. Brian stared, as the techs untied the ropes. He looked at the sealed plastic evidence bag which contained the clothes. *Why the killer would strip down the dead before carrying out his act.* Brian watched in disbelief as the medical examiner lifted the girl's ruins into the black leather body case. This customary shroud would protect her. He rolled her to the van, while an assembly of crows sat satisfied in the trees above. Brian gazed upward. *It's nature, the living feast on the dead. A perfect fucked-up world, indeed.*

Chapter 36

Good-bye, Alex

Lucifer parked the Honda a mile away from the residence of Alex Barnum. He followed the directions on the paper and made a cursory pass by the house. The killer wanted to survey the area and note any vehicles parked in the driveway or adjacent to the residence. He was pleased Spruce Street was quiet; only two cars propped on cement blocks made a home on the long narrow street. *That's far enough away.* Lucifer noticed the two vehicles weren't close enough to make a difference. He would trust his instincts and just walk toward his next masterpiece's home. He was ready to exit the car, when he glanced in the rearview mirror. Lucifer was surprised when he saw what stared back at him. The killer had spent the morning hours to prepare his personal looks for this event. Lucifer found an old set of hair clippers and used them to shave off all of his long wavy hair. He also rummaged through his closet and found several armed forces sweatshirts buried under an assortment of medical journals.

He found one he loved. It was red with an eagle, globe and anchor on the front. The words "*Always Ready*" were screen-printed in yellow above the insignia. It went well with the black tactical Law Enforcement trousers he purchased several weeks ago from a local military surplus store. The killer looked the part. If anyone happened to see him in the detective's neighborhood, they would see the portrait of a military man, carrying a green duffel bag.

Lucifer knew it would be easier to wait until darkness, but he enjoyed the dramatic and the mere thought of discovery drew a certain appeal. A muffled laugh escaped, as he remembered what his mother used to call him. *Drama King*. He knew this was a perfect description of his personality. Even now, if the slightest kink crept its way into his plots, the killer would become irrational, regardless if it affected the murder or not. Why else would he have strived so hard to create these masterpieces only he could enjoy? Sometimes, Lucifer would restructure how he approached and attacked a victim based on that alone. Today's task was to quell the rhetoric of Commander Alex Barnum. Lucifer knew the man wasn't your average, non-alert citizen. This was a Valentine police detective and a supervisor besides.

This is exciting. He popped the lid on the trunk of his car and grabbed the large olive green duffel bag. Opening the bag, the killer pulled out a dusty black baseball cap. He shook it out and chuckled at the design. There was an emblem of a naval ship embroidered in white stitching across the center. Lucifer didn't like to wear these types of accessories, but the cap fit with what he chose to wear and it was the appropriate compliment to complete this façade. *Time to get to work*. He placed on the cap and closed the bag. He slung the duffel bag over his shoulder, taking vigorous strides as he headed up the sidewalk.

* * *

Alex Barnum sat in a steel chair ridiculously small for his large frame. He peered out into the inquisitive and frightened crowd assembled in front of police headquarters. The citizens had made their way out for this significant mid-morning press conference. Barnum reached down with both hands to straighten his suit as he prepared for the day's media exposure. He wore his favorite; the expensive attire was charcoal gray and went well with his ivory-colored long-sleeved shirt. The tie was plain and dark navy with a gold Valentine Police tie clip to hold it in place. The suit wouldn't draw any attention from the media; it was the ideal choice for the Chief's press conference. He yawned. *Still fucking tired.* It was most in part to the damn guy who phoned in the middle of the night. His wife didn't even remember the legal counselor's name. *Maybe he left a message on my office voice mail.* Barnum would have to check the office after he was done here. *Hopefully this shit won't last long.* He was already covered in sweat as the sun's rays started to penetrate the fabric. He stood up when Chief Ralph Anderson walked out of the main entrance, and gave him a hostile wave. *I'm fucked, so, fucked.* The prestigious authority wore the dark blue uniform of the Valentine Police, which surprised his colleagues. The shirt was long-sleeved and had three yellow chevrons stitched on both sides halfway up the arm. Each colored chevron was an indicator the person had ten years of continued service in the department. He also wore a set of four-star insignia on each collar of the shirt. Only the executive of the department sported these designations. Chief Anderson stepped up to Barnum and signaled for the press officer in the crowd to start the event. Barnum leaned in to his supervisor.

"Nice monkey suit, Ralph."

"Thanks, where's yours at?" The chief hesitated. "Oh, you couldn't get the raspberry jelly stain out, could you?"

"Ha, fucking, ha. You and that damn Jeffers, think you guys are damn comedians," Barnum said, yanking his tie.

"Of course we do. "Alex, pay attention, it's time for the conference." Several news media stations gathered for the anticipated extravaganza. The pack of reporters wanted to hear the Chief discuss how he would solve all the recent homicides. Chief Anderson patted Barnum on the shoulder as he strutted to the metal podium. He shifted the dark, foam-covered microphone attached to it so it was perfect for his height. *I wish I were at Parma Point*, Barnum thought. He wasn't able to meet with the younger investigator for the latest attack by Lucifer, due to the fact; the chief decided the senior detective would be better suited to run interference for the line of questions from the news hounds. He also knew Anderson didn't have the ability to answer some of the queries that would be directed his way.

The various reporters had their television cameras and microphones perched in all directions. This was industry standard protocol for news stations, eager to soak up any tidbit they could use to propel their agency over another in coverage. Barnum gawked at his watch; he always hated these types of things. The conference went quite well, all things considered. The Valentine Law Enforcement leader finished his prepared statement and even addressed the latest murder at Parma Point. No doubt, the reporters not at this event would trample over one another to get to the crime scene. After Chief Anderson reported on the latest murder, he fielded questions from several of the media. Barnum heard the chief answer about ten questions before a young reporter from *Eyespot 5 News* posed a pointed question to the leader.

"Chief, I'm Lance Sheets from *Eyespot 5 News*. A few questions after hearing you, sir. You state your department still hasn't any valuable leads in this case and the offender could be anyone. Don't you believe, sir, this information may create mass hysteria among the citizens of Valentine and its adjoining suburbs? Secondly, sir, if this were the case, wouldn't our citizens be well within their rights to protect themselves? Most *importantly*, the need to protect their families? Maybe the ability to purchase firearms permits for everyone that qualifies would give some peace of mind to our citizens."

"Mr. Sheets, thanks for your multiple questions. I will address just a part of your inquiry. Our investigative team has been spending countless numbers of hours processing evidence at the scene of each murder. You misunderstood me, when I mentioned our evidence in the case hasn't resulted in linking a possible suspect. What I *said*, Mr. Sheets, is that we have many pieces of evidence the department is still evaluating before we release the information regarding a suspect. Do you understand the difference, Mr. Sheets?"

"Yes, my mistake, Chief Anderson," the young reporter scribbled a few notes on a pad of paper.

"Good, Mr. Sheets, I'm glad we have cleared that up. The next part of your question I will hand over to Detective Alex Barnum. He is the senior investigator for the department and our resident expert in this case. He also has witnessed these ritualistic murders, first hand. I trust he will be able to provide you answers to the remaining particulars of your inquiry."

Barnum wasn't surprised when the focus shifted onto him. He knew the man wasn't fond of him and figured at some point thatAnderson would throw him to the wolves. The Chief stepped aside and ushered Barnum to the microphone and flashed him a smirk. *Yeah, fuck you too*! Barnum cleared his throat. "Well, Mr. Sheets, to answer your question about the members of this community obtaining weapons permits, it's simply this: I don't believe giving everyone a weapons permit will reduce the propensity for the killer or killers to strike again. Like the chief explained, this individual carrying out these heinous crimes seems to study his victims and appears to know a great deal about their regular routines. You and everyone else here in Valentine have the right regardless of this investigation to apply for the proper weapons permit. The department handling the permits will review the application and appropriate training will be provided, prior to issuing the paperwork.

This is the way the city has always operated, and I don't anticipate any immediate major changes to our present procedure. The public can protect their families by being vigilant and reporting suspicious activity or suspicious persons in their respective areas. Listen, Mr. Sheets, everyone knows their neighborhood and what appears to be the normal environment of it. If any citizen feels something is out of place, call us and we will dispatch officers to investigate the situation. I think through the vigilance of the officers and senior leaders in the Law Enforcement agencies both municipal and county, we will get through this rash of murders and the perpetrator will be caught and prosecuted. Does this answer your mass hysteria question?" Barnum exchanged looks with the news reporter, as he shook his head in visible disagreement, but didn't bother to question the law officer. Chief Anderson shook Barnum's hand as he returned to the podium to conclude the speaking event.

"Ladies and Gentlemen, does anyone have other questions at this time that I haven't covered?" The crowd of media and public citizens seemed to be content with the answers they received. Chief Anderson continued. "If not, I appreciate everyone coming today. This will conclude the press conference. My staff or I will keep you informed of any breaking developments, should any arise." Chief Anderson and Barnum stepped away from the podium. Most of media dispersed after a few more cursory snapshots of the men. Barnum and Anderson were silent as they returned to the police station and headed for their respective offices. Barnum picked up his desk phone.

"Jeffers."

"It's me. The press conference just completed. How is everything going up at Parma Point?"

"How did you and Ralph get along?" Brian asked.

"He's a damn son-of-a-bitch, and you know it!" Barnum ripped open his desk drawer and withdrew a travel-size bottle of aspirin. "Other than that, fine," Barnum said.

"You two just need to kiss and make up," Brian jested.

"Fuck you." Barnum unscrewed the cap to the bottle and grabbed a handful of the small white capsules. He shoveled them into his mouth. "Well, anyway, I asked you how you were doing up there?" Barnum left the bottle open on his desk in case he needed more.

"I wish I could have been playing press secretary with you instead of being eaten alive by all these mosquitoes."

"Did you get identification on the victim yet, Jeffers?"

"Krista Meade. Apparently she's got a few shoplifting convictions after the age of eighteen, so it was easy to get the file on her," Brian said.

"Shoplifting, huh?" Barnum asked.

"Not a thing on her criminal history since. I could use a little help out here, if you could make it." Barnum knew Jeffers had been working non-stop with all of the recent homicides. He decided after he stopped for a quick lunch at home, it would be best to give the overworked detective a much-needed break. No way in hell was he going to tell Brian he was taking a fucking lunch break. The young Jeffers would tease him to no end if he used his hunger as an excuse. He thought of a more sensible explanation the man would believe.

"All right, I'll be up in about thirty minutes. I have to stop off and get some medication for my wife."

"Is Lorraine okay?" Brian asked.

"Jeffers, she will be fine. She has been sick and asked me to pick it up this morning." Barnum lied; His wife left town to stay at her sister's for the week.

"Okay, Boss. I will see you then." Jeffers hung up the phone.

Barnum dumped the rest of the pills from the bottle into his mouth and discarded the container in the waste-basket underneath his desk. "I can't wait to retire," Barnum said, loud enough for the administrative assistant, Cynthia Cornerstone, to hear him.

"You got a good five years left in you, sir," Cynthia jested.

Fuck you too. Barnum ignored her as he exited the station. *Time to stop off at home.* It was just a short drive to some peace and quiet.

* * *

The home on Spruce Street displayed many large trees in the front yard and was also lined with miniatures planted along both sides of the driveway. The house itself was of moderate size, made of brick, and was accompanied by a two-car garage. The backyard had a considerable sized patio leading to an Olympic-sized pool and a fenced-in Jacuzzi. His wife was a swimmer in college; Lorraine loved to spend her time in the water. The interior of the house had three bedrooms and two large bathrooms. The kitchen was recently redone in pearl tile; they had just put in a new enclosure, which made the walk to the pool and Jacuzzi easier for the aging couple. Barnum eased open the front door and bent over to pick up the scattered letters, the postal worker shoved through the mail slot. *Fucking Government employees!* He hesitated at the doorway as his nostrils were filled with the scent of cinnamon incense. *Wow! The sixties revisited.* He left this morning, long before Lorraine was up. Barnum knew she loved various aromas throughout the house, so the unique fragrance didn't surprise him. Barnum trudged through the hallway and stopped in front of the fridge and glared at the miniature chalkboard.

"Very funny, Lorraine." Barnum squinted, as he read the words written in pink. He threw open the refrigerator door, while he sorted through the stack of mail. Barnum shook his head at all the various health foods that replaced his usual fat-filled snacks. *Just fucking wonderful*. Barnum leaned down and opened the bottom shelf drawer. *Private stash*.

Hungrily, he lifted out the pack of half-opened ham slices. Lorraine scolded him for many years about eating so much "crap" food. He stopped the gym requirement long ago; the lack of exercise was a factor which led to the fifty additional pounds on his frame. He tried to change his habits as of late, but once in a while, the urge to dive back towards the dark side overtook his will power. Barnum used excuses when Lorraine found his supply of Ding Dongs. Now, he had resulted to ham and turkey, and in the long run, it was much better for him than a greasy double cheeseburger and the fries he typically ate at the local *Starburger* fast food restaurant. Still in possession of the ham slices and several letters under his chin, he reached down to the bottom shelf which was home to his worst enemy, but also the tastiest. *My dear Provolone. You haven't forsaken me at least.* He plucked out the cellophane-wrapped heart blocker, as he sang, *"A sandwich isn't a sandwich without cheese, and don't you belong in my stomach? Yes, please!"*

A scraping noise sounded behind him, but before Barnum turned to investigate, a strong sensation surged through the base of his neck. Within a few seconds, the police detective became dizzy and his arms and legs were useless. The compilation of mail, ham slices and cheese scattered across the glossy tile as Barnum crashed to the ground. His head recoiled from the hard surface and it was difficult to catch his breath. Barnum was still conscious enough to believe he might be on the verge of a heart attack.

"Help me! Someone—help!" Barnum cried. "Oh, my God, help!" He felt a numbing sensation consume his entire body and within a few seconds was unable to move or speak. His breathing was shallower and needed air seem to escape his lungs, in effort to find their own refuge. His head faced the open hallway as a pair of black boots walked into his line of sight. *Someone heard my plea for help, thank God.* A man appeared from the shadows and now towered over him. *Oh no.* Barnum eyes widened; his mouth opened to scream, but only a light squeal escaped. As the investigator slipped into forever emptiness, a voice called out to him.

"Hello, Detective Alex Barnum. My name is Lucifer. You have been chosen to join my collection of masterpieces. Be honored, Detective. Be *very* honored." The killer flipped the fifty-cent piece in the air a series of times before he caught it and stared at his palm.

"Heads it is," Shoving the coin back in his right cargo pocket, he leaned over and rifled through the soon-to-be-dead detective's pants pockets. He ripped out the golden trophy and slipped it into his duffel bag; Lucifer laughed like a madman who had just created an evil Frankenstein. When Detective Alex Barnum succumbed to the blackness, Valentine's most feared killer sculpted his masterpiece, and whistled while he worked…

Chapter 37

A Disturbing Phone Call

Brian Jeffers glared at his watch. *Where the fuck are you*? Waiting for his overdue supervisor, he was more than a little upset, since Barnum called and indicated he would be there within the hour. *That was three hours ago*. Brian had finished with the area and decided to give Barnum a follow-up call and tell him not to bother. He glanced to the lot; only one news media vehicle remained in the area. Most of the reporters seemed to have secured their exclusives and left in transit to their respective agencies. This new murder, along with Chief Anderson's press conference, would have most of the broadcasting morons in media havoc. Brian didn't even want to think about how the citizens were taking the news about the latest death.

He unclipped his cell phone from his belt, and scrolled to Barnum's number. After several rings, the voice mail system kicked in. *He always answers*. Brian waited a few minutes, and then tried a second time. The results were the same, Brian tapped the phone. *Maybe Cynthia will know where he is*. If anyone knew where Barnum was, it would be her.

"How are you doing? You about done?"

"I could be better. Just a few more minutes. A quick question for you?"

"Anything an older woman can do to help, my dear."

He almost laughed a little at that. The consistent stress drained him of many things; humor was close to the top on the list. "I was called by Barnum earlier and he told me his ass would be out to help me at Parma Point. Is he by chance still at the office?"

There was a slight pause. "He left a few hours ago. It seemed that he was in a hurry to leave, but didn't say anything to me."

"If he left a few hours ago, he *should* have been here…" Brian's voice trailed off.

"I would have thought so too. Give me a few minutes, I will phone dispatch and see if he got called for something."

"Okay." Brian didn't understand why Barnum wouldn't have called him, A few minutes later; Cynthia was back on the line. "Dispatch confirmed they didn't send him out. They did try to call him on the radio, but he hasn't responded."

This behavior was not like his supervisor, since, he just stood in front of the entire population of Valentine and acted as Chief Ralph Anderson's right-hand man. What was it that Barnum told him earlier? *Medication for his wife.* "Cynthia, I think he does patrol the southwest portion of the city once in a while. Do me a favor and have the marked units in that area, keep an eye out for him."

"Sure. Brian, you think something's wrong?"

"I don't know yet. He said his wife needed some meds. Barnum said she was sick."

"I will call Holly back and tell them to have the officers look out for him."

"Also, have a unit also drive by his house. If his wife is ill, maybe he decided to stay with her. He may have turned off his cell and radio— not smart, but could be a possibility."

"Sure, I will someone stop by and check if his squad

is parked in the driveway."

"I hope that damn guy isn't taking a lunch break somewhere," Brian said.

"You know him. Eating is his national pastime," Cynthia joked.

"You are *so* right about that."

"Anything else you need dear?" Cynthia asked.

"Yes, one more thing."

"Let me have it."

"I sent you an e-mail about a phone number for a medical institution I was doing some research on?"

"The wheelchair thing, right?" Cynthia asked.

"Yeah, that."

"I already called. The people I talked to were not very interested in a stolen wheelchair," Cynthia said. "The gentleman I spoke to, Mr. Wright acted like I was wasting his time."

"Well, hopefully we get some prints back on it. I figured *someone* would have interest."

"I can call back and speak to someone higher on the food chain, if you want?" Cynthia said.

"You have done fine. I do have some good news. We may have some extra help from the sheriff's office."

"Really?"

"I will tell you about it when I see you."

"Good, are you heading back to the office or your house? In case I find Commander Barnum," Cynthia asked.

"I was thinking of coming back to the office, but this has been a *long* day. I might just head home."

"I'll tell Commander Barnum to call you when we find him."

"Sounds good to me. "Take care." Brian ended the

call. He snapped a few more photos of the now-barren recreational area. He was about to walk the crime scene one more time, when his cell phone vibrated. Recognizing the number as Barnum's, he was quick to answer. "Well, there you are, *Bossman*! I have been waiting all damn afternoon for you!" Brian hissed into the phone. He waited for a response from his supervisor, but all he could hear was background music. Then something even stranger happened. The music was accompanied by a male voice, screeching out some of the words to the popular song, but added these several lyrics.

"You're so— dead, you didn't even know. You're so— dead I feel it my soul. You're so dead. I want to say— You're so dead. I'll make you pay—"

The cell was disconnected. A rush of icy cold surged throughout his body. Brian bolted to his unmarked unit and grabbed at the radio handset. "Dispatch, thirty-nine, two."

"Dispatch, go ahead," the female dispatcher responded.

"Listen, get a few units to 1222 Spruce Street quickly. I will meet them there," Brian instructed.

"Ten-four, sir, any more information available for this address?"

"This is the residence of Detective Alex Barnum. I just received a call from his cell phone. It sounded like he may have a medical emergency," Brian said.

He didn't want to divulge any more, due to the fact that the local media would be on scanner alert in search for their next hot exclusive. After a short delay, the dispatcher came back on the radio. "Thirty-nine, two, we have several units that have been dispatched to 1222 Spruce Street, sir. Any direction upon arrival at the

Death's Prescription   Jeffery Martin

scene?"

"Have all responding parties wait for me, before entering his residence; also have the closest unit in the area, call me on my cell phone ASAP."

"Affirmative, sir."

A few moments later, Brian received a call from Officer Sharon Dester. She was the first to be contacted to the scene at Spruce Street.

"Officer Dester, here. The dispatcher said you needed to talk to me."

"Dester, I just received a strange call from Commander Barnum's phone. I think he may be in serious trouble," Brian said.

"Sir?"

"In the background, there was some music playing. It was like hard-core rock music. Not like anything Barnum would listen to. All of a sudden in the middle of the lyrics, the line went dead."

"Detective, what do you think that means?" Officer Dester asked.

"I think someone went out of their way to call me from his cell phone. I don't know why, but it doesn't make sense."

"Sir, what do you need me to do?" Officer Dester said.

"When you get there, take a tactical position in the backyard of the house. Make sure whoever is in the house doesn't see you. Don't go inside the residence. Do you understand?"

"I do, sir."

"Good. If Barnum is in danger, the guy might still be inside. With you outside, that will limit his options of escape."

-216-

"The theory sounds good, sir," Officer Dester said.

"Well, I hope it's more than a theory, Dester. I really do. Good luck; I'll radio you when I get on scene," Brian said.

"Okay, sir."

Brian increased the speed of the patrol car. He believed Lucifer decided to go after Barnum; the bastard had the nerve to use the detective's cell phone to let Brian know. Lucifer seemed to always be one step ahead of the investigators, now he had rubbed it in Brian's face. He assumed his supervisor was already dead, but wasn't sure if Lucifer was still at the residence. Maybe for once, the police had the upper hand. *Maybe… it was at least a chance.*

* * *

Lucifer, satisfied with his latest accomplishment, gathered his tools and placed them in the duffel bag next to the newest trophy. Wiping off the cell phone, the killer placed it on the kitchen table and scanned the room. Content that he hadn't left any visible clues, the killer gazed upon his latest creation. *See if you can catch me now.* He laughed to himself. *It was a bold move to have dialed the other one.* Playing the rock music for the recipient was the perfect touch. It wasn't in his nature to inform the police just after and he wouldn't repeat the possible vulnerability. Lucifer just felt a last-minute urge to play a little with the dead man's coworker. A rush of adrenaline pulsed though his blood, which made him feel invincible. He slid out the rear patio door and left it open. Lucifer hiked through several backyards until he came upon an elderly couple at war with their patio cement blocks. They waved to him; the killer realized he still wore the military sweatshirt and baseball cap. He gestured back, crossed the sidewalk and spotted his Honda.

Opening the trunk, the madman stuffed the duffel bag under the spare tire. Lucifer double-checked the lid was secure, then stared down the street; He started the car, and sang the lyrics to the song he played earlier. *"You're so—dead, you didn't even know. You're so—dead I feel it my soul. You're so dead. I want to say— You're so dead. I'll make you pay—"*

He loved the melody; it was textbook for the mood of his last masterpiece. Lucifer turned the corner, but was surprised, when two Valentine Police units sped down the street headed in his direction. *They couldn't have figured it out yet.* Both patrol cars had on their emergency red and blue lights. As they drew closer, the shrill of the powerful sirens filled his ears. He maneuvered the Honda to the side of the road and watched them disappear from sight. *What a rush*! Once he was convinced they were a safe distance away, the killer eased back into traffic.

He laughed. It would be curious to know, if the Chief of Police would make another false statement, who was responsible for the lazy detective's demise. *Probably not again*. Turning up the volume on the car stereo, Lucifer sung the words to his newest and favorite song. This time he changed the last few words of the verse to make it his own.

"You're so dead. I'm glad to say— You're so dead. I made you pay—"

Chapter 38

Too Late

The two Valentine Police units which passed the Honda didn't realize how close they were to Lucifer. Officer Sharon Dester paid little attention to the Honda parked along the curb. Her sole focus was to get to the residence of a possible downed officer. Detective Jeffers told her: the man was in danger, and if she could make it in time, Lucifer wouldn't hurt anyone ever again. She turned up Spring Street; within a few seconds spotted the house. Positioning the patrol vehicle, Dester blocked the driveway. Exiting, she noticed an unmarked car in front of a brick two-car garage. A wooden fence ran the length of the property. She sprinted from the patrol car, and took shelter at the back of the garage. The barrier was small enough for her to peek over, but it was also sturdy enough to protect her from exposure to possible threats. She found herself in excellent position to observe the rear patio door. Once settled in, Dester clicked the external microphone on her portable radio.

"Thirty-nine, ninety-nine, to dispatch."

"Dispatch, go ahead with your transmission," the female dispatcher said.

"I'm in position at Spring Street on the west side of the garage."

"Ten-four. Detective Jeffers should be arriving at the scene within a few minutes," the dispatcher informed.

"I have spoken with him, dispatch. I have direction on how to proceed. Thirty-nine, one- hundred is parked in front of the residence monitoring the area."

"Anything to report from your location?"

"It appears to be quiet from what I can tell." *Too quiet*, Dester thought. "Dispatch, I did locate Commander Barnum's squad in the driveway."

"Copy that. Keep us advised to what's going on."

"I will," Dester said. The radio became quiet. Sharon Dester's heart took a series of leaps. A killer may be only a short distance away, and she may be called upon to silence him.

* * *

The other patrol unit sent to Commander Barnum's residence positioned his patrol car along the street in front of his house. The officer took a defensive stance, as he kept watch of the front door. Brian Jeffers raced up the road from the opposite direction, in hopes of cutting off any escape path, in case the killer had already departed. He maneuvered about fifty feet away and faced the marked unit. Brian radioed dispatch. "Thirty-nine, two, to dispatch."

"Go ahead, sir."

"I'm on scene with both units. Send additional officers to block off Spring Street from both directions. Also, place a few on all of the side streets in the neighborhood," Brian commanded.

"Affirmative, sir, anything else we can help with?" the dispatcher asked.

"I will be out on portable, so keep channel three clear of all traffic unless it's emergency transmissions."

"Yes, sir," the dispatcher said. "Hold on sir, while we tell the other units to free the channel up."

"Ten-four." Brian jumped out of his vehicle and turned on his portable radio. The crackled voice of the dispatcher boomed the speaker. "All units... be advised to keep channel three clear for thirty-nine, two and the officers on scene at Spring Street."

Everything is in place. Brian would have crucial un-interrupted communication with the two officers at the scene. He activated the portable radio.

"Thirty-nine, two, to thirty-nine, one-hundred," Brian said.

"Transmit," the uniformed patrol officer responded.

"This is what I need. "I'm heading up to the house. Give me some backup and let me know if anything seems to be out of place." Brian released the microphone.

"Sir, I haven't seen any movement in the residence at all."

"Good, let's go." Brian sprinted to the first available large tree. He darted to the next in the yard, and kept himself hidden from anyone in the house. He glanced back at the cover officer, who repositioned himself next to Barnum's unmarked vehicle.

"Sir, you doing ok?" The officer asked.

"Ten-four." Brian flashed the officer a quick wave to show him he was fine. He withdrew his sidearm, and he moved with due diligence as he approached the home. If Lucifer was in the house, the man would be armed and ready. He wasn't going to risk unneeded movement and be an easy target for the proven killer. Pushing the orange transmit button. Brian spoke. "Jeffers to Dester," Brian called the female officer by name; he didn't want to confuse her in this already high-stress situation by using the call numbers.

"I'm behind the garage, facing the rear patio door," Dester said.

"I'm at the front. Don't move from your location, until I give you the green light," Brian directed.

"Sir, he can't get by me this way."

"If the suspect is still in there, you're the one that will be in the best position to get the angle on his escape route." Brian let in sink in.

"I'm a little nervous*,"* Dester said.

You and me, both. "Hey, believe me; I know what you're going through." Brian paused. "Try to get off the best shot you can, okay?"

"Yes, sir," Officer Dester said.

"Relax, and you will be fine." Brian jumped onto the front porch. The other patrol officer approached from the opposite; he was almost to the cement slab as well.

"If that's even possible," Dester's voice cracked.

Brian crept along the length of the wooden structure, as he made it to the entrance of the house. He bladed his body, so it wasn't in the path of any attack. His heart pounded with so much turmoil; it felt like a compilation of drummer boys' had set off on a mission to spread their message. The other officer stepped up on the porch and now was just a few steps to the right of the door.

Brian moved with agility and quickness. The beating in his chest had returned to a more suitable state. He lashed out with his foot and delivered a strike with enough force to cause the bulky frame of the doorway to splinter and break away from the lock. Brian slipped inside. *So far, so good*. He motioned for his backup to stay by the entryway, while he moved onward. Brian crept towards the foyer; the strong pungent odor of burnt cinnamon flared throughout the soft tissue of his nostrils. He was unaware; *this* was the identical scent Barnum was exposed to when he arrived home. He stepped into the room. The only light into this area was from several small tears in the dark-colored window blinds. Brian trained his firearm on the stairwell that led to the second floor. He motioned for the second officer to provide cover, while he pulled out his tactical flashlight and scanned the area. The investigator needed to make sure Lucifer wasn't there ready to ambush the two.

When he felt the area was secure, he snuck through the living room in the direction of Barnum's kitchen. The other officer stayed hidden by the stairwell, so the front would stay protected; also it was an ideal place to watch for any unseen threats that could jeopardize their safety. Brian moved closer to the kitchen doorway. He heard a steady hum emit from behind the door. He remembered how Barnum complained to him about the constant noise of the refrigerator. Brian hoped this was the particular sound he had mentioned, and not some surprise the killer had left for his guests.

Tightening his grip on the firearm, Brian skimmed the light around room. *Nothing out of the ordinary*. Brian hesitated before he pushed open the wooden barrier. He peeked around the corner, as, the steady mechanical sound drowned out any verbal communication. His eyes widened; his heart raced as he stared in amazement. *Not again*. Even though light was still at a premium, Brian recognized the outline of his supervisor's body. The carcass was still clothed; Barnum was face down in the center of the slippery tiled floor. Several bloodstained letters, along with square-shaped pink pieces of meat were strewn around the corpse. The blood still poured from wounds as it seeped across the waxed floor and its progress stopped at the base of the wall. He stared at Barnum's upper back and observed pieces of the Commander's flesh had been torn off, and were now pasted onto the refrigerator. *Holy Fuck!* Brian clamped down on the button on his portable.

"Thirty-nine, two, to thirty-nine, one-hundred, I need you in the kitchen now*!"*

"I was just clearing the house," the uniformed officer said.

"Get the hell in here*."* Brian knew Lucifer was already gone. "Call for a crime scene team and medical examiner*."*

"Yes, sir," the officer replied, his voice faint. Brian holstered his sidearm and approached Barnum. *Fucking Bastard*! His hands covered his face and he froze in place. *Another fucking calling card.* The sound of footsteps against tile caused Brian turned to turn away from the horror.

The patrol officer stopped; his mouth was open but words were unintelligible. Once he regained his composure, he stammered. "I took… care of what you needed," he said.

"Yeah… well, I could use a little help here. Grab the police tape from the car and start—" Brian said, defeated.

"I will take care of it. I will also call Officer Dester to help."

"That will be fine. No need to fucking hurry *now*." Brian dropped to one knee and inspected Lucifer's latest artistry. The message that vandalized his supervisor's backside beckoned for Brian's attention. *Lucifer's calling.*

The words were handwritten but this time it wasn't engraved into the skin. This time, Lucifer made his sadistic design by removing flesh to create each word. Brian turned the body. Barnum's eyes were still open; a terrified look in them. Blood oozed from both sides of the detective's mouth. *Why so much blood*? Brian slid on a pair of plastic gloves. Yanking a pen from his pocket, he pried open the mouth. Brian gritted his teeth; all the muscles in his body tensed up when he realized why. The space reserved for the detective's tongue was now a cavernous abyss. The gap was filled in by the older man's broken teeth and a folded bloody white piece of paper. It was stapled inside the right cheek and it would be more than a challenge to extract without further damage. He fished in his pants pocket and pulled out a tactical knife. *Not the best choice, but it's all I've got.*

Placing the blade against the staple, Brian pressed outward on the metal, which caused it to loosen and free it from its iron captive. He continued to manipulate the blade until Brian was able to scoop it out of the dead man's mouth. He placed the stained square onto a clean spot on the tiled floor. Brian used the steel edge to open the paper and observed four miniature typed words, which said: *Look in the fridge.*

Even though the pieces of flesh covered the unit, he knew it held a tragic find. As Brian stumbled to his feet, he felt a slight breeze against his skin. Turning to find the origin, he discovered the patio door was ajar. Lucifer had murdered his supervisor and slipped out *again* unobserved. He had taunted the junior investigator and led Brian on the path he took well aware that there would be no way the investigator could catch him. *Fuck me!* Drained of usefulness, he sleepwalked to the fridge and did his best to ignore the gruesome sight, but instead focused on the magnetic chalkboard. He almost managed a quick smile, when he read the words scrawled on it. *No Damn Provolone Cheese. Lorraine.*

Brian shook his head; slow to open the relic appliance. It was filled with necessities, except on the first shelf was a hunk of cheese wrapped in cellophane. It was placed on top of a glass jar, which appeared to be filled with a murky substance. Brian glared wide-eyed at what floated in the viscous fluid. *It was worse*! Barnum's ripped-out fleshy tongue danced in the liquid as Brian clenched his teeth and slammed the fridge door with such force, all the multi-colored magnets dropped and bounced off the tile in various directions.

Trophy, think, trophy! Clearing his head, Brian kneeled over Barnum, and searched for the most important item who defined all law enforcement. Brian tore the clothes apart in hopes that it had fallen off, but he failed to find the important credential. Lucifer was in possession of Barnum's gold detective's shield and with it, he could utilize the badge to create even more havoc. He trudged into the living room and ignored the uniformed officer as he continued to make his way to the main entrance. He stepped through the broken door and collapsed on the cluttered steps. Brian bowed his head and buried his face in his hands. The investigator was on the verge of a breakdown. *Still loose and have no idea where he is headed.* He imagined what evil the killer still had in store for the city, but if the slaying of Barnum was any indication, mercy wasn't on the agenda.

Chapter 39

Almost Caught?

Lucifer arrived at the apartment and unpacked the olive green duffel bag. He took out the leather badge holder and placed in his pocket. He cradled his newest collection in both hands, and admired the gold and shiny five-point star. The word DETECTIVE was positioned in the center, as black engraved letters identified the badge holder. The center was surrounded by the blue outline of the Valentine downtown area. *This needs to be cleaned up.* Lucifer stopped in front of the sink and pulled open a drawer. *There it is.* His eyes lit up with anticipation. The killer removed a dry white cloth, along with a medium sized orange jar. The words *POLISH PERFECT* were printed on the face of the lid. He sat down at the table and uncovered the container. He dipped the cloth into the jar; when he was satisfied enough of the solvent was obtained, he rubbed the gold shield with the fabric. Lucifer smiled when he saw his reflection in the gold star. "Excellent, this is how you should look!" He took out the badge holder and clipped the shield back in its tight sleeve. He retreated to his closet that contained all of his collections. *A little housekeeping is in order.* Throwing his clothing in a pile, Lucifer grabbed a black garbage bag from a cabinet under the sink, and stuffed in all of the clothes. He ensured it was secured, so the stench couldn't escape into the air and alert other tenants to the contents. He tucked it between a nook adjacent the front door, and would make sure to dispose of it.

Gazing at the back of the doorway, the floral-designed calendar caught his attention. He flipped over the glossy page and studied several of the dates circled in black marker. *Time is running out*. He knew the effort spent on Commander dipshit cost him and he was also aware, the detective's murder wasn't flawless like most, but a kill was still a kill. Tapping one of the circled dates, his eyes narrowed. Three weeks were left before he needed to be in position to carry out the final stage of his revenge. It was a long time, but the man responsible for the transformation of Lucifer would soon be held accountable. After a quick shower, he stopped in the bedroom and removed a black suitcase from underneath the bed. Opening it, the killer surveyed the contents. A freakish grin crossed his lips.

Three suits, each wrapped in tan carriers were stacked on top of one another. The attire was used when the killer planned to create special works of art. He picked up the first and unzipped it. Lucifer inspected the dark blue Artole suit for any damage and was pleased when he discovered it was in pristine condition. Lucifer remembered how he picked this up the last time he visited Italy. This was, without a doubt, a power suit. Lucifer used it when in professional settings with people in his former occupation. He secured the bag and removed the second. This fine work was black and blue pinstriped and was designed by the Russian tailor *Restur Amaina.* The killer used this ensemble for one of his previous high-profile masterpieces. He inspected this as well; again it was in excellent shape. Lucifer was *very* thrilled when he pulled out the last carrier. This crafted piece was the killer's favorite. It was a German made limited design hand-woven *Gestalt* suit. This tan three-piece had a distinction which identified the owner as being successful. The modern style of the non-pleated pants was what attracted him to it. *Simply exquisite*. Placing it separate from the other two, he decided to use this when he visited the Jeffers residence. This outfit would look very professional with the gold shield. He pulled it out and hung it up on the single brass hook on back of the bedroom door. Lucifer would drop it off at the drycleaners to make it presentable. He needed to look his best, as this would conclude his masterpieces in the city. Then it would be onward.

Lucifer realized he needed cardboard boxes to pack all the necessary items he would take to his next city to continue his collection. A quick thought entered his mind. *Drive the Honda to check out the address of the final victims*.

He would take note of the neighborhood and what escape routes were available, should the killer need to utilize one. Lucifer figured that was a good idea, since he needed to stop at a local grocery store and get the boxes anyway. Lucifer grabbed the suit from the bedroom and exited the back of the complex. He had only taken a few steps when he stopped, mid-stride. Lucifer was surprised to see three Valentine Police cars parked in the barren lot of the adjacent apartment complex. He eyed the units as he resumed the pace to his car. One of the police officers exited his patrol vehicle and approached the now worried Lucifer. He realized the slight uniformed man had positioned his right hand on the butt of his service weapon. The man had a look of urgency in his eyes as he hurried his pace, even more. Lucifer slid his hand into his back pocket and removed a folding knife. *One well-placed strike would end this, but in the end, his reign would be over*. Taking a deep breath, the killer tried to remain calm, but his heart raced at an uncontrollable rate. He was unsure if the local police solved the murders and now were here to collect him, just like he collected his masterpieces. Lucifer fumbled with his keys as he tried to unlock the Honda. He heard it unlatch; the killer clutched at the door handle.

Almost free.

"Sir, excuse me. I'm Officer James Patters with the Valentine Police Department. I need to speak with you a second, sir."

Lucifer froze as he snapped the knife into the kill position. "Is there a problem? I was just going to drop off some clothes." With his free hand, Lucifer showed the patrolman the carrier.

"I can see that. I just need a few minutes of your time."

"Of course," Lucifer said. "Anything I can do to help the overworked and underpaid public servants in this community."

A quirky grin filled the man's face. "Yeah, you got that right," Officer Patters said. "We are searching for a man involved in robbing the grocery store down the street…"

"A *robbery*?" Lucifer asked.

"Yes. Several customers witnessed a man carrying a large knife, as he ran out of the store."

I have a large knife. "Was anyone hurt?" Lucifer asked.

"Nobody was injured that we know of. The night manager saw the individual running in *this* direction."

"Wow, this neighborhood is quiet," Lucifer said. "I never have had a problem living here."

"It is a quiet area, except for when it isn't." Officer

Patters nodded. "Sir, have you seen anyone around here you would consider suspicious?"

He loosened his grip on the knife. "Not that I can think of." Lucifer breathed a sigh of relief. The local police were looking for a second-rate criminal. This officer didn't realize Valentine's serial killer stood right in front of him. "Officer, I have been busy in my apartment all afternoon. I didn't have the chance to see many people today. What does the man look like? Just in case I happen upon him."

"The owners described the man as a white male about six feet tall. He is very thin, and wearing a red sweatshirt and blue jeans."

"I will keep an eye out for you."

"Thanks. Excuse me, sir. You live over there in the Brooke Shadow Apartments?" Officer Patters pointed to where Lucifer exited.

"I do, Officer. In apartment 13B. Is there anything else I can help you with?"

Officer Patters eyed him; his eyebrows narrowed, which warned Lucifer, he had become a little suspicious. "Do you have any identification on you, sir?"

Fuck! The killer again reached for the knife. "Did I do something wrong, Officer Patters?" Lucifer asked. *Come just a little closer.*

"Not at all. It's just that our department has been in a recent rash of, uh, incidents, and they require us to fill out paperwork on who we talked to, whenever we respond to a call for service."

Well, I didn't fucking call you. Lucifer's blood pressure rose, in realization, he lacked any other choice but to reveal his identity to the public servant. Again, he loosened his grip on the weapon, and reached into his front pocket and pulled out the black leather billfold that held his correct driver's license. He knew the fake identification utilized at the motor vehicle department office wouldn't fool this officer. Lucifer handed the thin plastic to the policeman.

"Here you go, Officer."

"Thank you, sir." Officer Patters stared at the driver's license and removed a green memo notebook. He glanced at the last name of the man and sort of laughed to himself. He scribbled the information into his notebook and handed it back to Lucifer.

"Is there anything else you need from me?" Lucifer asked coldly.

"Mr. Calling, looks like everything is in order. I think that's all I will need. Be careful though. We don't know how dangerous this man could be," Officer Patters said.

"Well, hopefully he is already gone from this area."

"That's what I hope too. The manager was very frightened, so his details were a little sketchy on the guy. The robber did shove a knife into his face," Officer Patters said.

Just like I would have done to you. "That sounds a little crazy."

"Just be careful, sir."

Lucifer nodded. "I don't know what I would do if someone ever flashed a knife in my face. I would run as fast as I could in the opposite direction," Lucifer managed a nervous grin.

"That would be the smartest thing anyone could do. I don't want to trouble you further, but if you see anything suspicious, give me a call, okay, sir?" Officer Patters handed Lucifer a business card.

He watched, Patters walk away and join his comrades. Several minutes later, all three of the police vehicles left the area and split off in different directions. Lucifer would have to move his schedule up and strike within a few days. Then the ambitious killer would leave Valentine and never return. *Oh, no. No time for this.* The familiar rant of his long dead mother was again present.

"*Lu-ci-fer, Lucifer, Lucifer! Some tough man you are! They are going to get you and put you in the electric chair, you sick bastard! They will kill you, like you killed your poor mother*!" Lucifer smashed his fist into the steering wheel.

"Stop, you bitch! You deserved everything you got, you two-timing slut!" Lucifer remembered the time he walked in on his mother and some dirty sloppy man engaged in rough sex. The man *wasn't* his father and his whore of a mother threatened to hurt him, if he told of her transgressions. This was the first time he felt hate for the woman. The killer reached into the glove compartment and pulled out the bottle of medication. He popped two pills; within a few minutes, the voice disappeared. He didn't want to lose concentration on what was planned for the Jeffers' girls. He drove the Honda through the city, until he found the address his next victims. Parking a block away from the residence, Lucifer reached under a newspaper on the adjacent set, and removed a set of high-powered night vision binoculars. He was careful to adjust all the car mirrors with his position. *No one is going to sneak up on me.* The killer focused in on his prey. Lucifer noticed the champagne-colored blinds were wide open; the strong lenses from the device made it seem like he was inside the house. He watched as three little girls jumped around and played in what appeared to be the family room. A few minutes later, their mother joined them and engaged in the fun as well. Lucifer's face formed an evil grin, as he planned what would be his ultimate masterpiece.

Chapter 40

Stalking Another

Lucifer returned to the apartment, to rectify a possible situation, which could ruin his plans. He would revisit the Jeffers's residence later, and finish his little late-night observation. He was worried; the police officer might come back after him, if the man actually paid attention to what was written in the green notebook. *It could be all over.* He fingered the smooth business card Officer Patters handed him and inspected the information. Lucifer needed to retrieve the policeman's green memo notebook, or the hope of his ultimate masterpiece would soon slip through the killer's grasp.

He snatched up a yellow note pad from the computer desk and jotted down the details of the meet and greet with Patters. He realized the officer appeared a little nervous. Lucifer could use this to his advantage. If the officer decided to forward the contact information to a competent supervisor, it wouldn't take long before they figured out who was responsible for the murders. Lucifer came up with a sinister idea; he booted up his computer and waited as the logon boxes popped up.

He accessed his favorite search engine. Lucifer typed in the words: *VALENTINE POLICE DEPARTMENT.* The search returned with the results he needed. *I must be lucky.* He was surprised to see the department with its own website. The page was well-constructed. The background was blue and a photograph of the city park with many uniformed officers around various police patrol units was the home page. He noticed a black word banner scrolled left to right, across the top of the screen.

Valentine Police is urging every one of its citizens to stay vigilant in their daily activities. The recent outbreak of violent crime against the faithful people of this community is being investigated by both city and county Law Enforcement. Remember to report any suspicious behavior you witness, regardless of how small it may seem. If this is an emergency, dial 911.

All of his "work" was an impact on this community; this was the desired result. He studied the left side of the webpage and laughed. In bold black letters the Police Department motto was on the bottom of the screen. W*e strive to make your safety our priority*.

Not lately, he thought.

He glanced over to the top left and located the yellow menu box, where there was an assortment of options for access to departmental information. He was interested in one section; the one needed for his plan of attack. Lucifer found the link and clicked on the yellow drop down box. He calculated his strategy, based on the information listed on the page. Lucifer inspected the business card with scrutiny. His eyes fixated on the slippery surface.

Officer James Patters- Badge/Call Sign #3927
Valentine Police Department
5150 Balboa Street, Valentine, NE 66599
Patrol SW metro district
Phone 997-236-1395

He gazed at the computer for quite a while and then typed some information into the search engine. Within a few seconds, the webpage popped up on screen. *Too easy, way too easy.* Lucifer reviewed the abundance of on-screen information. He grabbed a pen and wrote down the numbers that would give him a chance to retrieve the green notepad. Lucifer's lips curled into the sadistic smirk he would get when he was in the throes of evil. It was time to shop and the killer knew the perfect place.

This this was a critical situation, and it was time to act before the police became lucky enough to catch him. He couldn't risk exposure, not as he was about to finish his last work of art. He turned off the computer and exited the apartment complex.

* * *

Lucifer gaped at the of the twenty-four-hour discount store sign, as he stepped through the double glass doors. An older male uniformed city police officer was posted at the information desk engaged in a conversation with a sales associate. Lucifer waved to him. The brightness of the white lights made him squint a little. The police officer noticed this and smiled. He lifted his hand, "I know, those lights are bad on the eyes, especially when you walk in from the dark."

Lucifer passed by the counter and smiled. "Either these lights are too bright for me or I'm getting old," he joked.

"Sir, we all are getting older," the man nodded.

Lucifer continued on his way. He was shocked to see the store was full of customers. He scanned the aisles of the mega center, in search of the sports section. *Here we go.* The killer stopped in front of a three-shelf Plexi-Glass cabinet. He peered through the glass, astounded by the assortment of electronics that crammed the shelves. There were several different styles of car stereos, radar detector units, and on the last, three styles of emergency scanners. Lucifer bent down to get a closer look at which device he needed to hone in on the Police communications center. The killer found the correct one; he pushed the green button, which was reserved to contact the lowly-paid employees. He waited for several minutes, until he realized assistance wouldn't be on the immediate horizon.

Figures. Leaving the area, Lucifer scoured the other rows in search of someone to help him. He turned up the hardware aisle, and spotted a young female employee at the end of the row. She was having difficulty with the boxes that were too heavy for her small figure. He approached her; the red and white store uniform made her look like his candy striper victim from two years ago. *She is quite attractive.* She had mid-length dark brown hair, a girl next-door face, and a full chest.

"Excuse me, can you help me?" Lucifer used his masculine voice. The girl turned around and glared at Lucifer, upset. Apparently she was disturbed from her simple-minded duties.

"What do you need, sir?"

"I don't want to take you away, but I just need a little assistance in the sports section." Lucifer's face turned red.

"Can't you see I'm busy," the girl said with a smug look.

"I'm—sorry." Lucifer felt hot all over. He couldn't believe this. "Excuse me, I just needed one item from the secured glass cabinet and I waited for a while, but I guess everyone is busy somewhere else."

The girl pointed to the area, where Lucifer had been, prior. "Sir, there is a button on the counter in the section over there to push if you need help. *God*, haven't you been here before?"

"I pushed the button," Lucifer wrung his hands. "I

did wait."

"What?" The girl grabbed at the two-way radio, belt clipped to her waist. "Hold on, I will call Harold. He is the one over there tonight."

"Okay." Lucifer concentrated at the white lanyard that hung from the girl's crushable neck. *Fucking bitch, you so need to die!*

"Give me a minute. I need to finish this." The girl ignored him.

He leaned in closer, and inspected the plastic nametag attached to the lanyard. *If there was only time.* He decided something needed to be said. "Miss, I'm sorry, but no, I haven't been here before. I appreciate your help, even though you feel I'm wasting your time, you stupid little bitch. I will let you get back to your mundane ritual of stocking shelves; I know it will probably be the apex of your professional career. Thank you, *Mandy G.*"

Lucifer turned, not interested in any response that uttered from her useless chatterbox. *She should be gutted like a thanksgiving turkey.* He returned to the sports goods area. This time, a sales clerk appeared almost out of thin air. The man was tall and slim, with gray hair. The killer guessed the man was in his late sixties. His eyes widened as he greeted Lucifer with a sincere smile.

"Hi ya, my name is Harold. Mandy radioed me and told me you need some help over here."

Lucifer returned the smile. "She is correct. I would like to buy this one right here on the bottom shelf." Lucifer pointed to the item. He didn't have time for the employee to expound about how the other models were in comparison to the one he had chosen. Harold looked Lucifer directly in the eye. "Well, you know your devices; this is an 800 MHz, one hundred channel scanner.

Sir, this will work almost anywhere and pick up anything you want to hear."

"*Anything*?" Lucifer cocked his head.

"Yep. Well, almost." Harold winked. "You happen to be a cop or fireman or along those lines?"

Lucifer didn't even hesitate. "I'm a weather spotter. I live out in the country and nobody has one, so I was appointed to take the job."

"Well, that's mighty nice of you to do that for your friends, sir. I will run this up to register three and you can pay up there."

"Great, thanks." Lucifer nodded.

"You're welcome. Thanks for the business, sir."

"It was a pleasure, Harold. Do me a favor though. Tell Mandy G. she better start an attitude adjustment to-wards customers or she may receive complaints." *Not to mention a slashed jugular.*

Harold smiled and laughed. "Mandy is a rough one, she really is. Girls her age are all about that damn hip-hop music. They all want to act like punks, and you know what, sir? She's a pain in my ass as well."

She's always a bitch then. Lucifer laughed. "Touché Harold. I have to pick something else up while I'm here. You said register three, right?"

"Just to the left over there," Harold said.

A few minutes later, Lucifer exited the store. He would make sure to program the scanner first thing when he returned home. The killer had finished the first phase in preparation for retrieval of the notebook. Later he would begin the second portion, which involved how Officer Patters spent his patrol shift. Within a day or two, this problem would be solved; his identity still undiscovered. Lucifer was excited again, as he reached into his pocket to grasp the fifty-cent piece. Another masterpiece was on the edge of creation and he couldn't wait to get to work.

Chapter 41

Becoming Clearer

Brian Jeffers sat on the front steps of Alex Barnum's house as afternoon turned into late evening. He was awakened from his trance-like state, when the halogen bulbs from the familiar County Medical Examiner's van pulled into the narrow driveway. Only a few marked patrol units were left at the scene; the staple of them were busy on adjacent streets in search of the suspect. Brian stood up; his legs felt rubbery from the inactivity. Dr. Sanderson stepped in. "I'm sorry about Commander Barnum. I cannot believe the audacity of this killer—he slaughtered one of your own. I can't imagine what you are going through right now."

"I don't see how he can spill so much blood at each scene and *still* leave no evidence." Brian wobbled to his feet.

"His luck will run out. Sooner or later he will be caught," Dr. Sanderson said.

"I hope the hair sample found in the bathroom of the Daltry or prints on the wheelchair will lead us to him."

"Have you heard anything about that yet?" Dr. Sanderson asked.

"The wheelchair thing didn't pan out like I hoped. The lab tech I know still hasn't called me about the results either. Meanwhile, Lucifer is on a fucking rampage and who knows when it will end?"

Sanderson was a close associate to the forensic specialist, and the respect from academia throughout the country made it impossible to have information kept from him. "I might be able to find out more for you with the hair sample and the wheelchair. Let me look at the scene here to do the necessary protocols and I will give the lab a call," Dr. Sanderson said.

"That would help a lot." Brian patted the man on the back.

"I can't promise you anything, but I know someone who may speed up the analysis of the sample." Dr. Sanderson unzipped the body bag. "Also, I wanted to let you know, I found positive identification Propaganician was used on the victim Krista Meade. I'm sorry I didn't get you this earlier."

"You've been here every time I needed something; it's been greatly appreciated, really. Those hair samples are *all* I have to identify this guy. This might be our only shot to get that bastard." The man just nodded his head in agreement, as Brian escorted him to the kitchen, where the now-bloated detective lay. Brian opened the refrigerator and showed the medical examiner the mutilated tongue.

Doctor Sanderson studied the contents of the jar. "The murky film in this container definitely looks like formaldehyde."

"Formaldehyde? Where do you suppose he's got that?" Brian grabbed the container.

"I will tell you one thing for certain. This substance is not available through normal channels and obtaining it would create a paper trial. I would say more so than his paralytic drug of choice."

"It's like this guy has his own laboratory," Brian said.

"He may have. Why do you think he left the appendage in the refrigerator for you?"

If there was one thing Brian knew for sure about the demented Lucifer, it was to expect the unexpected. There appeared to be no rhyme or reason other than Lucifer's desire to kill. "Doc, I wish to *God* I knew that answer, I really do."

Sanderson retreated to conduct his coroner duties as Brian muddled through to process the murder scene. *It isn't just difficult, this is fucking impossible.* He had known Barnum since he'd been hired; on occasion he even visited the house for a weekend barbecue. He felt guilty now for his brashness towards the supervisor. The Chief would have to assign another detective to this murder; Brian was too tired. He left the house, prepared to finish the day with the people he loved and was only a few blocks away when he received a call. "Brian, it's Chief, how are you holding up?" The man was always was sincere; he cared for his people, even with his political position as Valentine's Law Enforcement leader.

"Ralph, this past week has been hell. I need you to send someone else over here to process this mess. Are you heading out to Alex's house?"

"I will send Jacobs to take over. Okay?"

"Thanks, that will work," Brian said.

"I won't be coming there, Brian. I'm heading out of town to see Alex's wife and give her the death notification in person."

"Barnum told me she was sick," Brian said, now a little upset his supervisor had lied to him.

"Not that I was aware," Anderson said. "She apparently left town this morning for a relative's house. Cynthia found the address of her sister."

"God help her, when she finds out." Brian sighed.

"God help us *all.*"

"We're not going to be able to keep his death out of the media, you know that," Brian said.

"I know. When I return tomorrow, I will be releasing another statement on his murder. Brian, I know finding Alex was hard for you, but son, I really need you more than ever now. We need to find this lunatic, before he kills any more people."

"I'm doing my best." Brian sighed. *And it wasn't even close to good enough.*

"I can see you are, but the mayor called me a short time ago and is livid that we still don't have a suspect. Talked about the feds…and takeover.

Brian imagined that conversation was more than likely one-sided, and didn't envy the chief's position. "I may have a lead with the hair sample I found in the Daltry Hotel bathroom, but other than that, our killer hasn't left us anything to go on."

Brian heard a pause, then a deep sigh. "I have never seen anything like this ever. The public is losing faith we can protect them. *I'm* beginning to wonder if we can. This person just killed one of our own. This enrages me so much, son," Anderson said.

"I don't get it; you would think he would want to stay away from the police at all costs."

"That's why this latest murder scares me. It really scares me."

An idea popped into his head. "Ralph, I was just thinking, when I arrived here and found Alex's body, Lucifer removed his tongue. It seems this killer usually just takes from the victims, but *this* time he purposely left the tongue for me to find."

"That doesn't make a lot of sense. You're right. That's his first time doing that."

"He ripped it out. I think there is a reason behind it."

"Besides the obvious reason that he's a sick bastard?" Anderson said.

"Besides that. I wonder something; how did the press conference go downtown?" Brian asked.

"Fairly well… as press conferences go."

"Did Barnum ever talk to the media during it?" Brian asked.

Chief Ralph Anderson paused. "Now that you mention it, yes there were a couple of questions he answered for me," Anderson explained.

"Really?"

"He was better suited to answer a couple of them, due to my lack of knowledge on the subject matter. Why, do you think him answering a few questions is relevant to his murder?"

"I don't know, but I think it's possible," Brian said.

"Son, if that's the case, this killer could have all of us in his sights."

"No, that's not it." Brian needed to see the video of the entire press conference, but there might be something Lucifer may have seen that attracted him to his latest victim. "Do me a favor, Ralph, have Cynthia pull the video from the press secretary's office and I will stop by and take it home and review it. Maybe Alex said something that triggered Lucifer to go after him."

"I will tell her to pull it for you. Give me a call on my cell no matter how late if you do find anything."

"I will."

"Good luck, Brian; I think we need some right now."

"I'll keep you posted on that, along with the hair sample issue as well," Brian said. "Ralph, tell Lorraine I'm sorry this happened."

"I will." Chief Ralph Anderson disconnected.

Brian knew the killer was drawn to Alex Barnum for a purpose, and he was convinced it started with something from the press conference…that had to be the connection; it just had to be.

Chapter 42

Ego of a Madman

"*Ladies and Gentlemen, I'm Commander Alex Barnum of the Valentine Police Department. I have been asked by Chief Anderson to give you this statement on a recent outbreak of homicides that has been occurring since approximately six days ago. We have had five murders that appear to have some similarity. A single killer, or multiple killers with the same method of operation, is operating in the city of Valentine. All the deaths have been within the city jurisdiction and haven't spread to the outlying county areas as of this time. The killer or killers have been leaving their calling card on each victim. I'm not going to explain the details on this, but will say this person or these people have a definite agenda. The chief wants to urge everyone to be vigilant in his or her daily business, but not to panic. The Valentine Police Department, along with the Dunlap County Sheriff's Office, will work in joint cooperation to bring this killer or killers to justice. Chief Anderson wants every citizen to know that Law Enforcement will be stepping up the number of patrols and officers per patrol unit throughout the city. We will do everything we can to limit this killer or killers' chances to strike again.*

The Chief has also informed me he will address the local news himself tomorrow morning for his press conference on the current events of these tragic homicides. He is very confident the Law Enforcement in this community is more than capable to stop these senseless murders. He also wanted me to express his deepest sympathies to the families of the victims. I as well want to personally convey my condolences. If any of the news media wants to address questions to the press secretary, they may do so tomorrow. I will not be able to field any questions on the subject matter at this time.

I repeat, if media personnel contact the press secretary tomorrow, the Chief will be able to address any of your individual concerns at that time. No questions will be answered until then. This will conclude all official statements from the Valentine Police Department regarding this matter. Thank you for your cooperation."

Brian had retreated to his work hideaway to review all of the press conferences in conjunction with the killings, and although the one outside the police department didn't yield anything of substance, the statement given by Commander Barnum at the Daltry Hotel provided him deeper insight. Brian clicked on the second e-mail attachment of the press conference. Cynthia Cornerstone suggested he go over the transcripts of both, rather than watch the actual videos of the events. *She was a lifesaver.* Brian scanned through the second document. *Not much here.* He grabbed a print out of the first attachment. The statement given at the Daltry Hotel gave him a strong sense Barnum was pegged as a target because of what was said. Brian believed Lucifer would have paid attention to every word Barnum said. Why else would the killer strive to make him a target? He reviewed the text and underlined key phrases that might have some relevance. Brian understood the connection.

"Ladies and Gentlemen, I'm Commander Alex Barnum of the Valentine Police Department. I have been asked by Chief Anderson to give you this statement on a recent outbreak of homicides that has been occurring since approximately six days ago. We have had five murders that appear to have some similarity. A *single killer, or multiple killers* with the same method of operation, is operating in the city.

All the deaths have been within the city jurisdiction and haven't spread to the outlying county areas as of this time. The *killer or killers* have been leaving their calling card on each victim. I'm not going to explain the details on this, but will say this person or these people have a definite agenda. The chief wants to urge everyone to be vigilant in his or her daily business but not to panic. The Valentine Police Department, along with the Dunlap County Sheriff's Office will work in joint cooperation to bring this *killer, or killers* to justice. Chief Anderson wants every citizen to know Law Enforcement will be stepping up the number of patrols and officers per patrol unit throughout the city. We will do everything we can to limit this *killer or killers'* chances to strike again. The Chief has also informed me he will address the local news himself tomorrow morning for his press conference on the current events of these tragic homicides. He is very confident the Law Enforcement in this community is more than capable to stop these senseless murders. He also wanted me to express his deepest sympathies to the families of the victims. I as well want to personally convey my condolences. If any of the news media wants to address questions to the press secretary, they may do so tomorrow. I will not be able to field any questions on the subject matter at this time. I repeat, if media personnel contact the press secretary tomorrow, the Chief will be able to address any of your individual concerns at that time. No questions will be answered until then. This will conclude all official statements from the Valentine Police

Department regarding this matter. Thank you for your cooperation."

Brian believed he had discovered what made Lucifer set out after his former supervisor. The key phrase that stood out for the investigator was "*killer* or *killers.*" Lucifer placed his signature on all of his victims to include Barnum. He took pride in all the victims. Lucifer wanted *everyone* to know that it was he and he alone.

This statement infuriated the assassin. Several times, Barnum indicated more than one killer might be at large. Brian realized Lucifer took offense to this, and targeted the senior police investigator. The killer removed the focal point responsible for the offense, which was Barnum's tongue. *Now, this does make some sense*. Brian reviewed all the underlined phrases. Lucifer went after Barnum based on his *ego* alone. Brian was cognizant Lucifer was not just a ruthless killer, but an egomaniac to top it off. The tired detective was about to head off to bed when the desk phone rang.

"Hello."

"This is Dr. Sanderson. Sorry to call you so late."

"No problem, Doc." Brian hit the speakerphone button. "Hey, I hope you have some good news for me."

The medical examiner took a deep breath. "I have something, but it's not good news, by any stretch of the imagination."

"Why would it be? That would be almost a miracle to ask for." Brian rubbed his bloodshot eyes.

"The forensic lab just sent me the results of the hair sample you found in the drain. Nothing for prints on the wheelchair, though, sorry," Sanderson paused. "The DNA hair fibers that you collected are *not* from your killer, they are from his female victim, Tamia Stevens. I matched it with a sample I took at the autopsy. The hair probably got stuck deeper in the drain from the last time she used the bath in the hotel room."

Brian hoped the hair might be a link to the killer, but now that was dashed with reality. "So we still have nothing?"

"It appears that way. I'm sorry to disappoint you."

"I do appreciate your follow-up. Thank your friend at the lab."

"Also, I checked Alex Barnum's system for the paralytic drug Propaganician. He had twice the amount of all the other victims in his tox screen." Sanderson's voice appeared worried as he relayed this to Brian.

"Twice the amount. Hmm, it doesn't surprise me," Brian said.

"The killer is an expert with this paralytic, Detective. He did this on purpose."

"I think so too. I will contact Chief Anderson and let him know."

"Don't give up…you will get him."

"I wish I was as sure as you." Brian clicked off the speakerphone. He'd figured Lucifer used twice the amount of Propaganician on Barnum to make a point, and it did. Brian sat at his desk half awake, and within a few minutes had drifted off to sleep; unaware he was being watched. Through the half-drawn window shade, a muscular man conducted surveillance on the investigator. Lucifer stared with compassion at the man as he formulated his final masterpiece. He ran the fifty-cent piece through his fingers as a sinful sneer spread across his face. *Just a matter of time*.

Chapter 43

Officer James Patters

Lucifer dimmed the lights of the Honda. The alley adjacent to Brian Jeffers' residence was the ideal location, and the dilapidated garage was icing on the cake. The shelter lacked an overhead door, but that was soon rectified by covering the getaway car with an assortment of refuse found throughout the abandon property's dumpsters. Leaving just enough of the driver's side door clear, the killer snuck into the front seat and turned on the scanner. Lucifer became preoccupied with the radio traffic and listened to the various calls for service from the Valentine Police dispatch center. Most of them were of little significance as he paid close attention to the radio protocol. After thirty minutes, he overheard the dispatch center broadcast a communication for his prey's call sign. Lucifer's eyes gleamed with anticipation. *Ready to die, James?*

"Dispatch to thirty-nine, twenty-seven." A crackling sound of the dispatcher's voice sounded over the scanner.

"Thirty-nine twenty-seven, go ahead with your communication." The male voice of Officer Patters responded.

"I need you to meet with thirty-nine, forty-seven, at 1777 Mackey Ave, to assist with a dispute. Do you copy?"

"I will be en route to the location. Thanks."

"Keep us advised," the dispatcher said.

"No problem. I will radio you once I'm on scene,"

Officer Patters said.

Lucifer opened the glove box and pulled out a city map of Valentine. Within a minute, he found the street. *Should only take fifteen minutes to make it there.*

     * * *

Lucifer pulled up to the corner of Mackey Avenue, where two patrol units were parked under the broken streetlight. The vehicles sat in front of a one-story residence and appeared to be on pause. *This is the place.* Lucifer switched off the headlights. He figured the lack of illumination would make it close to impossible for anyone to identify him. The killer wanted to maintain his distance, just in case Officer Patters was able to recognize his Honda. He didn't want to underestimate the policeman's memory, mostly because of how suspicious the man was of him when they first met. If Lucifer made one slip-up, his passion for his art would be forever spoiled.

He sat there and thumbed the fifty-cent piece, until his target exited the house. *Finally.* Glancing down at his watch, he took a deep breath. *Patience, and this will be done.* The moonlight's reflection bounced off the timepiece. *Forty minutes?* He smirked when the policeman exited the house, in escort of a handcuffed scruffy overweight male. The officer threw the man into the rear of one police cruiser. *Careful, that could be a lawsuit.* A few seconds later, a second officer emerged from the house; the two conversed as Lucifer watched the interaction until the second officer jumped in the patrol car and sped off.

Officer Patters returned to his car and left the area in the opposite direction. The killer waited for several seconds, then pulled away from the corner. He flicked on the headlamps, staying a close distance behind his prey.

Lucifer checked all of his safety equipment to ensure compliance with the local regulations. *Can't get caught now.* He tailed the unaware officer for several blocks as he kept part of his attention trained to the scanner in the hopes the man would not be needed somewhere else. The sun would rise in a few hours; Lucifer knew he needed to return to the Jeffers' home for continued surveillance. He activated his turn signal, ready to delay this hunt, when a crackle from the scanner, caused him to flash a sadistic grin.

"Thirty-nine, twenty-seven, to dispatch." Officer Patters voice was broken but Lucifer could still hear.

"Dispatch, go ahead with your radio traffic, sir."

"I will be on break for thirty minutes at Tommy's Twenty-Four Hour Deli. I will be available by cell, should anything urgent come up."

"Okay, enjoy your break." The scanner went silent.

Lucifer smiled to himself. The all-night eatery was just a few blocks away. He was familiar with the lay of the land. The patrol car turned the corner, while Lucifer slowed down and watched him pull into the darkened rear lot. He passed the area and continued to drive a few blocks down the street, until he found a spot in front of a drycleaners. The killer punched the release button on the trunk and removed his backpack from underneath a dark wool blanket. He gawked; the white letters sewn into the fabric stared back at him. *BHA,* Lucifer thought. *That damn place.*

He shook off this memory and continued to rummage through the backpack, until he found the "slim-jim." It was a piece of flat steel about three feet long with a small notch at one end and a black rubber shroud, a few inches in length on the other. This was held to get a steady and firm grip. The person would then take the other end and insert it between the molding of their driver or passenger side window and the thin layer of metal which surrounded it. This led to the internal locking device of most vehicles. The instrument would have to be jiggled; if done in correct fashion, access would be almost instantaneous. It was designed to bend and its purpose was used to unsecure car doors of forgetful motorists whom left their keys locked inside.

Lucifer had used the tool once, and was a little nervous he hadn't had much practice to develop more expertise with it. Tucking it inside his jacket, the killer snuck through the deli's lot and observed several cars parked at the back of the restaurant. The cozy concrete building was of cheap construction, as the rear of the restaurant didn't have any windows which faced the parking lot. There was one way in; the rear door appeared to be broken, or at least the boxes stacked against the metal barrier gave it that appearance. This was a safety violation, but the local inspectors deemed it worthy for continued business. Lucifer dodged between several vehicles and took note of the patrol vehicle's location—flush at the rear of the structure. Lucifer scanned both directions, and when he was certain it was safe to move onward, crept to the front passenger's side door. The dimness of the lot and the starless night made it next to impossible for anyone to see him. He didn't realize it at first, but the rear windows of the patrol car were tinted enough, Officer Patters would almost need to have a flashlight. He lifted out the slim-jim and took another glance, mindful of any unwanted onlookers. Placing the flat steel tool at the base and between the black plastic window mold of the passenger's side door, Lucifer wiggled the tool in various directions, and the lock disengaged. He eased it open and slipped inside.

Lucifer inspected the interior and opened various compartments, which could hold the precious green notebook. His quest for the notepad ended in failure. He pushed on the mechanism, certain what needed to be done. Climbing out of the passenger side, he cracked opened the rear door and left it ajar. Lucifer surveyed the seats; a black steel cage barrier was bolted into the floor of the patrol car. This separated the front seat from the back, but the cage possessed holes large enough to slip through a syringe of his concoction. *Convenient and deadly*. Lucifer opened the backpack and extracted the hypodermic *"What a beautiful night."* The killer crouched down against the floor and waited in anticipation to seal the fate of his next victim.

* * *

Officer James Patters sat at a wooden table in Tommy's Deli. It was a surprise to have the company of twenty other customers at this time of day. He was a regular for the past few years and Tommy's menu was simple but exquisite. *Meatball sub.* The mixture of American cheese and Italian meat, smothered in melted provolone was like a jaunt in his own personal heaven. Patters was delighted the business was open twenty-four hours a day and since he worked a majority of overnight shifts, it was his number one stop. Not to mention the owner, Tommy Parine worked the midnight shift, and served his customers just like the other employees. Officer Patters admired Tommy for his commitment to his family. Tommy made the choice to work at night, so he could be off during the day with his children. Tommy had been in the business for fifteen years; his restaurant was very much a staple of

Southwest Valentine.

The interior of the deli was quaint, with most of the tables, covered in red and white checkered design. In the center, stood a state-of-the-art video jukebox, which housed over ten thousand songs. It was complemented by a ten-person dance floor, which most of the time, seemed to have more patrons than the allotted number. The walls were stonewashed white, as two brown ceiling fans hung to provide a better airflow for the overworked air conditioner. The long open deli counter had a variety of specialties displayed for the daily onslaught of customers. Officer Patters finished off his chocolate shake, as Tommy was behind the counter, engaged with inventory. He was a short, middle-aged heavyset man with long black hair. Several scars littered his face; the apparent result from a disastrous fire. Tommy never told him any of the particulars, and Patters never pushed the issue. Tommy winked at the patrolman, as he rubbed his hands against a red apron. "Hey, James, how is your meatball sandwich, my friend?"

He winked back. "Excellent, as always, Tommy. You know I don't eat anywhere else if you're open."

"Much appreciated, James my boy, much appreciated, since we're always open." Tommy laughed.

"That's true," Officer Patters said. "You know what I mean."

"Hey, I know. I'm just messing with ya," Tommy rubbed his forehead. "Say, James, everyone is talking about these murders lately. Do you guys have any good leads?"

"I wish to God I could answer you, but I know about as much as you do," Patters lied. He knew the small business owner didn't want to know what the ritualistic killer had done to the bodies.

"James, a lot of my customers are really scared. Some of them are talking about not leaving their homes after dark," Tommy said with sympathy.

"Tommy my friend, be assured, the chief is doing everything he can to have extra patrols out during the evening hours."

"You're just repeating what the news conference said, James. I figured *you* would at least shoot straight with me."

Shit! He liked Tommy, but he didn't want to say too much.

"Tell your customers to carry on with their business and not be consumed by the murders."

"That's all the customers keep talking about. The damn murders!" A few of the customers looked over to see why the owner was louder than usual.

"The person responsible for these deaths will be caught. I promise you." Patters portrayed the look of confidence, even if though he wasn't sure if the statement was true.

"The police always say things like that. I just hope you're right and you guys catch this damn guy." Tommy turned his back, and returned to the inventory.

"Don't lose sleep over this, Tommy. You just concentrate on making those great sandwiches you do so well. I won't let anything happen to you, partner."

The man whirled around. "Ha! You can't guarantee that!" Tommy said. A smile again appeared on his face. "Can you?"

"Hey, buddy, I gotta go. Lunch time is over for me. I will see you tomorrow night." Patters waved on his way out.

"Take care. Have an uneventful shift tonight."

Officer Patters turned the corner towards his patrol car and jerked out the keys. The Valentine Police Department didn't believe keyless entry devices were needed or cost effective, so they issued out individual keys to each officer. He inserted the dull silver into the driver's side lock. *It's almost too dark out.* The interior overhead light wasn't set to turn on; it was pitch black. He slammed the door. *Ouch, must be getting old, or these sandwiches are getting to me.* He rolled down the driver's side window to get some fresh air. *Ah, feels nice.* Turning the ignition key, he rubbed his face. *Tommy, I will protect you. I promise.*

Flipping on the inboard radio unit, Officer Patters reached out, and attempted to unhook the radio handset. His actions were cut short by a deep sensation in the back of his neck. "What the hell?" Officer Patters cried out. He spun around and looked through the cage. He panicked in disbelief when he saw the intruder's face. "What did you do to me, asshole?" Officer Patters attempted to grab his firearm from his holster but his fingers felt weighted which made *any* movement a challenge. *I can't move.* Numbness coursed throughout his body as the policeman was forced to take short gasps in order to catch his breath.

* * *

Lucifer cocked his head and watch Patters succumb to the drug. Patters fell forward as the impact caused the horn to sound.

We can't have that! The killer pushed on the door and climbed out. He stood next to the driver's side window and scanned the area. *Empty Streets... Good.* Reaching in, Lucifer moved the officer off the steering wheel, pushing him further back into the seated position. The killer locked eyes with the man; the elixir had done his will. The man was seconds from the afterlife. Lucifer glanced down at a rectangular bulge in the officer's right front shirt pocket and this gave him a slight sense of relief.

Lucifer unsnapped the pocket and removed the green notebook. He thumbed through the pages. *No time for any mistakes.* Lucifer was halfway through when he found the information. He slid the pad into his left pants pocket. *Thank God.* He laughed and reached into his other cargo pocket and pulled out the second item he purchased at the discount store. This was a duplicate of the green memo notebook Patters filled out, the night he questioned him. He tucked this back into the officer's pocket.

Patting the dead man on the head, the killer turned and shook his head. *Not exactly a masterpiece, but it will do.* Lucifer whistled his favorite song as he sauntered away. It was time to move on to the final installment of his Valentine collection.

Chapter 44

Identity of a Killer

Lucifer revisited the Jeffers' house after the Officer Patters ordeal. He spent the last hours of darkness in review of the layout of the home, along with the activity around the neighborhood. He was surprised that with all the recent murders, the streets were absent local law enforcement. *Oh well, Lucky me*. He figured the area was quiet and other areas of the city were considered more vulnerable than Palmer Court. Their thought process for the lack of security would also prove to be a false reality when they found the bodies.

Lucifer needed to concentrate on the getaway. He retrieved several cardboard boxes from the all-night grocery store. The clerk was happy to get rid of the boxes, and Lucifer slipped him a twenty just for the inconvenience. *Things are falling into place.* The killer spread the cardboard throughout the, floor space but saved one just for his collection. Lucifer opened the hideaway and turned on the light. He ogled his glorious assortment and determined the next place he rented would need to have a much more spacious area devoted for his work. This would be essential, since his ensemble would have *many* more additions. He removed the items from their shelves and filled the box.

The killer wrapped each treasure with newspaper and enclosed them in bubble wrap. He didn't want any to incur any damage on the journey to the next community. When he finished, Lucifer grabbed a black marker from the computer desk and labeled the box *FRAGILE*.

He could never be too careful if some police or patrol deputy stopped him on his trip. They would think the box contained precious breakables and not bother him.

It's already mid-morning. He loaded up the boxes in the trunk of the Honda, but left his box of evil treasures in the back seat, along with the backpack. Lucifer dressed in the suit he most admired for this victorious day. He reached into the closet and removed a lone tie. It was made of black silk with no distinguished designs. *Keep it simple*. It was essential to do just that. The proud killer looked at himself in the mirror, confident he was ready to create his final masterpiece. He grabbed the leather case, gold shield, and slipped it through his belt loop.

Reaching out, the killer scooped up the fifty-cent piece from atop his desk and placed it in pants pocket. He looked at what remained and spoke out to no one in particular. "At least someone can use them." He would replace the items, once he found a new place. Lucifer took one final look at the apartment, as he shut the door forever. *One final stop!*

* * *

Lucifer smiled at the sign. *Do-It-Yourself Storage* was the perfect name for him, or at least, it was, for the tools of his trade. The company, who came up with the idea, made it sound much more like an advertisement than a small business. The storage units were brick with white garage doors. Lucifer wondered who thought of this type of design. He drove along the circular road that led up to his rented shed. The number 210, once painted black was now less than visible on the cracked wooden frame. All that remained was the outline. He pulled out the key and slipped it into the garage door type lock. The sound of metal greeted Lucifer as he lifted the door, unveiling his private Utopia. On the right side of the caged wall, two medium-sized black briefcases were stacked in one area, which appeared reserved just for them. On the left, there were two large containers positioned side by side. One was made of pinewood, about two feet long and one foot in depth. It appeared to be handmade from the way the wood was just slapped together. The other was made of gray plastic; it appeared to be about seven feet long, with just about a foot of depth. Lucifer knelt down next to the briefcases and picked up the first.

Opening it, the meticulous killer examined the rubber banded empty syringes that filled the case to the brim. *Just how I left them*. Lucifer seized the other and followed suit.

This contained a multitude of steel cylinder vials stacked upon one another. They were all labeled in red letters with the word: *PROPAGANICIAN*. He pulled out three from this suitcase and three empty syringes from the other. Lucifer emptied the contents of the vials into each and discarded the empty ones in a garbage container next to the shed. Closing the briefcases, he placed them in the rear of the car. Lucifer grasped the backpack and eased the filled syringes into the bag. He stepped inside the storage unit and surveyed the other crate. The man inspected the contents, delighted to see two sets of rusted leg irons. Stolen several years ago from a hospital mental ward, the killer knew someday they would fulfill a purpose. *Almost like destiny*. He ran his gloved hand over the rusted metal. *One small set…and one just a little larger*.

Lucifer stuffed the chains into backpack and kept it open for *one* last item. He fumbled further and collected several brown folders. As he reached for the last item, his arm banged against the crate, which caused the folders to fall. A piece of worn yellow paper floated from the documents and landed outside the shed. He scrambled over and snatched it off the ground. The killer's eyes fixated on the faded print.

Dr. Lucas Calling,

We regret to inform you Bourne Hospital Administration has determined your medical practices a liability to the organization. The board members have decided to offer you a fair severance package for the commitment and perseverance that you have shown. You can appeal the Administration's decision if you disagree with the findings that were sent to you in the previous communication. We wish you luck in finding a suitable organization that can accommodate and advance your career with experimental medications. Unfortunately this organization cannot risk further litigation with this type of treatment protocol.

Cordially Yours,

Dr. Samuel P. Longnecker

Medical Director, Bourne Hospital Administration.

Lucifer stood frozen for what seemed like eternity, before he shoved the tattered document back into the binder. The former physician hadn't seen the letter in such a very long time. He remembered the day he was sent the correspondence and the extreme anger he felt toward Samuel Longnecker. This son-of-a bitch had cost him his research and medical license. The man used Lucas as a scapegoat, when Samuel was just as responsible for the failed experiments. The Director of the Bourne Hospital Administration destroyed *any* hope to resurrect his career. *Soon, dear Samuel, you will get what you deserve*. Lucifer closed the storage unit. He knew this fateful letter changed his path forever. The day Dr. Lucas Calling was escorted out of the hospital by security officers was the day Lucifer the "collector" was born. He shifted the car into gear. *It's time for another creation.*

Chapter 45

A Visit from Hell

Brian Jeffers sat in his crouched over his desk. Sarah had come down a little before dawn and ushered him upstairs for a little more relaxed rest. He flipped several black and white photos of Alex Barnum into a folder; the speakerphone buzzed and the voice of Cynthia Cornerstone filled the room. "Brian, there is a call for you on line three. It's Toby from Calmine County."

"Patch him through." Brian hadn't talked to his friend for several days and was anxious to see if Toby had found anything.

"Hey, dude, I wanted to call and see how you're doing? The sheriff just left me a voice message about what happened."

Brian replied with scratchiness in his voice. "Hey, thanks, I think I may have found out why he killed Barnum though."

"What? Toby asked.

"I believe Lucifer went after Barnum because he reported to the media that more than one killer was responsible for the homicides." Brian paused. "I think that signed his fate."

"It makes more sense than anything else. Everything you have explained… and I have seen, indicates he likes being in the spotlight.

Brian sighed. "I am fucking worried; this lunatic's gotten himself a badge."

"He stole your boss's credentials?" Toby asked. "That wasn't in the intel report."

"I'm sure they forgot to add that juicy tidbit. Yeah, he's got em, and God only knows what he's going to do with them. I have spent most of the morning sending out alert messages to other Law Enforcement agencies notifying them of the missing credentials."

"I wish there was something I could do," Toby said.

"Hey, without your info on the paralytic drug issue, we may have never suspected that was part of his sick protocol."

"I guess so," Toby said.

Cynthia Cornerstone rushed into the office. "Brian, I got some bad news."

"Hey, partner, I got to go." He cupped the receiver and whispered to the shaking woman. "You okay?" "Cynthia approached him. "What more bad news are you bringing me now?"

Her eyes watered. "I just received a phone call from Sergeant McGough of the Southwest division. One of his officers was found dead in his squad car."

Brian stood up. "Did he say what happened?"

"McGough doesn't know. He said the officer was found behind Tommy's Deli," Cynthia said.

"Who was it? Brian asked.

"His name was James Patters," Cynthia said.

"I don't know him. What does McGough think happened?"

"He thinks the guy might have had a heart attack." Cynthia sat down in a chair in front of Brian's desk.

"Really?" Brian said.

"That's what he thought," Cynthia replied.

"Hmm, nothing suspicious about the death at all?"

"McGough doesn't get that impression."

"He doesn't, huh? Well, is Officer Patter's body still

at the scene?" Brian asked.

"McGough said someone from the coroner's office had already been there and they were going to do an autopsy as soon as they could." Cynthia tapped the desk with her nails.

"It could be death by natural causes, but with what's been happening in this city, I somehow doubt it."

"What are you thinking?" Cynthia leaned forward in her chair.

"Believe me, when I say, you don't want to know what I'm thinking."

* * *

Lucifer stopped the vehicle in the alley. He parked adjacent to Sarah Jeffers' minivan, close enough to block the driver's side door. The killer didn't consider any of them would escape, but it never hurt to be prepared. The Venetian blinds were closed. *Didn't even see me pull in.* Stepping out of the Honda, he grabbed the black briefcase. He strutted up the sidewalk, and opened his suit jacket and exposed the shield. If anyone were watching from the cluster of houses, this would diminish their curiosity. Lucifer pushed the yellow oval doorbell. A few seconds later, he heard the voice of a young girl. "Mom, I'll get it." This was Melissa Jeffers, the oldest of the girls. Melissa slung open the door; a large bald man stood in the doorway. The stranger flashed a gentle smile. She looked at him for a second, blinded by the sunlight's refection from around his waist. She shielded her eyes and pointed to the shiny metal. "My daddy has one exactly like that, Mister. Do you work with my daddy?" Melissa crossed her arms. "Hey! I've seen you before!" Lucifer widened his eyes; he was mesmerized by the heart necklace which hung from the girl's collar. He spoke in a soft tone. "Well, yes I do. I was going to meet him here to talk about something important about work. You know, little girl, *grown-up* kinds of stuff."

Melissa's shot him a look of disapproval. She knew that meant her dad would be busy with this man and not be able to spend time with her. "He's not here. I'll tell Mom you're waiting for him."

Lucifer pushed through the open door and grabbed a hold of the young girl. He spun her; the killer placed her into a headlock. Reaching over, Lucifer covered her tiny mouth, so she couldn't warn the others. Melissa lashed out with her feet to fight the large man, but he was too strong. He forced her deeper inside the hallway, and spoke. "Don't worry, little girl, I will make sure he gets the *message*." Lucifer slammed the door shut. He reached into his suit pocket and pulled out one of the syringes. Then Valentine's serial killer forced the needle through the girl's soft flesh. Grasping the plunger, he emptied the contents into her, until the struggle was over. Melissa became limp in his arms, as the sound of footsteps from above, alerted the killer, to the location of the next victim.

The tender voice of Sarah Jeffers floated down the stairs. "Melissa, honey, is everything okay? Is someone here, baby? I have to pick up Alyssa and Victoria from daycare. Honey, who's here?"

Lucifer dragged the body to the corner of the staircase; just out of sight of the inquisitive Sarah Jeffers. The female protector hurried down the staircase; safety not on her agenda. The killer heard the mother mention that the younger siblings were not at home. He felt a little cheated they would not be included in the festivities; more importantly, he wouldn't be able to finish his masterpiece the way he wanted. "Too bad," he whispered. The madman would just have to make do. He slipped out; his massive figure surprised Sarah Jeffers. Lucifer's eyes locked on the woman as he worshipped *all* that she was. So supple and delicate. And now she would be his… forever. He cleared his throat. "Hello. Let me introduce myself. My name is Lucifer, and you have been chosen to be my next masterpiece."

Chapter 46

The Ultimate Masterpiece

Sarah Jeffers stared in unexpected horror at her first-born daughter who lay helpless in the corner. Tears welled up in her eyes; rage filled her heart. "What did you do to my baby, you bastard? Mother Fucker!! Who are you!" Sarah didn't realize she was too close, which proved to be a painful mistake. Lucifer smiled, formed a fist, and struck her in the center of the face. He cackled. "Uh, oh! That hurt!" The sound of crushed bone filled the room. Sarah fell backward and almost toppled over, as blood flowed from her disjointed nose. "Fuck you!" My husband is coming!" She spat; a stream of crimson spurted from her mouth.

Sarah tried to regain her balance, but her vision was blurred due to the power of the strike. Turning to run, she screamed. "Get out! Why us?'

Lucifer hurled himself at her. The majority of his weight landed on her chest, causing her small ribs to splinter. "Why not you, dear Sarah? Death comes to all." He snickered.

She felt all the air leave her lungs due to the heaviness of her attacker. She tried to scream from the pain, but the strong hands around her throat stifled the cry. Her hands went around his, in effort to loosen the madman's death hold.

"Yes, fight me! A kill should be earned!" Lucifer clenched even tighter.

"Please, stop!" Sarah squeaked. Realizing there may be one way to escape, Sarah brought her hands down toward the crotch of the killer. "Please…my children." Hoping this cry for mercy would be a slight distraction, she clutched at his groin, and with one swift movement, yanked down as fast and as tight as her waning strength would let her. The force she generated ripped his pants and pocket, which caused the man to howl.

"Shit… you bitch!" Lucifer was oblivious as the fifty-cent piece spilled from his possession and rolled, finding a home beneath a leather chair. "Now, you die!" Lucifer felt the pain in his genitals, which made him roll away and gave the woman a few precious seconds to get up and run to safety. She stumbled to her feet as blood cascaded along her neck and trailed down her body.

The kitchen was just around the corner. She squinted; the cordless phone was on the table. If she could get to it, Sarah would be able to get help. She limped towards the counter; the extreme blood loss causing her to fall. Her will to survive forced her to her feet. She was close enough to reach out for the white handset, but her luck had run out.

Lucifer, even in intense pain, managed enough power to lunge at her which forced her onto the tile "The one that didn't get away, my lady!" He spat into her face. The pressure of his weight drove Sarah's already-broken face into the surface of the hard floor. Gripping Sarah's hair with both hands, the killer slammed her into the tile several more times, until she didn't fight any more.

Sarah raised her head one final time. "Wh—y"

Lucifer, a little out of breath from the struggle, reached into his now-dirty suit coat and pulled out the second syringe of Propaganician. He injected its contents into the back of Sarah Jeffers' neck and smiled. Leaning in, the killer answered. "Just because…just because." He gazed down at the tanned arms of Sarah Jeffers and focused on the left hand. Lucifer knelt down, obsessed at the wedding ring. *What a perfect piece.* Reaching down, the killer ripped the diamond from her hand. *Mission accomplished.* Lucifer limped over to the briefcase.

He removed both pairs of leg irons from as well as the last item he had removed from the storage shed. Lucifer flipped over the package that held his tools and opened the elongated leather pouch. He ogled at the surgical utensils which would assist him in another work of art. He hadn't used these since the time he killed the used car salesman who sold him that piece of junk. He was happy to finish his spree, with these fine instruments. He held the scalpel blade in his hand and rotated the blade until it was in position. It was wonderful to be able to grasp such a fine piece of advanced cutlery. Lucifer ran his fingertips along the steel beauty, worshipping the blade that once saved lives. Now, it had another designed purpose. Lucifer, overjoyed, raised the weapon over his head and plunged it deep into Sarah Jeffers.

Chapter 47

Straight Through the Heart

Brian Jeffers tried to reach his wife on the cell phone but was diverted to Sarah's voicemail. *Probably low battery*. He would stop by home, when he finished the notes on Barnum's murder. As he evaluated the documentation, the cell on his desk vibrated. Brian picked it up and scanned the number. It was Pamela Marquis. She was a mid-fifties widow and the daycare provider for the Jeffers' girls for the last several years. Confused, he picked up. "Hey, Pamela, what's going on?"

"Brian, Alyssa and Victoria are still here. I have tried both Sarah's cell and home number. She didn't answer either. Have *you* heard from her this afternoon?

It was unlike his wife not to pick up the girls on time. "No, I tried to get a hold of her as well." Brian shuffled the papers on his desk and shoved them in a folder. "Pamela, did she tell you what she and Melissa were planning for the day?"

"She didn't say, just something about picking up some winter clothes for the girls."

"Hmm, I know those two like shopping, so I wouldn't be surprised if they were still out doing that," Brian joked.

"She told me to look for her around early afternoon. It's almost five o'clock in the evening," Pamela said, in a matter-of-fact tone. Brian hadn't realized how fast time passed; it had him more than a little worried.

"That is late," "Pamela, has she ever been *this* late before?"

"Never. She is always on time to pick them up. I hope everything is okay."

"Give me some time and I will be over to get the girls, okay?" Brian ended the phone conversation before the daycare provider could say any more. He dialed his home number, after three rings the machine picked up. He waited until the message prompt. "Sarah, pick up the phone if you're home, baby. Pam just called about being late to pick up the girls. I tried to call your cell several times, but it must be dead. I'm on my way."

* * *

He pulled into the alleyway; Sarah's minivan sat it the driveway. He felt relieved, and removed the file folders out of the back seat. He glanced at the rear window of the minivan and noticed though it was dirty; one of his girls had used the glass to send a personal message. He leaned in and smiled as wiped at the large heart scrawled out in the dust. The words *I Love my Daddy,*

M.J. were inside of the design. *Well, so much for being a teenage drama queen.* Turning towards to the back of the house, Brian observed that it was wide open. *What the fuck, ladies?* He *always* told his family to lock the door, no matter how safe the neighborhood appeared. Brian stressed this more, since the recent murders. Pushing the door open, the home appeared way too quiet. "Sarah, Melissa, you guys here? Dad's home! Honey, I have to pick up the girls. Pam is pissed you didn't get them when you told her you would." Brian waited for someone to answer, as he stood in front of the coat rack. Again, he was greeted with dead silence. Brian's pulse raced and he didn't understand why, but he felt scared.

Reaching down, the detective undid the leather thumb break on his holster. His hands fumbled to remove the weapon. Brian walked through the hallway that led to the kitchen. A pool of dark crimson stained the hallway floor. "What the hell? Sarah! Melissa! You guys here? Sarah, honey, I'm home. Is anyone here?" Again there was no response. Brian moved closer to the kitchen; his face lost all color.

"Oh, *no*! Please, *God,* no!" He peered down at a thick crooked line of blood that led from the hallway through the kitchen and to the front of door of the family room. Brian squeezed the gun so tight; the butt of the weapon left its imprint into the palms of his hands. He was afraid to follow the trail any further, but didn't have a choice. As he approached, Brian heard the familiar sound of the two heavy-duty ceiling fans whirling at top speed. *It's a little chilly, why would they be on?* When he pushed the door, Brian smelled a strong putrid odor. Stepping through, the law enforcement officer and devoted husband was mortified. Each appliance had a naked bloodied body attached, as Sarah and Melissa were suspended upside down by what appeared to be leg irons. They were connected to the strong base of both rotary devices. The blades spun at their normal pace, not being disturbed by the excess weight. The bodies hung there like slaughtered animals in a factory, as blood from their ripped-open torsos dripped onto the once virgin-white carpet. Brian lost all sense of where he was, collapsed to the ground and loosened his grip on the firearm. It bounced on the carpet and landed a short distance away. "Why, God? Why?" Brian cried with guilt; he managed to get to his feet and stumble to the power switch and end the devious rotation. He approached his two loved ones; and recognized Lucifer's handiwork. On the back of both females the words which had terrorized the community were sculpted so deeply into the flesh, Brian could almost see the organs.

Glaring at the markings, he screamed out like Lucifer was in the house, even though he was gone. "You murdering bastard! This was my wife and daughter!! Why them? Why did you have to pick them, you son-of-a bitch! I will hunt you down and kill you. I promise you! I fucking promise you!" Brian Jeffers, drained of all his strength, crumpled to his knees on the bloodstained carpet and wept like he never had done or would ever do again..

Chapter 48

A New Home

Lucifer had driven west on Interstate 280, since he left Valentine hours ago. The steering wheel was gripped between his hands with such fierceness, his knuckles had turned white. His pocket was ripped by the Jeffers' bitch. The killer didn't anticipate she would be able to put up much fight, but she had. Now his trophy was somewhere inside that house. He knew if the Police found it, they would possess his identity. He held it in his bare hands many times; his fingerprints were all over. Lucifer looked up and saw the outline of a city. The gas tank of the Honda was on empty, so this would be an appropriate place to stop.

Lucifer glanced up as the name of the city on the sign caught his eye. He smiled to himself. *This must be destiny.* Driving onto the ramp, the killer stopped at a road-side gas station; only a few cars were parked at the pumps. He pulled into the dusty lot and alongside the "full service" lane. In a few seconds, an older heavyset man with gray coveralls and a red baseball cap appeared at the doorway. The man waved at him to roll down his window. "I'll be with you in just one minute, sir." The voice was very gruff; and it was accompanied by a slight southern drawl. Lucifer waved back to acknowledge the attendant. While he waited, the killer couldn't take his eyes from his torn pocket. The more he obsessed, the more, Lucifer was lost in this train of thought.

The attendant greeted him. "Hi, there, sir. Would you like the car filled up?"

Lucifer managed a very weak smile. He stared at the name patch. "Well, yes, thank you very much, *Harlow*. I have been driving for hours and was wondering if the city has a nice hotel to stay at?"

Harlow wiped off the windshield. "Lots of hotels in the city, my friend. This is just the outskirts of it here, sir."

"Oh, I didn't know that." Lucifer played dumb.

"Indeed it is, sir." Harlow checked the s tires. "There are too many of those big, well-to-do fuel centers in the city. I like to keep it small and friendly."

Eccentric old man. "About the motels in town…" Lucifer tried to get the man back on track.

"Oh— sorry." Harlow took off his cap and ran his hand through his white hair. "Well, I guess the best motel for the price would be the Stone Motel. The others are way overpriced, if you know what I mean, youngster."

Lucifer liked the man's honesty; a trait Lucifer lost in himself years ago. He decided to probe a little more. "Say, Harlow. My name is Patrick Vain and I was interested in finding a new place to live."

"You are? Well plenty of nice homes in this community," Harlow said.

"Great. Hey, I just came from a large city and was looking for a place not so intimidating. How big is this place, Harlow?" Lucifer cocked his head.

The man appeared to be impressed this traveler engaged him. Harlow smiled. "Well, Patrick, this city is growing but we have about one hundred and fifty thousand people who call us home."

Perfect. He could stay here for a while; maybe even create more masterpieces when the time was right. He smiled back as he opened the driver's door and stepped out. He sauntered up to Harlow; the attendant was almost finished. He stuck his arm out. "Well, I guess I may be staying a while. Why don't you point me in the direction of the motel you were talking about?" Harlow shook Lucifer's hand with a strong firm grip; he pointed down the road.

"Thank you, Harlow. I'm sure I'll be seeing you again.

"Pleasure to have met you."

Lucifer started the engine and pulled away, when the older man, again stopped him. He rolled down the window. "What were you saying?" Lucifer put on his trade-mark fake smile to show interest.

Harlow approached the open car window. "Patrick Vain, I just wanted to welcome you to Dementia. That's all I needed."

"I hope Dementia will enjoy having me here," Lucifer said as he drove away. He gawked at the blue flyer on the passenger seat. *One week is all you have left, Samuel.* The medical conference at the Paladium invited Samuel Longnecker to be a guest speaker for his recent success in paralytic treatment protocols. Lucifer reached over, and crumpled the flyer. *There was planning to do.*

Epilogue

Fifty Cents

Brian Jeffers struggled with sleep in the weeks that followed the murders of his wife and daughter. Brian hated Lucifer for taking the two from him. The bastard had also "*collected*" his wife's diamond ring. He wasn't sure what the killer had taken from his daughter Melissa… this just made him angrier. Dr. Sanderson also informed him, the officer found dead in his patrol unit was another victim of the madman. The killer had injected the man with the Propaganician as well, but for some reason, the familiar calling card was absent. *No rhyme or reason.*

After the funerals, he decided to take an extended leave from work. He wanted to be with his other daughters, Victoria and Alyssa. They needed him now more than ever. Brian remembered explaining how a very bad man hurt mommy and their big sister and they were now safe in Heaven. The girls seemed to have accepted that, and in the last few days they were back to laughing and playing with each other. They would have a few episodes once in a while late at night and climb in their mommy and daddy's bed. They felt safe with Brian around to protect them.

He was in the process of moving out of the beautiful home he and Sarah shared for so many years. He couldn't live *here* without her. He found a smaller place in the suburbs of Valentine; in a week, they would leave this place. A fresh start somewhere else might be good for all of them. He had just packed the last of the boxes when something under the black leather chair in the hallway caught his eye. He bent down and reached underneath, pulling out a worn, silver fifty-cent piece. He inspected it and had to grin when he saw the engraved date. The year on the coin was 1971. *What a weird coincidence.* It was made the same year he was born. He didn't know where it came from, but figured it might bring him good luck. *I could use some luck for a change.* Brian placed the fifty-cent piece in his right pocket as he finished the rest of the house. He didn't realize how very close he was to the identity of the man responsible for taking his wife and daughter away from him.

The End

Author Bio

Jeffrey Martin is currently a Federal law enforcement officer in the Midwest. Using a strong law enforcement platform, he creates terrifying tales in the suspense/thriller and horror genres. Works in progress include, *Weaving Evil, Death is Only a Click Away, Death Map, Death Harvest* and his first full length horror novel, *Raining Blood.* When not working and writing, Jeff enjoys spending time with his wife and three daughters. Learn more about Jeff by visiting his website at

http://www.jeffreymartinsnovels.com

Lightning Source UK Ltd.
Milton Keynes UK
UKHW012154241122
412814UK00004B/38